CLAIMED BY CIPHER

Grabbed #5

Lolita Lopez

Night Works Books
College Station, Texas

CLAIMED BY CIPHER

Prologue

Splinter Stronghold
22.7 Miles Outside Willow's Tears
Planet Calyx

P AIN IS WEAKNESS *leaving the body.*
Wracked with agony, Terror repeated the mantra that had been drilled into his brain from the first day at the academy. The sizzling arc of electricity ripped through his body, causing every muscle in his body to seize violently. When it finally—mercifully—stopped, he twitched and jerked for a few seconds before managing to suck a harsh, almost sobbing breath into his lungs.

Sagging in his metal bonds, he clenched his good eye shut and ignored the relentless ache in his shoulders. How much more of this unending torment could he take? It shamed him to admit that he didn't know. He had lost track of his time in captivity some time ago. He thought it might have been thirteen weeks but he couldn't be sure. What he did know was that his body was slowly beginning to fail him and his mind wouldn't be far behind.

Before he let even one secret slip, he would find a way to end his own life rather than betray his brothers-in-arms. His honor would accept nothing less. His desperate need to protect his friends demanded it.

Since being taken from the scene of the crash, he had been moved four times, always under heavy sedation and chains. There had been no chance of escape and no sign of rescue. In the first few agonizing days of his captivity, he had been in the care of Devious, one of the Shadow Force's long-term undercover agents. Though the torture he had suffered under his friend's hand had been horrendous, Terror had trusted that Dev wouldn't kill him. He had been optimistic that Devious would find a way to get word to Torment about his location.

But that hadn't happened.

After three weeks in the main Splinter camp, he had been trucked out in the dark of night to a new place—and then another and another. This new installation seemed to be underground in the old mine shafts near Willow's Tears. The cold, dank wetness of the place assured him of that. The sooty purple dust that coated everything was evidence of the clean-burning fuel that had been mined here in decades past...

A heavy hand smacked his face, the sting of it bringing Terror back around to reality. "You still breathing or do you need another jolt get you going again?"

He lifted his weary head and stared at the pock-faced man who had been trying to get him to talk for over an hour.

"You know I can keep this up all night." The interrogator motioned toward the battery array he had arranged in the cell.

Terror simply blinked his eye and waited for the threats to continue.

As if understanding that pain wasn't going to loosen Terror's tongue, the man switched tactics. "I know you're hungry. I know you're cold. Give me something useful—just the tiniest piece of actionable intel—and I'll make things more comfortable for you in here."

Although his empty belly ached and his dirty skin desperately needed a good washing, Terror rejected the tempting offer by lowering his face and focusing on the floor. Muscles tense, he waited for a blow or another round of the electricity but neither came. The interrogator surprised Terror by unhooking the electrodes and winding up the cables. Certain this was some sort of trick, he mentally and physically steeled himself for an even more painful experience.

He consoled himself with the knowledge that none of the Splinter interrogators were as sadistic or cruel as Torment. There was a reason men broke the moment Torment walked into their cells. A lifetime in a Kovark prison cell or a quick hanging as a convicted Tier One Terrorist was preferable to even ten minutes under Torment's skilled, punishing hands.

The door to the cell was jerked open, the rusted metal squealing and grating, and the Splinter interrogator jammed his head into the hall. "Hey, Bruno, get D.D."

Terror perked at the mention of this new person. He imagined another pair of evil hands torturing him. They hadn't yet brought in a wetworks man to cut at him. Maybe that was next on their list of horrors. Razor blades, knives, chisels—there were all sorts of heinous tools of the trade to cause gruesome injuries in the hopes of motivating him to break his silence and talk about the undercover operatives, the long-term mission plans for Calyx and the current operations underway to neutralize the Splinters.

He suspected they had avoided causing him traumatic injuries so far because of the infection risk and the odds of killing him before they had extracted every last bit of information from him. Now that he had proven he couldn't—wouldn't—be broken, the Splinters might have decided it was time to step it up a notch.

When the interrogator stepped aside to allow a new person to enter the cell, Terror fully expected to be greeted by a much bigger, more menacing and dead-eyed specialist. What he actually spotted coming through that door perplexed and surprised him. It wasn't a man at all. It was a woman holding cleaning supplies.

Small like Vee's Hallie, the younger woman entered the cell and glanced around the interior. She seemed totally composed and calm as she scanned the dimly lit space. The leather satchel resting against her hip caught his eye. It didn't move much as she took more cautious steps into the cell. Whatever was in it was heavy.

The long dark braid she wore fell to the small of her back. From his vantage point, her hair looked black as night, certainly the darkest he had ever seen. Garbed in dark gray cargo pants and an oversized men's shirt over a cotton tee, she gave off the impression of coming from an all-male household. Not much of her skin was visible in those boyish clothes but what he could see was tanned and smooth. This was a woman who spent more time up top than down here in the shafts.

Young and sweet, she looked totally out of place among the hardened Splinter terrorists who inhabited this place. Was she a daughter? A niece? A sister? He considered what he knew of the cultures of these rural people. She might be a wife to one of his captors or even a mother to little terrorist babies.

His interrogator tapped her shoulder, waited for her to look at him and then pointed to the long coils of wire and the batteries. "Tidy that up."

She nodded and crossed the cell. Terror noticed the way she didn't spare a single glance for him, probably because he was stark naked and in chains. She seemed focused on the task given to her and was completely oblivious to everything else. A flicker of hope hit him. This was the sort of situation he could easily exploit. She was a tiny little thing and could be easily overpowered if she got close enough to him.

"You like her?" The interrogator mistook his keen observation and tactical planning for sexual interest. "She's even prettier up close. Ripe for the plucking, if you know what I mean."

Terror's gaze skipped from the interrogator who made a crude gesture to the young woman who had her back turned to him. She didn't stiffen at the suggestive remarks or acknowledge them in any way. Either she was very used to being talked about so nastily or…

"Don't worry about her," the man said with a dismissive wave. "There's a reason we all call her D.D. Deaf and Dumb," he spelled out cruelly. "She's in her own fucking world most of the time—but that's the way some men like them."

Terror considered D.D. for a moment. *Better and better*, he thought as that flicker of hope flared stronger. If she couldn't hear him, she would be even more easily overtaken.

"How long's it been since you touched a woman, Terror? You've been in our hands for more than three months so it's been at least that long since you've felt the slick squeeze of a wet pussy around your dick." Coming closer, the interrogator motioned toward the woman. "Look at her. I mean—really look at her. That tight little ass? Those perky tits?"

Terror looked at her but not at her ass or her tits. He sized her up as his ticket out of here. What would it take to turn her against these people?

"She's never been fucked. I know that for a fact. How would you like to be the first one to sink balls deep in that virgin pussy? I can make that happen. I'll let you breed on her all you want."

Terror found the offer distasteful in the extreme but he feigned interest. Without saying a word, he glanced at his interrogator and held his gaze just long enough to show he was considering the offer. The man smiled, showing his brown-streaked teeth, and nodded.

He left Terror's side and moved toward the woman. When he drew near, she glanced at him, this time with apprehension. The interrogator leaned down and spoke slowly. "Clean the cell. Clean him. Understood?"

She nodded.

"Bang on the door twice when you're done." He held up two fingers. "I'll have Bruno let you out."

She nodded again. From the way she reacted, Terror confirmed his suspicion that she could read lips. What was it like for a deaf person in this bizarrely backward society on Calyx? If she had been born to his people, her hearing would have been fixed in-utero. The routine prenatal tests run on pregnant mates would have alerted her parents to the birth defect and allowed a skilled surgeon to make the necessary improvements to her ears. Here, though, she had no doubt been treated like a pariah.

Still not meeting his curious stare, the young woman finished tidying up the cell. He watched the methodical way she wiped and swept the space before unrolling a hose in the corner and turning on the faucet there. She brought the hose toward the center of the room and stood in front of him.

Their gazes finally met—and Terror's stomach did a wild flip. She had the bluest eyes he had ever seen, bluer even than those common in pureblooded Harcos males. Her bright white teeth bit into a plump lower limp. Holding the hose in one hand, she used the other to make a gesture. Brow furrowed, he tried to figure out what she was asking. It was some sort of sign but for what?

Exhaling with frustration, she pointed to his body and then the hose before nodding and shaking her head in an exaggerated way. He understood finally. She was asking for permission to clean him. The simple act of seeking permission surprised him. Since being captured, he had been at the total mercy of others. To have this small choice to make felt somewhat liberating.

He gave her a firm nod and waited to see what she would do next. After testing the water on her hand, she made a shivering motion to let him know it was cold. She waited to see if he would change his mind. When he didn't make any move to stop her, she carefully sprayed his body. The frigid blast made his teeth chatter and his heart stutter, but he was happy for the chance to be clean.

Careful not to openly watch her, Terror used his peripheral vision to keep track of D.D. She wasn't skittish around him and that raised his suspicions. He wasn't the sort of man who inspired calm in women. One look at him—with his ruined eye and puckered, scarred eyelid—and most of them blanched.

But she wasn't looking at him with fright. Her gaze was almost clinical. What was she thinking? Was she counting the many scars marking his body? Was she trying to figure out how they had been caused? Knives, shivs, bullets, fire, shrapnel...

Fuck, he had long ago lost track.

As she set aside the hose and grabbed soap and a rough looking washcloth from her satchel, he began to form a new opinion of her. This situation was too neat. She was too beautiful and too enticing to be true. This had setup written all over it.

Starved for affection, weak with hunger and frail from torture, Terror was a prime target for a black widow type agent. He had trained enough of them in his many years in Shadow Force to know how she would operate. This vulnerable woman with her hearing impairment and angelic face would find a way to get under his skin. She would provoke those protective instincts so strong within all Harcos males—and then she would strike.

There was only one thing for him to do. He had to strike first. With his arms chained overhead and his ankles bound with shackles, he couldn't move but his time would come. When it did, he would take it without hesitation. He would snap that fragile neck of hers before she even had a chance to gasp with fright at being caught by him.

Forced to endure the bizarre and unsettling sensations of being washed by a strange female, he kept his gaze fixed on the far wall. She didn't try to touch him inappropriately or even to arouse him. Her skin never made contact with his because she kept the rough cloth between her palm and his body.

Although thorough in scrubbing him, she never once let her hands get anywhere near his genitals. She seemed to be going out of her way not to make contact with the more intimate areas of his body. Part of that he chalked up to virginal fear. If she was as pure as the interrogator had said, it wasn't surprising that she shied away from him.

But, as an agent for these terrorist assholes, she was

badly trained. Using "accidental" sexual touch was the easiest way to ensnare a man. She was failing miserably on that count.

Because he hadn't been touched with a gentle hand in weeks, Terror couldn't stop his body's natural response when she climbed on a crate positioned behind him and began to wash his hair. Without his usual monthly visit to the barbershop for the close trim he preferred, he had gotten rather shaggy. Her short nails scratched across his scalp, swirling along his skin as she massaged the woodsy-scented suds into his dirty hair.

Shivering arcs traveled down his neck, along the curve of his back, through his legs and out through the soles of his feet. His cock throbbed to life, the full length of it growing erect and pointing toward his navel. Even before being taken from the crash site, it had been weeks since his last visit to one of the poppies on a nearby pleasure ship. On edge and desperate for stimulation, he clenched his teeth together and tried to think of anything but the way he wanted those warm hands of hers to glide down his chest and into the nest of curls crowning his dick.

She stepped away from him, taking her body heat and the pleasant scent that accompanied her. A few seconds later, ice cold water splashed over him. He sucked in a sharp breath of shock but welcomed the cooling effect it had on his raging libido. The last thing he needed was to let his dick control him.

As his erection faded, he hardened his thoughts toward the tempting siren with her dark hair and big blue eyes. She was trouble—and he needed to view her as merely an obstacle in his path to freedom. He would step on her and over her if it meant getting out of here and finding his way back to the *Valiant.*

She retrieved a towel from the satchel and wiped down his slick skin. When she produced a small tin from the leather bag, he narrowed his eye. She held it up for him to sniff. He caught the scent of something antiseptic. Certain the scrapes and cuts he had collected over the last few weeks could use some help in healing, he nodded to confirm that it was all right for her to treat them.

Swiping her finger through the ointment, she applied it to the wounds on his body. Like the other times she had touched him, she never lingered. She simply did what was necessary and moved on to the next scrape. When she was finished, she wiped her hand on the damp towel and tucked away the salve.

While she dug around in her bag, the door to the cell opened. A man he recognized as his jailer Bruno appeared in the shadowy entrance. "Hey, Dum Dum, you finished jerking this asshole off or what?"

With her back turned, she didn't hear the ugly remark. Before Terror could make a movement that would garner her attention, the bastard in the door pulled an orange, one of the native fruits these Earth-descendants had brought in their generational ship and cultivated on Calyx, from the pocket of his hooded sweatshirt. He threw it at the woman. It bounced off the back of her head and caused her to lurch forward.

Rubbing the back of her head, she spun around and glared at the asshole. She made an outraged gesture and a strange noise that Bruno mocked with jerky movements before shouting, "Hey, retard, hurry it up! Your step-daddy wants you to make a supply run so get moving."

Jaw visibly clenched, she shot the finger at Bruno. The cruel jailer laughed harshly and slammed and locked the cell door. Wincing, she rubbed that spot where the heavy fruit had ricocheted off the back of her head and pivoted toward the corner where it had rolled. Unable to see her when she was behind him, Terror relied on his highly-trained senses to keep track of her.

When she returned to his field of vision, she held the orange in her hand. Bending down, she retrieved a black object from her boot. With the a few graceful flicks of her wrist, she produced the gleaming blade of a knife from the folding handles. He recognized the style of the knife from the Blue Shores community along the ocean. The people there had been islanders back on Earth and had fostered and protected their culture here on Calyx. It wasn't uncommon to see the knives—*balisongs*—sold in the open air markets in the seaside city.

Considering the way she wielded the weapon, it was clear she was handy with a blade. Perhaps she wasn't totally helpless. Somewhere along the way she had learned some self-defense techniques. After watching Bruno abuse her, he had a bad feeling she had been hurt and bullied her entire life.

The strangest pang invaded his chest as he imagined a

smaller, younger version of D.D. suffering at the hands of others. Annoyed by the flare of concern, he pushed it aside. *She's the enemy. She's one of them. She wants to kill you. Don't be fooled.*

She cut a slit in the top of the orange and then expertly peeled the rind from the juicy flesh. The citrus scent that tickled his nose made Terror's mouth water. It had been so long since he had eaten anything but the watery broth and stale bread they infrequently provided. To watch her peel and eat the fruit in front of him was yet another torment.

But she didn't take a bite of the plump orange wedge that she plucked from fruit. She held it up to him, eyebrows raised questioningly, and waited for his reaction.

Terror wavered with indecision. What if the fruit had been injected with poison or a serum that might loosen his lips? What if Bruno's cruelty had been planned? He felt sorry for her, didn't he? Now she was offering him this bit of food with a shy, nervous smile. Was this the way she planned to enthrall and eventually trick him?

That endearingly sweet expression she wore confounded him. He needed to know if it was real or an act. To do that, he would have to embrace the cold bastard within him—and be exceedingly mean.

Parting his lips, he leaned forward as far as his chains would allow and lowered his head. She took a timid step toward him and brought the orange segment toward his mouth. This close, he was able to inhale the clean, earthy scent of her and to see the deep flecks of color in her blue irises. The light freckles dusting her nose and cheeks drew his interest.

D.D. pushed the cool, plump flesh of the fruit between his lips and waited until he had sunk his teeth into it to drop her hand. She pulled back as fast as an inquisitive child touching a stove for the first time. His eyelid drifted closed as he relished the succulent citrus flavor washing across his parched taste buds. It was like tasting fucking sunshine.

When he had extracted every last bit of the delicious juice from the pulpy meat of the segment, he balled it up with his tongue—and spit the entire soggy mess right back into her face. Startled by the chewed up fruit and saliva splattering her cheek and eye, she yelped and jumped.

In that moment, Terror understood that she was more complicated than he had ever imagined. In times of shock, it was difficult for any agent, even the best trained, to mask a true response. Provoking a real reaction with such a disgusting deed had been the easiest way to tear away her mask and see what was underneath.

But there was no irritation or anger in her expression. No, there was only confusion and hurt written on her face. The raw sincerity of it made his gut clench. And there was something else, something haunting in those brilliantly blue eyes of hers that he couldn't quite decipher. Perhaps she wasn't an agent after all. Perhaps she simply was an innocent, naïve young woman who had been pressed into Splinter service.

With his own face a stony mask of indifference, he watched her carefully. Would she prove herself to be just as nasty as the people she lived with and worked for? Would she lash out or injure him for his ugly stunt?

She reached up and slowly wiped the soggy mess from her face. Still holding the partially peeled orange, she carried the chewed up fruit to the dented bucket used for refuse and dropped it inside. She retrieved a handkerchief from her bag, wiped the sticky juice from her skin and turned her back toward him.

Senses on edge, he inhaled measured breaths and listened carefully. She stepped just beyond his line of sight again but he could feel her moving around behind him. Remembering that wicked looking knife she had so masterfully wielded, he started to doubt his estimation of her as an innocent. He had been in captivity long enough that he might be losing his touch.

Terror stiffened when she poked his back. Wondering what she was playing at, he held his breath and fully expected the sharp bite of that blade at any moment. When her fingertip began to tap against his skin, he frowned. Flummoxed by her odd behavior, it took him a few moments to recognize the taps as the elementary signal code he had memorized his very first year at the academy.

D.

E.

V.

I.

O.

He didn't have to pay attention to the next few taps to figure out that she was spelling Devious. Thinking of the undercover operative, Terror experienced a rush of hope. If Devious had put this strange creature in contact with him surely that meant his rescue was imminent. He just had to hold on a little while longer. He had to keep fighting.

The pressure of her finger disappeared. He heard her crouch down but couldn't see what she was doing. A few moments later, she was walking away from him and then he heard the scrape and jangle of metal as the chains holding his wrists high overhead were finally lowered. He hissed at the horrendous pins and needles sensation that traveled from his fingertips to his shoulders but figured that he should just be glad he could still feel anything.

With freedom of movement for his upper body, Terror collapsed to his knees as D.D. scurried to grab her bag and the cleaning supplies she had brought with her. He instantly tested his chains but realized she had given him only enough length to sit, sleep or reach the exposed hole in the corner where he was forced to relieve himself. It wasn't much but he was grateful for the chance to rest.

She banged twice on the door and exited without casting a single look his way. It wasn't until the cell door had been locked again and the lights were switched off to plunge him into darkness that he caught the enticing scent of the orange again. Reaching behind him, he patted the cold ground until he felt the soft handkerchief she had used to clean her face after he had spit in it. His fingertips moved to the left and he felt the segments of the orange laid out for him.

Grabbing the package left for him, he dragged his

chains to the wall and leaned back against it. He stretched out his aching, tired legs and placed the handkerchief on his thigh. One by one, he savored the orange pieces. They would probably upset his stomach after eating such thin, bland food for weeks but he didn't care. He was starving and refused to waste the chance to ingest even one extra calorie.

When the last succulent morsel was gone, he closed his eye and rested his head against the wall. In a moment of weakness, he brought the handkerchief to his nose and inhaled deeply. Behind the citrus notes lingered the smell of leather and grass and that barely floral hint that he had detected on her.

Hating himself for being so pathetic, he lowered the handkerchief but continued to clutch it in his fist. Refusing to think of those big, beautiful eyes, he turned his thoughts to Devious. The covert operative had been framed for a serious murder and publicly tried as a traitor to gain him sympathy and entrance into the Splinter faction.

Years and years of building trust and earning his reputation as a loyal member of the terrorist group had taken their toll on Devious. There had been a few times during his captivity in Devious' stronghold where Terror seriously questioned which side the man was on these days.

Of all the people Devious might have chosen to serve as his contact, why this girl? As an asset, she was an interesting but fairly useless choice. Assets were supposed to be the invisible eyes and ears of the Shadow Force. Unable to hear, there wasn't much intel this woman could gather.

Unless…

A glimmer of an idea began to form, one that intrigued and unsettled him. How far would Devious go to keep tabs on the many strands of his tangled web of terrorists on this planet?

As Terror began to sift through his memories of Devious' status reports, he made a decision on D.D. He wasn't going to snap her neck, after all.

Chapter One

U NFAMILIAR CHIRPS AND croaks filled Cipher's ears as he crept quietly through the darkness. The forests on Calyx were strange to him, especially this high up in elevation. Most of his life had been spent on warships or on deployments in the worst sort of sandy, hot, miserable places. This lush planet was a mystery that he wanted to explore, but so far, most of his days had been spent on the *Valiant,* The City or the settlements where nature had been pushed to the far edges.

Vaguely, he wondered if he would come across any of the predators he had been warned about in his briefing. His hand drifted to the holstered weapon at his hip as his gaze swept the shadows. He hated night vision goggles and avoided them whenever possible. Wondering just what might be surrounding him, he slipped them into place, dragging them down from the top of his head, and blinked until his eyes adjusted.

His heart rate ticked up a few notches as he noticed all of the beady eyes staring back at him. Everywhere he looked, there were animals watching him. Most of them seemed small and unlikely to bother him, but there was one set of eyes shining out from the low vegetation of a bush that drew his concern. He noticed the strange sound in the background of all the chirping insects and croaking frogs. It was a deep, growling hum.

A warning.

Not in the mood to tangle with some wild animal that wanted to rip out his throat, he kept moving. His steps were deliberate and unhurried. He didn't want to spook the animal or give it a reason to chase him. Gradually, the growling faded into nothing, and he relaxed his shoulders. Keeping the goggles in place, just in case, he continued on the path indicated by the GPS unit on his wrist.

The mission tonight was a simple one. He was meeting with a Shadow Force asset who had intel needed to plan Terror's rescue mission. It had been only twenty-seven hours since Torment had received the photos of Terror, alive but in captivity. He was being held in an abandoned mine, deep in the wilderness. The asset, a miner from a long line of miners, had the necessary maps and the explosives skills that were likely to be required.

He didn't often take missions like these, but sometimes the Special Response Unit where he served as the chief engineer loaned him out to the Shadow Force. Once, he had considered taking an offered spot on the elite team of covert operatives, but he had seen too much of their handiwork to ever be comfortable in their ranks. He had a moral code, and it wasn't compatible with their directive.

The unit on his wrist vibrated to alert him that he was closing in on his destination. The map included with his mission briefing had shown him a small cabin tucked away beside a stream. It was located high up the mountain, higher than any of its neighbors. The next closest cabin was more than two miles away. He likely could have been dropped down right in front of the cabin by his flight crew, but he hadn't wanted to rouse any sort of suspicion. It was imperative he get the mine maps and secure the help of the asset without alerting the Splinters holding Terror captive.

When he neared the edge of the tree line, he crept forward carefully and used a wide trunk as cover. He surveyed the area, noting well-worn paths in the dirt leading up to the rickety porch and another leading behind the cabin, probably to the stream nearby. He tapped the side of his goggles to change to the infrared setting and searched the area for heat signatures. There was only one inside the cabin. It moved back and forth. Pacing. Waiting.

Certain it was safe to move forward, he tapped his goggles, turning them off, and slipped them up to the top of his head. He let the moonlight above guide him forward, his boots crunching on twigs and dried grass. There was one window on the cabin, the glass illuminated by the flicker of a lamp or candle. The closer he got, the more he worried about the rundown shack. It had been sturdy once, but now, after years of neglect and the abuse of the environment, it was sagging and decrepit.

His focus was so intent on the cabin that he didn't even notice the thin, clear string until his boot had already hit it. Something rattled off to his left, and the light in the cabin window was instantly doused. He crouched down, hand on his weapon, ready to defend himself is necessary.

The hinges on the door squeaked, breaking the stillness of the night. He held his breath and listened, ready to draw his weapon if he heard the unmistakable click of the practically ancient firearms used by many of the settlers on the planet. Instead, he heard something he hadn't been expecting at all.

"Redwood?"

It was a woman's voice. Small. Nervous. Startled that the asset wasn't a man, he stood quickly. His gaze moved to the open doorway where he could only see the vague outline of a person. "Driftwood," he called out, his voice steady and strong and hoping to put her at ease.

"Careful," she urged. "You've hit the security lines." A flashlight switched on and illuminated the zigzag of clear fishing lines with silver cans dangling from them. "This way." She used the flashlight to show the path he needed to take.

He followed the guiding beam of dim light until he reached the porch where there were more lines stretched along the stairs. He hesitated at the base of them. In his culture, a man didn't walk into another man's home when his wife or daughters were there alone. Different settlements on the planet had different rules about these kinds of things. Some were much more conservative and patriarchal. Others were more progressive and relaxed. Not wanting to start off on the wrong foot, he asked, "Is your father home?"

"Right over there." The flashlight beam bounced to an area off to the left. There were two simple headstones visible. "Right next to my mother."

He was glad for the darkness and the way it lessened the awkwardness. "I'm sorry."

"There's nothing to be sorry for," she assured him. "It was an honest question. And," she added hurriedly, "before you ask, there's no brother or uncle or cousin or husband. It's just me."

He grimaced. Too many horrible things could happen to a vulnerable woman alone in the woods. Considering how young her voice sounded and the Shadow Force's reputation for breaking the rules when it came to their assets, he couldn't ignore the very real possibility she was just a kid. "How old are you?"

"Old enough to die saving your friend, apparently."

"I've seen kids die in war. There isn't a minimum age for dying."

"Nineteen," she said. "Is that old enough for you?"

He swallowed hard, wondering if that was meant to be flirtatious or serious. Erring on the side of caution, he chose not to follow up with the remark that burned the tip of his tongue. "Yes."

She waved her flashlight to beckon him inside. Skipping the questionable steps altogether, he used his superior size and strength to hop straight to the very top. He heard her sharp intake of breath, and he worried he had scared her. The porch whined under his weight, and he wondered if he was about to crash through weathered wood.

"Come inside, sir."

His gut clenched. She was being polite, but his brain

went straight to sex. Like so many of his kind, he had a dominant streak that yearned to be set free with a mate, but he refused to capture a woman in the Grabs. Occasionally, he would visit a poppy, but it was rare and only when he felt so on edge, he couldn't handle it on his own.

So, hearing this woman with her sweet, gentle voice call him sir heated his blood. He mentally chastised himself. She didn't ask for him to come here to seduce her. She was cooperating to help save one of his own.

"Watch your head," she urged, aiming the flashlight at the door frame. "You're a lot bigger than I expected."

He stifled a groan at the sinful image her words conjured. *Stop. Thinking. With. Your. Dick.*

Ducking to clear the door frame, he stepped into her cabin and shut the door behind him. This close, he caught the earthy, woodsy scent of her. She moved quietly, her footsteps silent on the floorboards. Anticipation built as he heard her strike a match. What did she look like?

A lamp flared to life. She had her back to him, but he could see the dark braid trailing down her back. She was absolutely tiny. Smaller than any of the other women who had been Grabbed by his friends. As she lit another lamp, more details were revealed to him. She wore ill-fitting men's clothing that had been patched and mended too many times. It hid her slim body from his interested gaze, and he tamped down the irritation at being denied.

When she turned toward him, he sucked in a surprised breath. She was beautiful. Her smile was shy but warm, and her eyes were bright and curious. She walked toward him,

her bare feet making no noise on the old wooden floorboards and threadbare rugs, and held out her hand. "I'm
Brook."

He cleared his throat and hesitated before taking her
small hand. "Cipher."

"Cipher." She tried out his name and grinned mischievously. "I wonder if I can solve you?"

He couldn't help it. He smiled like an idiot at her little
joke. Had he ever met anyone so adorable? She was sweet
and innocent and pretty and—*fuck. Fuck.* Of all the ways to
meet the only woman who had ever turned his head, it had
to be like this. She was an asset. She was off-limits.

"You can make yourself at home," she said, gesturing
to his headgear and the backpack he carried. "Do you want
something to drink? Was it a long walk?"

"Not that long," he replied, taking off his gear and placing it on the table that seemed to serve as the place she ate
and worked. "Water, if you have it."

"I do." She took a glass jar from a shelf and poured water from a pitcher into it. "Straight from our well," she said
as he handed it to him. "It's clean. Daddy was very careful
about where he drilled. It's one of the reasons he built so
high up the mountain. He wanted us clear of all the
pollution from the mines."

"You've lived here your entire life?" He sipped the surprisingly cold water and enjoyed the taste of it. "This is
good."

"I was born in that bedroom back there." She waved
her hand behind her. "My mother died when I was six, and

I spent the rest of my time following Daddy around the mountain and the mines."

"You were working in the mines as a child?" His protective instincts flared to life. He couldn't imagine allowing his daughter to climb through dirty tunnels and breathe in the dangerous dust kicked up by the constant chipping and digging.

"Your people send little boys to war at the same age," she countered with a shrug. "Life is hard for some of us."

"We go to the academy. It's a school. We're educated and trained. It's different than working in a mine."

"I wouldn't know. I didn't go to school."

It wasn't the first time he had met a woman from this planet who had never seen the inside of a classroom. To his mind, it was a complete waste of resources on a planet where sharp minds were desperately needed. How many girls denied the right to an education would have accomplished great things if they had only been born somewhere else?

"So, they told me that you want to see some maps of the Drowning Door?"

He frowned. "Drowning Door?"

"The mine used to be called Pit Seventeen, but after the accident, it got another name." She walked to the far wall of the cabin where someone had built a tall, wide cabinet with row after row of small but deep cubicles. The grid held dozens of maps, and she plucked the correct one and brought it back to the table. "The mine was bought out by some scumbag from The City who thought he knew better than the colliers."

"Colliers?" He slid onto the long bench opposite her at the table.

"Miners who belong to families that have been here since the first mines opened hundreds of years ago," she explained and moved two of the lanterns closer for better viewing. "They're experts."

"And what did the experts tell the scumbag?"

"That he was playing with fire," she said sadly. Rolling out the maps, she slid her pale hands across the yellowed layers of paper. "This mine was in three sections at the time but the accident happened down in the deepest part. The ventilation wasn't adequate, and the gases built up until a spark caused a horrific explosion. The owner had been warned about the gases and that there was water behind this wall here." She tapped a spot at the bottom of the map. "The explosion blew a hole in the rock, and the water gushed up and out and flooded the lower level. The workers on the top level dropped the emergency gate—a solid metal door—and sealed the water and most of their fellow miners behind it. Two hundred and seven miners died." She paused, and he glanced at her face, losing himself in the glow and flicker of the lamp on her skin. "My mother was one of them."

"I'm sorry," he said, genuinely sympathetic to her loss. "That must have been very hard for you."

"Harder for Daddy," she admitted. "I was so little I didn't really understand what had happened, and I still had my father so I wasn't alone. But, Daddy, on the other hand…" She shook her head. "He was all alone with a little girl he had no idea how to raise."

"And that's how you ended up in the mines with him?"

"Yes. He couldn't leave me here, and he didn't trust anyone to watch me." She eyed the window of the cabin with mistrust. "These woods aren't safe for anyone. Haven't been for a long time." Her gaze flicked to his. "The moonshiners and their stills bring all sorts of lowlifes up here, but it's the skin traders hiding out in the woods who are the most dangerous."

"Skin traders? Out here?" All intel he had seen claimed the sex traffickers operated mainly in The City.

"They move their victims through the old passes up to the flattops," she explained. "You can see the lights from the ships at night. I guess it's easier to land them up there where it's flat." She shrugged. "They mainly steal girls from the farms down in the valley. They say the farm girls fetch higher prices. They're healthier."

Cipher's stomach soured at the thought of young girls being ripped from their families and sold into sexual slavery in the far wilds of the galaxy. He had the same feeling when he watched the Grabs. Seeing his fellow soldiers and airmen chasing down terrified women, snatching them up and locking collars around their necks twisted his gut. As far as he was concerned, the sooner the old traditions died, the better.

"Anyway," she said with a little sigh and moved aside the top layer of the maps. "This is the most detailed map I have of the first level where they're holding your man."

"How recent is this?"

"Two years," she said, tapping the date scrawled in the lower corner. "It was my father's last job. He was hired to go in and lay some precision explosives to backfill the lower levels and make the top level safe for use."

"Your father worked for the Splinters?" His hackles raised at the idea that he was working with the enemy now.

"No, it was some bigwig out of The City. He came up to Black Pit Number Six where we were working and convinced the boss to loan out Daddy for the job. We went, did the work and left. Later, we found out the Drowning Door had been taken over by new management, so to speak."

"Do they know you have these maps?"

"They might. Daddy gave them his originals, but he always made a copy for himself."

He studied the map in front of him. It was useful but limited. He needed to know the proper layout of the mine to plan their attack. "Is there any way to get an updated, more detailed layout of this top level?"

"Don't you have scanners that can see deep inside the ground?"

Their advanced technology was no secret. "We do, but the Splinters have sensors all around the mine. They'll know if we use it. We need more recent intel, but we'll have to get it the low tech way."

She hesitated and dragged her lush lower lip under her top teeth. The sight inspired wild thoughts that he quickly shoved aside. "There is a way."

"But?" He sensed she was less than enthusiastic.

"I could go into one of the ventilation shafts to get into the air flow ducts here," she reluctantly suggested. "The metal ducts run above the reinforced ceilings. They house the lines for the fire suppression system and also carry cool air when the pumps are working. They're a tight fit for a grown man, but I'm small enough to get through them. I should be able to see into each area of the top level through the air flow registers."

Cipher hated the idea. It was very risky, and if she were seen or heard, Terror's captors would know an attack was imminent and either move or kill him.

"I know," she said quietly, as if sharing his thoughts. "It's dangerous."

"Very," he agreed.

"But it's the only way to get the information you need, sir."

Sir. His eyes closed briefly and wondered how the hell he was going to get through the rest of this meeting if she kept calling him that.

"If you expect me to lay explosives before the mission to free your man, a ventilation shaft will be my only way inside," she reasoned. "It might be better if I get in there and make sure the shaft and ducts are clear. It would be a disaster if I find out too late that I can't get my explosives where they need to be."

He quashed the immediate urge to reject her suggestion. His intense and unexpected attraction to her clouded his thoughts. *She's not yours. She's an asset. Use her.*

That was the problem. He wanted to use her assets but not in any way that the Shadow Force or his superiors would approve. He wanted to tie her up, take her back with him and keep her safe in his quarters. He wanted to hold her on his lap and comb his fingers through her dark hair while plundering her mouth. He wanted to hear her call him sir while begging him to let her come.

The loudest stomach growl he had ever heard interrupted his filthy thoughts. Across from him, Brook glanced down with embarrassment. "Sorry, I didn't have dinner tonight."

He frowned. "If you need to cook, don't let me keep you from eating."

Not even the dim light of the lamps could hide the deepening flush of embarrassment on her face. "There's nothing to eat." She lifted her gaze to his. "I ran out of scrip two days ago."

"What is scrip?"

"It's the payment we get for working in the mines. You can only spend it at the company store. The prices are outrageous, but we can't get supplies anywhere else on the mountain. I wasn't able to catch any fish this morning, and my traps were empty." She shrugged as if it were a common occurrence. "Just a few days of bad luck, but I'm sure tomorrow will be better."

Unwilling to let her starve even a minute longer, he reached for his pack and unzipped the long pouch on the side. He pulled out the emergency rations and piled them on the table. "This is enough food to last someone your size at least two weeks. You rehydrate them with water. That's all you need." He grabbed another handful of supplies from the pouch. "These packets are drinks. You pour them into a large glass of water. They're flavored like fruit, and they provide vitamins and electrolytes and other things you need."

She tried to push it back toward him. "I can't take your food."

He placed his hands over hers, feeling the soft heat of her under his fingers. He fought the strong desire to stroke her skin. "I'll refill my pack when I get back to my ship. You need these."

She hesitated before finally nodding. "Thank you, sir."

"You're welcome, Brook." At the sound of his deep, husky reply, she lowered her gaze. It was a naturally submissive pose that inflamed his alpha instincts and set his body on fire. *Want. Need. Take.*

She stood up to make herself a meal, and it broke the spell. She rummaged around behind him and returned to the table with utensils, a bowl, another glass jar and the pitcher of water. Taking her seat, she asked excitedly, "Which should I try first?"

Amused by her enthusiasm for rations, he picked through them until he found the one he wanted. "This is my favorite."

As he handed it over, their fingers touched, and her eyes shot to his, widening briefly as if she felt the same spark. She took the packet and set about making her first ration meal. When it started to bubble in the bowl, she almost bounced in her seat. "This is amazing!"

Had he ever been so pure? Even after everything life had done to beat her down, she seemed to embrace new and interesting experiences. Compared to her, he was a bitter asshole—and he didn't like that realization.

"It's a chemical reaction."

"I know," she murmured, her eyes fixed on the bowl. "I've just never seen it with food."

"But you've seen it in the mines?"

"Some of the sprays used to clean the ore and prep the walls for explosives bubble." She poked at the hot reconstituted dish of protein and vegetables in a tangy sauce. She brought her finger to her mouth and tentatively flicked her tongue at it. "Oh! This is delicious!"

She's going to kill me. If he saw her tongue one more time, he was going to lose it. His misbehaving cock was already pressing uncomfortably against the fly of his tactical pants. He shifted carefully and hoped she hadn't noticed as she was busy emptying the drink packet into her jar of water. She seemed disappointed when it didn't bubble or steam.

"Stir it," he recommended. "It makes it more palatable."

She followed his direction and noisily clanged the spoon against the sides of the glass. She glanced at him as if to silently ask if she had stirred enough, and he nodded. Before he could warn her about the taste, she grabbed the glass and took a long drink. A moment later, she put the glass down and made a terrible face while reluctantly swallowing. "It's awful!"

"It's an acquired taste."

"I've tasted heads and tails that were better than this!" She pushed the offensive glass away from her.

"What are heads and tails?"

"Moonshine," she explained, picking up her fork and diving into her dinner. "There are four different phases that come out of the still. The foreshots are poison. The heads smell gross and taste terrible. The hearts are the good stuff. Then comes the tails which is bitter and sharp."

"I had no idea moonshine was so complicated."

"It's complicated and dangerous." She seemed as if she wanted to shovel the food right into her mouth, but she eyed him before neatly taking a small bite.

"Like explosives," he remarked, looking away from her and back to the maps. "You're comfortable with them?"

"It's all I know. I was laying line with Daddy by the time I was seven. I started measuring out the powders and grains at eight. When I was ten, he taught me how to make the pastes and pack the tubes. The math came next. Figuring out what kind and how much explosive to use and where to place it to get the result you need." She gestured to a leather journal on the table. "My notes if you want to see them."

Needing to see if she was capable of the work that might need to be done, he opened the journal and thumbed through the pages. Despite her lack of formal education, Brook understood chemistry, math and physics. Her calculations were neat and clean. Her drawings were detailed. From the first job to the most recent in the journal, she showed a knack for numbers and chemicals.

"You're very good at this," he remarked, still turning pages. "If you were allowed to go to school, you could have been an engineer."

She snorted. "Mountain girls don't become engineers. They mine until their daddies marry them off and then they make babies and keep a home. That's it. That's the life."

"You're not married," he pointed out and closed the journal.

"Are you?" She didn't even try to hide her curiosity about his status. "Or Grabbed? What do you call it?"

"Mated," he said, clearing his throat. "Some of the men on my ship have chosen to follow your ways, though. They've had marriage ceremonies after a successful Grab."

"The fixer who hired me for this job gave me a choice," she confessed, seemingly desperate to talk about her options.

"Oh?"

"I can either take a pile of credits and a transport ship to the colonies with all the papers and permits I'll need."

"Or?"

"Or I can let one of you take me as a mate."

He swallowed hard at the thought of her wearing a collar and kneeling at his feet. The thought turned ugly when he thought of another man claiming her. A jealous flare burned his belly as he imagined another man seeing her smile when he came home or listening to her moan and whimper while she writhed beneath him in their bed. That jealousy soured to fear for her when he considered some of the men who might take her. She was so sweet and gentle, and the wrong man would break her and ruin everything special about her.

"You should go to the colonies," he said gruffly. "Take the money and run."

She frowned. "You don't think I would be a good mate."

He thought she would be a wonderful mate, but refused to say it aloud. Instead, he grunted. "You couldn't handle a man like me."

"Oh." Her reply was soft and small. "I see."

She didn't, but he wasn't about to explain what he meant. She would be safer far away from this mountain and the men on his ship.

"Go to the colonies and get work as an apprentice. You'll make a good life for yourself there. You can make your own choices for once."

Her expression serious, she nodded. "Yes, sir."

Her obedient reply sent another wave of need through him. He wavered for a heartbeat, wondering if she wouldn't be safer with him. Safer, maybe, he allowed, but she had her entire life ahead of her and should be allowed to make her own decisions without the pressure of men like him.

"Tell me about the mine." He brought their meeting back on track. "What are all these different areas?"

"Ventilation shafts. Backfill access. Drilling platforms. Ore shaft. Ore removal. These lower levels are all blocked off by the earlier flooding and the blast Daddy arranged to make it safe for use." Her finger pointed out the various places she described before sliding to the top of the map. "There are access points to the ventilation shafts here. They're small and covered with grates, but I can wiggle into and out of them."

He didn't like the idea of her dangling by a rope or dragging herself out at the end of her excursion. Too much could go wrong, but if the dimensions on the map were correct, she was the only person he could imagine being small enough to fit through the shafts.

"Can you get into them tomorrow?"

"Yes."

He reached for his pack and withdrew the communication device he had brought with him. He showed her how to power on the unit, find the satellite signal and contact the Shadow Force unit on his ship. "You will contact us before you go into the mine and when you make it back to the cabin."

"Yes, sir."

He handed her another device. "This camera will capture images."

"How?" She turned it over in her hands, marveling at the small size and thinness. "This tiny thing is really a camera?"

"It is." He held it up and snapped a photo of her curious face. He showed her the screen on the back. "See?"

"Oh, this is fantastic!" She happily examined the device and the image he had captured of her. "How do I get the images off this and up to you?"

He taught her how to upload images to the communication console and send them to the Shadow Force unit. He
made her practice using her own photo. Torment had
asked him to get identification of the asset, and this was an
easy way to do it.

"This probe is flexible. It has a tiny lens at the end that
can capture clear and detailed images if you're access is
very small."

"It's tinier than my finger!" She seemed astounded by
the piece of technology she held. Her expression turned
serious. "I can do this," she assured him. "I won't let you
down, sir."

"No, I'm sure you won't," he agreed. Reluctant to leave
her alone in this cabin but aware of the time crunch he was
under, he finished up what he had come here to do. She let
him take the maps and thanked him again for the rations
before walking him to the door. Staring down at her,
wondering if this might be the only time he would ever see
her, he said, "Brook, be careful. Your life is your own, and
if you aren't comfortable risking it, you can change your
mind. Do you understand?"

"Yes, sir."

"Promise me that you will abort your mission if it's too
dangerous."

"I promise, Cipher."

With a final, clipped nod, he turned his back on her
and left the cabin. Every step he took tried his willpower.
Every fiber of his being screamed for him to turn back,

snatch her up and bring her back to the *Valiant* with him. Somehow, he managed to muscle through that dark desire and make it back to the rendezvous point.

As the ship lifted away from the planet and ascended to vast coldness of space, he couldn't help but feel that he had just made the worst decision of his life.

Chapter Two

BROOK LEANED BACK against the locked door and tried to slow her racing heart. In all her days, she had never felt what she did right now. The moment she had heard his voice in the darkness something inside her had flared to life. Commanding. Strong. Patient. His voice promised safety and security.

When she finally saw his handsome face, she had been struck by an unexpected realization. The reason no man had ever interested her was because she had been waiting for *this* man. Cipher. The sky warrior who came to her for help in saving his friend.

The man who had turned down her clumsy attempt at hinting that she was interested in more from and with him.

Groaning with embarrassment, she pushed off the door and started tidying up the cabin. What did she expect? That a man who could have any woman he wanted would take her? All the painful memories of teasing and bullying from her childhood reared their ugly heads. She had always been too skinny, too short, too dirty and too poor. Her hand-me-down men's clothing never fit correctly. Unlike the other girls she knew from the mining camps, she had never blossomed with curves.

Standing by the table, she let her hand drift down the front of her body, gliding over her small breasts and flat belly. Her hips weren't any better, and her bottom wasn't the sort that turned heads. Plain. Boring. Simple.

Maybe he was right. Maybe her future was in the colonies. Yet, the idea of going so far away where she knew no one terrified her. She had been alone in her cabin for seventeen months. She was used to the silence and emptiness that surrounded her. She never felt lonely here.

But the colonies? She would be utterly alone. She wasn't sure she was brave enough for a new start like that. Where would she live? Where would she work? Would she make friends? Find someone to love her? Would she ever have the family she yearned for so deeply that it made her stomach ache and her chest constrict?

Feeling dejected and overwhelmed, she finished tidying up and locked away the rations and equipment he had left her in a secret cabinet. She couldn't risk someone breaking into the cabin and finding any evidence that a sky warrior had been here. Even though the drink was terrible, she made herself finish it rather than toss it out and waste it. She gagged at the end of it and wondered if all of their food tasted like this.

As big as Cipher was, she didn't think that was likely. He didn't look like he had ever missed a meal. She couldn't help but wonder what he looked like under his uniform. She had seen naked men before, but she doubted she had ever seen one that compared to him. The men who stripped out of their soiled mining clothes and jumped into the river near the outlet of the pit to rinse off the grime and sweat of a hot day were wiry and lean. She suspected Cipher had muscles in places she had never even imagined.

Feeling ridiculously hot but foolish for her infatuation with a man who would never want her, she doused the lamps and moved through the pitch black of the cabin to the bedroom. She peeled out of her pants and socks but kept her shirt before sliding under the frayed and faded quilt her mother had made so many years ago. She curled onto her side and closed her eyes, listening to the soothing sounds of the forest until she finally fell asleep.

In the morning, she woke early, before sunrise, and immediately started hacking. The dry cough that plagued all miners had started to wake her more mornings than she cared to count. Like everyone who worked in the dust and damp, she expected to die young of Purple Lung. There was no use worrying about it. It was something to accept as inevitable.

She had another one of Cipher's rations after she changed into clean clothing for the day. Not wanting to lose her nerve, she contacted the spaceship as instructed, grabbed her small pack of climbing gear, her mining helmet and the camera Cipher had given her. She locked up the cabin and trudged off into the cool darkness, working her way down the trails until she reached the ridge just above the Drowning Door.

Low on her belly, hidden under brush, she surveyed the area. From her position, she had a clear view of the ventilation shaft she had chosen as her entryway into the mine.

This one had been all but forgotten. Brush had grown overtop and dirt was mounded against the sides. There were other shafts, easier to access and wider, but they were too close to the front of the mine's opening. She would rather deal with the tight squeeze of the smaller shaft than risk running into the men patrolling the front of the mine.

There had been rumors up and down the mountain that the Splinters had taken it over and were using it as a base. Always too nosy for her own good, she had investigated those rumors for herself shortly after hearing them. It hadn't taken her long to determine the rumors were true. She had counted less than twenty men that first day. Unable to stay away for long, she had come back every few weeks to check on the situation.

Not knowing what to do with her information, she had gone to the only person her father had ever trusted—an older woman down the mountain in Yellow Moss Holler named Miss Kay. Her father had never been political, but he had done small jobs here and there for the Red Feather. They were a secret group who worked against the planet's oppressive government. Sometimes, the Red Feather worked with the sky warriors who patrolled above the planet and were locked in a protracted civil war with the so-called Splinters.

Miss Kay had taken her information and relayed it to someone else above her in the chain. Soon, Miss Kay started asking her to go to different spots around the mountain to get a better look at the mine. She counted vehicles and men, noted the numbers of deliveries and their shapes and sizes. For her work, she was given a few pieces of extra scrip to use in the company store. There wasn't as much work in the pit where she was employed so the little bit of extra income had kept her from starving the last few months.

And, now, here she was, scooting forward on her belly to the entrances of the ventilation shaft. Miss Kay had introduced her to the Red Feather fixer named Danny who had given her the chance to escape life on the mountain. All she had to do was help the sky warriors obtain enough intel to plan their rescue mission and, possibly, plant some explosives as a diversion. If she did those things, she would be given a new life in the colonies or as a mate to one of the sky warriors.

Just not the sky warrior she had embarrassingly flirted with last night.

Her face flamed as she replayed the memory of her awkward attempt to show her interest. She hadn't ever flirted before, hadn't ever wanted to really. She had felt impossibly naïve and silly, but there was no going back to change her first impression. Not that it mattered anyway. He had been abundantly clear that she wasn't the sort of woman any of their men would want.

Ignoring the stab of pain at that thought, she listened carefully before cautiously lifting the grate covering the forgotten vent. She placed it on the grassy area to the right and covered it with twigs and leaves to make sure it wouldn't glint in the sun and rouse suspicions. Peering down into the shaft, she noticed the lights that were supposed to illuminate the space had long ago died. She wasn't afraid of the dark or tight spaces so it didn't bother her as much as it might have someone else.

With her small pack almost flat on her back and the camera Cipher had given her dangling around her neck, she put on her helmet and tucked one leg and then the other into the shaft. Her boots found the rusty rungs lining one wall of the shaft. Slowly and trying to make as little noise as possible, she descended down into the darkness until the pale light of sunrise faded to nothing and the black silence of the shaft enveloped her.

At the end of the ladder, she stepped onto the flat platform and crouched. She flicked on the lamp attached to her helmet, expecting to see the turn of fan blades. Judging by the amount of rust on the blades, they hadn't been maintained. She gave one of them a push, and it didn't budge. Glad that she had one less problem to handle, she stepped back and unzipped her pack of climbing gear. She quickly pulled on the harness and ran her fingers over the ropes and anchors inside the pack to reassure herself she had everything she needed.

Ready to descend deeper into the ventilation shaft, she squeezed through the space between the two large blades and moved into the ventilation duct. The chipped stone walls of the duct were dirty and damp. Air wasn't moving properly anymore, and the humid, dank wetness was allowing mold and mildew to breed. Her knees and hands slid in the slippery gunk, and she grimaced at the foul smell surrounding her.

While the smell and feel of the duct was disgusting, she was more concerned about what she would find up ahead. If the shaft didn't have proper airflow, was there a blockage ahead? A cave in?

When she reached the end of the straight duct, she had a choice to slide down one incline to the right or the other to the left. She flatted out on her belly and let her head hang over the edge the platform. She closed her eyes and breathed in deeply from each side. On the right, the air felt warmer and smelled of decay and death. To the left, the air seemed cooler and fresher.

She settled on the left and shimmied until her feet were hanging over the edge of the platform. She maneuvered her pack off of her back and onto the stone floor in front of her. Using the lamp on her helmet, she looked along the walls until she found the metal anchors permanently fixed to them. She took her time fixing her anchor ropes and tested them three times before sliding back and rappelling down the shaft to the next level. It was a nearly straight drop, and she didn't look forward to the climb out that awaited her.

At the next level, she reached across the shaft to the square access window into the actual metal ducts that carried air through the mine's upper section. She tacked her ropes to the metal wall of the duct using a magnet and carefully wiggled out of her harness, boots and belt. She couldn't risk the metal clanging or scraping against the bottom of the duct as she crawled. She put her things inside her helmet and placed them next to her ropes.

Although the camera would take the photos she needed, properly surveying the ducts and rooms below would require pencil and paper. She reached into her pack for both and then cracked a glow stick from her pack. It was rated to last twelve hours, but from her experience in the mines, she knew it was more like eight. Nothing that came out of the company store was worth a damn.

Holding the stick between her teeth, she used her body length as a measurement. She carefully counted the lengths until she reached the first bend in the duct. After scribbling the measurement on the paper, she followed the bend into the next length of straight ductwork.

The metal surrounding her was slick with mildew and stank of rust. The smell made her gag at first, but the slimy film made it easier for her to move without making noise. The fire suppression system supply lines ran the length of the duct works. The pipes were old and failing, dripping water steadily into the ducts. She wondered why the men living in the mine didn't seem to care about the mold and mildew and filthy water dripping down into their living spaces.

As quietly as possible, she eased toward the first register. The grille was caked in filth, but she was able to see into a dimly lit room below when she pressed her face against the metal slats. Inside the room, there were stacks of canned and dry goods and medical supplies. She worked the tiny finger-like probe between the slimy grates to get a clear recording of the room's contents before continuing her journey.

The next grille was over a room packed to the brim

with weapons. Certain Cipher would want to know exactly what was in this makeshift armory. Worried the photos she was taking might be inadequate, she wrote down any numbers or designations she could see on the crates of weapons and hastily sketched the others that were mounted on wall racks. The thought that Cipher might be injured if she failed to bring back the best intel made her extra diligent in her note taking.

Satisfied she had captured everything in the room, she moved along to the third register. Even before she reached it, she could hear voices. She hastily tucked the glow stick into her back pocket to block the light from reaching the grille. Holding her breath, she eased forward until she could see into the room.

A strange smell tickled her nose. Rather, it wasn't strange in the sense that it was unknown. It was strange in the sense that it didn't belong here. The smell of damp hay wafted out of the room below, and it made her slightly woozy to breathe the barely there scent.

Down in the room, men who looked similar to Cipher in size carted silver crates out the door. All of them wore masks, and she understood that whatever that faint smell was, it was dangerous.

"Hey, Doc!" One of the masked men below shouted. "What's the street value on this?"

"None of your business," another man answered, his voice muffled and angry. "And don't fucking call me doc!"

Not sticking around to breathe in whatever was in those canisters, she snapped pictures while holding her breath and moved along until the voices and the smell faded.

After making her notes, she continued her survey. Room after room after room yielded information. Most were quarters. One was a kitchen and mess hall. There was a communal bathroom and shower area that was surprisingly clean considering the state of the mine. The laundry facility wasn't much but she took photos and notes anyway.

When she followed the duct along the lower portion of the horseshoe shape, she discovered the more important areas of the Splinter outpost. The first three registers overlooked a large space that seemed to be use as their logistics center. The walls were covered in digital boards and screens. Tables in the center of the room were piled with models and projections. Certain this was the most helpful intel she could gather, she took her time and made sure she was thorough gathering photos and scribbling notes.

Once she moved beyond the logistics area, she discovered the cells. The stench filling the ducts made her stomach pitch violently, and she bit her arm to keep from vomiting. She overpowered the urge to retch and slithered forward in the goo and grime until she could see into the first cell.

When she saw the naked corpse hanging from its wrists, she gasped and shut her eyes. Like a scared child, she hid her face. It wasn't the first dead body she had seen, but it was the most gruesome.

Summoning her courage, she forced herself to look. It

was a man. Or had been. A sky warrior if she had to guess. His bloated body and mottled skin made it hard to determine what he had looked like in life. He still had his sandy hair and a scraggly beard. If there were markings or tattoos on his body, she couldn't see them anymore.

Was this the man Cipher wanted to rescue? No, she decided quickly. It couldn't be him. Their man was confirmed to be alive only days ago. This man—whoever he was—had been dead for a long time. A week or more, if her prior exposure to death and her understanding of decomposition was correct.

It felt wrong to photograph the corpse. She didn't like the idea of betraying the privacy of a dead man, but she was sure that the sky warriors would want to identify him if they could. Maybe he had a family, a wife and children. They deserved to know he was gone.

When she was finished, she closed her eyes and murmured a prayer for his eternal peace. She hadn't been raised religious like the farmers in the valley, but she had always found comfort in the idea that there was a place where souls rested after the suffering of this world.

Determined not to let Cipher's friend die like this man, she crawled as quietly as possible. The middle cell was empty, but up ahead, there was an occupied cell. The harsh bellow of pain confirmed it.

Eyes wide and stomach trembling, she reluctantly moved forward. A man was being tortured somewhere in front of her. Whatever they were doing to him must have been utterly depraved. He shouted in agony, his voice hoarse as if he had been screaming all day.

Not sure if she could stand to see what was happening, she hesitated at the grille. The idea that this man was alone and suffering gave her enough courage to finally look.

And she instantly wished she hadn't.

Dangling by his ankles, the man had blood running down his feet and legs and dripping from his fingers. The bloodied pliers on a silver tray of horror filled in the blanks. They had torn out all of his finger and toenails.

The torturers weren't stopping there. She watched, terrified, as his tormentors attached metal clips to his genitals and tongue. Her panicked gaze followed the cords attached to the clips. They led straight to a generator. Before she could even process what they planned to do, the monster closest to the generator flipped the switch.

The captive sky warrior jerked like a fish on a line. His entire body snapped, and an inhuman growl erupted from his throat. She gulped down a sob and pressed her fist to her mouth, painfully smashing her lips against her teeth to stifle the cry that threatened to escape.

What can I do?

The fire suppression system.

Desperate to stop the torture, she risked her life without a second thought. She grabbed the pipes above her and pulled until her muscles screamed and her vision swam. Gritting her teeth, she felt the first spray of brackish water hit her face. She closed her eyes and kept pulling until her arms were shaking.

Finally, the old pipes cracked. The loss of integrity

caused the pressure in the pipes to burst other segments down the line. Water that smelled like a latrine in summer began to flood the duct. She kept her eyes closed and mouth shut as the water rushed around her, spilling through the grilles into the rooms she had surveyed.

Down below, the heinous assholes who had been enjoying their work shouted as they got a taste of electrocution. She grinned evilly as they screamed. The water pouring over her might be filled with bacteria that would make her sick, but it was worth it to see those two suffer.

The sky warrior—Cipher's friend—showed his incredible strength and determination as he sat up while still dangling from his ankles. She hadn't even known it was possible for any person to use their muscles in that way, especially not a person who had been starved, beaten and tortured. He used his bound hands to knock the clips from his body, dropping them into the water and ensuring the men who had been hurting him wouldn't be walking out of that cell.

As if he had some sixth sense, he turned toward the grille where she watched. She gasped at the gnarly, puckered scar where his eye should be. This man had known so much pain. It didn't seem fair that one man should be expected to survive so much.

He might have been blind in one eye, but he zeroed in on her. Maybe he could see the shadow of her or the faint light of the fading glow stick. Somehow, he knew she was there.

She wanted to reassure him that he wouldn't suffer much longer. For a brief moment, she wondered if she could rescue him, but he was too tall and broad shouldered to fit through the grille or the duct. She wasn't strong enough to haul him out of the shaft either.

No, he would have to stay. Hopefully, his rescue wouldn't be too far away. Still, she felt like crying as she waved at him through the grille and then started her slow slog through the water and filth. The thought of saving him fueled her trek out of the mine's duct work and into the ventilation shaft. She ignored the burn in her arms as she dragged herself up the vertical incline to the first platform. She thought of the degradation and cruelty he had survived as she climbed rung after rung after rung.

When she finally emerged from the ventilation shaft, the sun had started its glide toward the horizon. After replacing the grate and covering her tracks back into the woods, she finally dropped down onto her bottom and hung her head between her bent knees. Exhausted and shaking, she allowed herself only a short break to drink deeply from her canteen and a moment to relieve herself in the bushes.

Her break finished, she clambered to her feet. Soaked in dirty water and covered in slimy filth, she stumbled home, determined to do whatever she could to save the one-eyed soldier.

Chapter Three

*I*S *BROOK STILL in the mine?*

Troubled thoughts occupied Cipher's mind as he worked his way through a pile of circuits that had been accumulating in his office. The smell of solder tinged the air as he tried to occupy his mind with menial tasks. All day, he had been in a cantankerous mood. Raze had finally called him on his bullshit and excused him from SRU physical training for the rest of the day.

According to Torment, Brook had sent a message before leaving her cabin. There hadn't been a single word of communication since. He glanced at his watch for the thousandth time and let loose a frustrated sigh. Where was she?

The worst images flashed before his eyes. Had she been captured? Was she being tortured? Raped? What if she had gotten hurt in the mine? Was she bleeding out in a shaft too far underground for anyone to hear her? What if she had run into a pocket of gas or a flooded section? What if her exit point had been blocked by a cave-in?

He hissed and snarled an expletive as the tip of his soldering iron burned his finger. He glared at the offending wound. He hadn't burned himself like this in more than ten years. Cursing his carelessness, he set aside the iron and grabbed an instant ice pack from the bottom drawer of his desk. He cracked and shook it before pressing the cold gel against his aching finger. It would blister and rupture and be a nuisance for the next few days.

"You okay?" Raze hovered in the doorway of his office. The boss's gaze drifted to the ice pack. "You burned yourself?"

Cipher nodded, in as much disbelief as Raze that he had done something so stupid.

"Okay. That's enough." Raze stepped inside the office and shut the door behind him. Leaning against it, he asked, "What the hell is wrong with you today?" When he didn't immediately respond, Raze guessed, "Is this about the errand you ran last night?"

Because this area wasn't secure, Cipher kept to the coded language. "Yes."

"Is it about the package that needs to be picked up?"

He shook his head. "The package is still where we were told it would be."

"The courier then?"

Calling Brook a courier seemed like an insult. She was going far above and beyond the expectations. "Yes."

"Is he not trustworthy? Not up to the job?"

"She," he said and finally met Raze's gaze.

The bastard smiled. "Oh, I see."

Groaning, Cipher dropped back in his chairs and tossed aside the ice pack. He rubbed his face. "That's never happened to me."

"What? Attraction?"

He nodded. "It was…instant. Strong."

"That's how it was with Ella." Raze narrowed his eyes. "You've really never been attracted to a woman like that?"

He shook his head. "I was starting to think something was wrong with me. I've enjoyed time with other women, but it never felt like this." He noticed his knee was jumping up and down and consciously stopped. "See what I mean? I'm a mess."

"She must be some woman."

"I think she is," he admitted. "She's too brave for her own good. She's going to get hurt, and she's all alone down there." He rubbed his face again. "She didn't even have food. I left her all of my rations, but what happens when she runs out?"

"She does whatever she's been doing to survive," Raze reasoned. "She'll probably be on a trip to some new place before she runs out, Ci. Unless you've got other plans…?"

"No." His answer came harsher than he had intended. "She's young. She should have the chance to live her life."

"Did you ask her what she wants? If you trust her to handle this errand, shouldn't you trust her to make her own decision about her future?" Raze pinned him place with a stare. "What if she feels the same way about you? Maybe she wants to be a wife, to have a family, to live somewhere safe where she's protected and will never go hungry again."

"Maybe," Cipher conceded.

His counsel given, Raze switched topics. "You hear

about the cargo ship that crashed near Willow's Tears?"

Cipher nodded. "Any survivors?"

"A few," Raze glanced at his watch. "That crew was lucky to fall so close to one of our medical missions."

"Vaccination campaign?"

"Yeah. Also basic dental and medical," Raze said. "It was a team from the *Mercy.*"

"Do they know what brought it down?"

"Mechanical malfunction is what I heard." He winced. "There will be hell to pay for the mechanics who cleared that ship for flight."

Cipher hummed in agreement.

"I'm headed back to quarters," Raze said. "We're off rotation until they call us in for the errand. Don't stay here playing with your toys too late. You're no good to me fatigued."

"Yes, sir."

Alone in his office, Cipher kept his mind on the tasks at hand and off of the pretty miner who had turned his world upside down. He didn't want to let himself think about the possibility that Raze was correct. He had been alone so long. It was the life he chose when he made the decision never to Grab.

He was fine with that decision most of the time, but some nights, staring at the ceiling in his cramped quarters, he yearned for a partner in life. He wanted what Venom and Raze had with their mates. He wanted someone to greet him after a dangerous mission. He wanted someone to care about him in the way only a woman could. He wanted all the secret touches and smiles.

And he wanted children. Daughters only, if he had his way. Curious and bright little things that would never be taken away from him and thrown into the meat grinder of the military industrial complex. Loving and kind girls he could help raise into strong, intelligent women who could follow their dreams and be whatever the hell they wanted to be—doctors, engineers, teachers, scientists, wives and mothers.

His watch vibrated with an alert. It was Torment calling him down to the Shadow Force sector. He fought the urge to leave his desk a mess and run. He tapped a quick message to Torment and tidied his office before heading to the elevator.

When he arrived at the Shadow Force sector, he used the chip implanted in his wrist to gain access to the highly classified unit. Pierce spotted him as he came through the second set of doors and waved him toward the war room. He found Torment there, leaning over the brightly illuminated table where holograms hovered.

Next to him, General Vicious stared at the same holograms. Terror was his best friend, and the two men had been through some serious shit straight out of the academy. Vicious had never given up hope that Terror was alive. He had insisted that his best friend was too much of a miserable asshole to die in captivity.

"Sir," Cipher greeted his superior officer with a salute.

"Specialist," the general replied in his deep, rumbling voice. "You prepped the asset very well."

"Your girl did exceptional work today," Torment remarked. "She's thorough and deliberate. She would make a hell of a recruit into our local assets training program. She's got the making of a first class operative."

The idea of Brook being thrown into the dangerous world of covert operations made his chest constrict. Hiding his emotion, he calmly replied, "She didn't seem too interested in that sort of work."

"Too bad." Torment flicked his hand at a hologram file and sent it to the screen on the wall behind him. "She orchestrated a diversion to protect Terror, killed at least two of theirs and got out of the mine unseen."

Cipher's incredulous gaze jumped to the screen. He couldn't see anything but a blue haze. The sound of breathing and something sliding accompanied it. "Was she recording the whole time?"

"She must have hit the record button on accident. There was plenty of battery life, and honestly, the video intel is much more helpful than the still images."

A mangled shout of pain filled the war room, and Vicious visibly tensed. The video jumped as if Brook had been startled. She seemed to hesitate before finding the nerve to keep moving. When she reached the next grille in the bottom of the duct, she maneuvered the camera probe into place.

Cipher wanted to look away from the screen, but he forced himself to watch as those pieces of Splinter shit tortured Terror. He estimated Terror had lost twenty percent of his body weight, most of it muscle mass since he had always been so lean. There didn't seem to be an inch of skin that wasn't bruised. There were scabbed and still oozing cuts and shallow stab wounds. Burns dotted his limbs. They had even taken his toenails and fingernails.

Behind the camera, Brook gasped as the assholes down below started to torture Terror with electric shocks. The camera's view shifted, and he couldn't see anything but darkness. Her heavy breaths and desperate groans filtered through the speakers.

Just as he realized she was pulling on something, the high pressured hiss of water echoed in the duct. Pipes clanged, and water splashed loudly. The camera's view turned misty and droplets of water clung to the lens. She turned in the duct and looked down into the cell.

The two torturers who had been working over Terror flopped like fish as the current of their poorly grounded generator zapped them. Terror used what strength he had to lift himself into a sitting position while still suspended and ripped free the clips they had used to electrocute him. He seemed to know she was in the duct because he looked right at the camera. It wasn't clear from the recording, but the movement of the lens convinced Cipher she was waving at Terror.

The recording continued playing in the background as Torment drew his attention back to the table. "She uploaded extremely detailed drawings and measurements along with a message."

The recording on the screen stopped as Torment flicked his fingers and sent another file to it. Cipher stiffened in shock at the sight of her. She was covered in filth from head to toe. Whatever she had encountered in the ventilation shaft and ducts had been far worse than he had expected. Thinking back to her reluctance when she proposed going into the system, he felt extreme guilt in sending her down there alone.

"I don't know how much longer your man has," she said urgently. "You have to get him out as quickly as possible—or else he'll end up like the dead man."

"What dead man?" Cipher asked, his gaze still focused on Brook. He wanted to bring her to his quarters, strip her down and wash her before feeding and cuddling her in his bed. The urge was so strong he could practically feel her soft skin on his.

"Devious."

Cipher tore his gaze away from the screen. "I thought he was deep undercover with the Splinters."

Vicious nodded gravely. "He was."

"You don't think Terror…?" He couldn't finish the thought.

"No," Vicious answered forcefully. "He would die before he betrayed a single one of us."

"The mole?" he guessed.

"That's my concern," Torment acknowledged. "There have been too many coincidences on the ship and in the field. There is a double agent on the *Valiant*."

"How do we even start to narrow the list of thousands of men and their mates down to a workable number?" he wondered aloud.

"We're working on it," Torment said.

Cipher understood that meant he wasn't going to learn any of the details until they needed his help. Whatever the plan in the works was, it likely violated privacy regulations and other laws meant to protect the men who served. He wasn't looking forward to implementing it.

"How soon can you mount your rescue?" Vicious asked as he leaned forward on his hands and studied the schematics the computer program had created from Brook's intel. His massive forearms rippled, and not for the first time, Cipher wondered how the general managed not to harm his delicate mate when they were intimate.

"We're going down tonight. After the crash so close to their hideout, they'll want to relocate. I want us in that mine before sunrise."

Cipher glanced at the still image of Brook on the screen. "Does she know?"

"I sent orders before I messaged you. She will be planting explosives to cause a cascade of failures. The Splinter forces will evacuate through the front of the mine—the only working entrance and exit—and we'll slaughter them. They'll bring Terror out with them when they flee or we'll go inside to get him. Either way, he's coming home with us."

He had no doubts about that. He did, however, have concerns about Brook. She had just spent nearly twelve hours in a cramped tube, crawling and climbing. Even if she managed to rehydrate and fill her belly with rations, she might not be able to recover in time for the precise work of planting explosives.

"You're worried about the asset?" Torment noticed his pensive turn. "Don't be. She's tenacious. She wants off that mountain. She'll do whatever it takes to get what we promised her."

"That's what worries me," he grumbled.

Vicious cocked his head as he looked at him. "Holy shit, Cipher. I never thought I'd see the day that you were lovestruck."

Cipher frowned. "I'm not lovestruck. I'm just concerned for her. She's young and small and underfed and alone and…" His voice trailed off as Vicious grinned wider and wider. Growling, he said, "It's not like that. I barely know her."

Vicious shrugged his massive shoulders. "I saw Hallie for a few seconds before I knew she was the one. I ran her down, collared her and brought her home. When you know, you know."

"I'm not going to run her down and collar her."

"You don't have to," Torment interjected. "We offer all female assets the same deal. In exchange for their help, they can choose a man interested in having them. If she's interested in you and you're interested in her…"

"No." Cipher slashed his hand through the air to put an end to the discussion.

Vicious smiled. "You know, there are vacant quarters on the same floor as Venom and Raze. I could have them reassigned before you touchdown tomorrow morning."

Cipher groaned and rubbed his face. "Can we please

get back to the mission and stop worrying about match-making?"

Both men nodded, but he could tell this was far from over. Once the general had his mind set on something, it was impossible to sway him otherwise. Torment was sneaky and underhanded. The two of them working together would be nothing but trouble.

Yet, as Cipher helped Torment plan the assault, he couldn't help but wonder if this was exactly the sort of trouble he needed.

Chapter Four

COUGHING INTO HER bent elbow, Brook took one last look around the cabin. If she survived planting the explosives, she would leave the mountain forever today. She had packed those few precious items she couldn't bear to leave behind in her pack, but there were so many more important things she wanted to take with her. The quilt, especially, was hard to leave, but it was too heavy and bulky to fit in the one bag she had been allotted to bring.

Knowing she was on a strict schedule, she blinked back the tears that burned her eyes and left the cabin. She traipsed through the darkness, letting the moonlight guide her feet on a path she committed to memory. As she trekked toward the Drowning Door, she ran through the list of tasks the man called Torment had given her. Place explosives. Set timer. Move to a safe distance. After explosion and the completion of the mission, meet at the rendezvous point.

She had been hoping to speak with Cipher again, but it had been the other soldier who had answered her transmission. Torment lacked the warmth and kindness of Cipher. He had been all business, and it had been painfully clear to her that she was expendable to him. Beyond planting and successfully detonating the explosives, she was of limited use.

Glad for the long walk to mine, she tried to work out the nervous energy vibrating through her body. Shaking, sweaty hands would be dangerous while handling the explosives. Last night, after bathing and having a double serving of rations, she had calculated and recalculated the amount of explosives she needed. Then, in a surge of anxiety, she had redone the calculations seven more times, just to be sure.

The explosives were neatly packaged in her pack, ready to be assembled and placed once she was in the ventilation shaft. She had a timer, but also planned to place a secondary line as switch. She wanted redundancies in place.

As she drew near to the ventilation access, she placed her backpack holding her belongings on a tree branch. She checked her watch. Of all the things she had ever been given by her father, the watch was her most precious. He had saved for years to get one for her. It was waterproof, shatterproof, illuminated and even had a glow function. It had all the bells and whistles, and she had never needed them more than she did right now.

She set a timer for the moment the explosives were due to detonate. Low on her belly, she crawled forward and scanned the area she needed to access. There was just enough moonlight to let her see that it looked exactly the way it had when she had left it. Even the small stones and twigs she had placed along the edges of the grate were right where they should be.

Satisfied her entrance hadn't been discovered, she exhaled a steadying breath and crept forward. Resolute in her intention *not* to die today, she carefully removed the grate, buckled her helmet in place and climbed into the shaft. Balancing on the second rung, she hauled the grate back over the top of the shaft. She couldn't risk an unexpected patrol finding it gone and stumbling onto her existence.

Down and down she descended, following the same route she had taken yesterday. Before she secured her anchor ropes, she checked her watch and was relieved to see she was ahead of schedule. Hooked into the harness, she climbed backwards down the sharp incline of the shaft until she reached the the section directly below the duct system she had accessed the day prior.

She swung herself across the shaft, paying no mind to the unending black drop below her. She racked her ropes into place and ratcheted her harness to give her the stability she needed to work with the explosives. Taking her time, she measured the spot where she intended to plant them and marked it with chalk.

The hand cranked drill she used to bore the hole was freshly oiled and spun as quickly as her arm could rotate the crank. It was quiet work, only the sound of her breaths and the twinkle of falling rock echoing around her. She stopped to measure every fifty rotations, marking the width and depth until she finally reached the required specs.

Inhaling a steadying breath, she retrieved the first set of explosives and packed them into the hole. She didn't set the timer just yet or activate the backup trigger switch. There were still two more sets of explosives to place, both farther down the shaft. The cascade effect of the three explosions would cause the desired outcome.

Checking her watch, she calculated how much time she had left to place the remaining explosives and get out of the shaft. She would have at least seventeen minutes of leeway, if she stayed on her current course.

She loosened the harness lock and lowered herself to the next spot. She repeated the same process, being deliberate in her drilling and measurement and placement of the explosives. Satisfied with the second, she moved down to the third and completed the task the same way.

Heart racing, she checked her watch and saw that she was still slightly ahead of schedule. She swallowed hard before setting the timer on the third explosive pack and activating the backup trigger. When it was done, she climbed her way to the second and first packs of explosives and did the same.

Dry mouthed and anxious, she freed the ropes she had racked earlier and swung across the shaft. Her legs trembled as she climbed up steep rock wall to the first platform. Her shaking hands fumbled with her anchor ropes and hooks, wasting precious seconds she needed to get clear of the blast radius. She ignored the fear building in her gut and moved methodically through the shaft to the access ladder.

Her heart raced so fast now she could practically feel it slamming into her ribs and sternum. Her ears were filled with the sound of pounding blood, and she fought to catch her breath as she climbed higher and higher.

When she reached the grate, she hesitated. Was that a footstep? She hastily switched off the light on her helmet and listened. *Crunch.*

Someone or something was out there. Dried leaves and dead twigs crunched under something heavy—a boot or paw. In that moment, she would have gladly faced off against a mountain lion or a wolf, anything but a man.

Frozen with indecision, she decided to wait. With every passing second, she brought herself closer to being trapped in the blast. If she moved the grate and climbed out, she was either going to be an early morning snack for one of the massive predators on the mountain or a new torture victim for the Splinters.

The footsteps grew louder and closer. She gripped the rungs and prayed her death would be quick. Closer and closer. Louder and louder. She squeezed her eyes shut and waited for the inevitable.

Snort.

Her terrified gaze snapped to the grate where two big, rusty brown eyes stared back at her. *Shit!* It was a bear! A huge, stinking and very curious mountain bear.

Now she was faced with another predicament. She didn't have the strength to lift the grate with a massive bear paw planted on top of it. If the bear thought he had his next meal cornered, he would stay there until he figured out how to move the grate. Once that happened, his razor-like claws would shred her in one swipe.

She glanced down the ladder and wondered if she had

enough time to make it back to the ducts she had flooded yesterday. She could, conceivably, hide in the ducts toward the front of the mine until the explosions detonated and then jump down into main level of the mine once all the Splinters evacuated out of the front entrance. One quick glance at her watch told her that idea was impossible. She was fast, but she wasn't that fast.

"Please, Mr. Bear, go away," she whispered urgently. "I will give you all the food rations in my pack if you will let me out of here."

The bear snorted against the grate again, and she flinched away from the wet blast of foul air. He scratched at the grate, his claws clanging against the metal. She wrapped her arms around the ladder and silently cursed at the universe for teasing her with a chance to escape the mountain only to be eaten alive by a bear.

The bear had its yellow teeth hooked around the metal grate, slobber dripping down onto her helmet and shoulders, when it suddenly stopped. The bear unhinged its jaws and let the grate fall with a clatter. It rose up on its paws and sniffed the air. With a lumbering growl, it stepped away from the grate and trotted off into the woods.

Crying and shaking, she grasped the slippery, dented grate and moved it out of the way as quietly as possible. Like a groundhog searching for predators, she lifted her head through the hole and scanned her surroundings. The musky stench of the bear still lingered, but there were no other signs of trouble.

Quickly and overwhelmed with relief, she climbed out

of the shaft, replaced the grate and checked her watch. Her stomach dropped. She had less than four minutes to get to the spot she had picked!

Terrified the bear was out there waiting for her and worried that whatever had drawn him away might be a danger to her, she headed into the woods in a burst of speed. She snatched her backpack from the branch where she had left it and sprinted away. The threats to her life seemed to be mounting. The explosives. The bear. Whatever had caught the bear's attention.

Sunrise had just started to lighten the horizon. From what Torment had explained to her, his men would already be in place by now. That meant Cipher was somewhere on this same mountain or hovering nearby in one of their invisible crafts. The concern she had for herself was only surpassed by her concern for him.

When she reached the old tree she had chosen as her lookout spot, she jumped as high as she could and grabbed the closest branch. Swinging up her leg, she hooked it over the branch and hauled herself up onto it. She stood on the branch, balancing precariously, and hopped to the next branch. The muscles in her arms and chest burned as she climbed to the correct vantage point, but she pushed away the pain and kept moving.

Seated on a thick, sturdy branch high on the mountain, she panted and checked her watch. Twenty-three seconds! She snatched her mine pack into her lap and grabbed the secondary switches. If the timers failed, she had to be ready.

She kept the blinking switches capped and glanced at

her watch to check the countdown one last time. Eleven seconds!

Switches in hand, she stared down at the back end of the Drowning Door and counted silently. Ten, nine, eight, seven, six, five, four, three, two, one...

The ground rocked beneath the tree. A few seconds later, another wave of rumbling struck and then another. She flicked off the secondary triggers and stuffed them into her pack. She retrieved a pair of small binoculars and trained them on the visible ventilation shafts. Smoke and dust billowed out of them.

She looked toward the front of the mine. Already, men were running out of the entrance. Clouds of purple and black dust followed them. She searched the distance for Cipher and his fellow sky warriors, but a sudden shift in the ground below had her scrambling to stay on the branch she had chosen.

When she had taken the job, she had warned Miss Kay that an explosion in an old death trap like the Drowning Door was a risk. There was no telling how much erosion the water had caused or how much destabilization her father's blasts had caused years earlier. It was all a best guess scenario.

My best guess was wrong.

Somewhere in the mine, the blasts had triggered a cave-in. The amount of dust and smoke pouring out of the vents and the front of the mine could only be explained by a collapse in one of the sections. The top of the mine—the sloped hillside below, hadn't shifted so the cave-in must have come from lower down in the second or third abandoned levels.

Panicked and worried for the one-eyed man, she turned her attention to the front of the mine. More of the Splinter terrorists were racing out of the mine now. She scanned them, desperately hoping to see the man who needed to be rescued.

There!

Stumbling between two Splinter men, he emerged from the mine's entrance just as naked as the day he had been born. Bruised and bloodied and covered in soot, he struggled to stand on his own two feet. One of them looked badly swollen, and she ached for him, wondering how any person could be strong enough to survive that kind of suffering.

A blast of red shocked her. She gasped as the men on either side of the one-eyed sky warrior dropped to the dirt. Their heads had been obliterated by bursts of plasma. Suddenly, all around the kidnapped man, the Splinters fell. Precision shots killed them as easy a sniffing out a candle.

Until there was only one left.

The harsh looking man who had been left alive reached for a knife at his belt, probably to slit his own throat, but he was quickly shot in that hand. Before he could grab the weapon holstered on his other hip, he shouted in pain as a second shot rendered that hand useless, too.

Sky warriors dressed in black uniforms rushed forward and took control of the scene. Just like that—it was all over. Days of planning, and the mission was competed in seconds of high-risk activity.

She sagged against the tree trunk and let the tears come. Relief, fear, pride, anxiety—the emotions flooded out of her. She had accomplished something truly great today. She had helped free a man. She had made it possible for him to be rescued without injury to any of his comrades. Other than Miss Kay and the men who had helped her plan it, no one would ever know what she had risked or done here today. It was a secret she would take to the grave.

It was a secret that was going to buy her a new life.

As she climbed down from the tree, she considered the decisions awaiting her. She could take the offer to become a mate to a stranger. She would have a home, a husband and the family she craved, but would she be happy? Was she capable of learning to love a stranger? What if he was more like Torment and less like Cipher?

It was a chance she couldn't take. The thought of being tied to an unkind brute was too much for her to risk. There was also the realization that someday Cipher would find a woman he liked well enough to keep. She wasn't sure she could handle seeing him with another woman. He wasn't hers—had never been hers—but her heart had set itself on having him.

To the colonies it is.

Away from the mountain. Away from the mines. Away from the sky warrior she had stupidly become infatuated with. Away from the only life she had ever known.

She trudged along her new path, arcing off to the left of the mountain and using the compass on her watch to guide her to the coordinates of her rendezvous point. The longer she walked, the more unwell she felt. She brushed her hand to her forehead, feeling the heat there.

Do I have a fever?

The heat radiating off her forehead wasn't only from the physical exertion of the hike. Her throat burned when she swallowed, and she noticed a strange ache in her joints. She felt queasy and could barely handle drinking the water in her canteen.

The water!

That foul water she had been showered with while trying to create a diversion was the likely culprit. All her life, she had been trained to never drink unknown water, to smell it and boil it first. As much as she had tried not to get that water in her mouth, some of it undoubtedly had made its way inside her.

Hoping the ship coming to pick her up had a medic on hand, she trudged forward, her pace slow and her steps heavy. She grew hotter and more nauseated and had to blink and close one eye to focus on her compass. She hadn't veered off course yet, but it was only a matter of time if she wasn't careful.

Feeling a surge of nausea, she braced herself on the nearest tree and heaved up the water and remains of her morning rations. Her head pounded as she retched into the grass, and she fought the desperate need to curl up on her side on the ground and sleep.

"You have to keep moving, Brook," she urged aloud. "You have to keep moving, Brook."

"Now, come on, honey, don't be so hasty. You can sit a little while with us."

Feverish and sick, she hadn't been paying attention to her surroundings. She spun around and came face to face with four leering men. She could smell them despite the distance, and her stomach soured at the stench of alcohol, sweat and filth. Skin traders.

The one who seemed to be their leader smiled evilly, showing off brown and broken teeth. "Sweetie, you lookin' mighty sick. Why don't you come back to our camp over there and let us give you some first aid?"

The true meaning wasn't lost on her. Nervous but trying to project confidence, she stood as tall as she could despite the stomach cramps. "Thank you, but no. I'm meeting some friends."

"We can be your friends," another man insisted and stepped closer.

"I'm not interested in new friends."

"You hungry? We just killed us a bear! Might fine eatin' if you're interested."

"I don't eat bear meat," she said, eyeing the men slowly moving into positions around her. Like all skin traders, they had their tactics down pat. "You shouldn't either unless you plan to cook it a long time."

The leader waved off her suggestion as if he weren't the least bit worried about catching worms and dying. Instead, he said, "How about a nice, soft bearskin rug? You can sleep on it in front of our fire tonight. How's that sound, honey?"

"Like a bad night's sleep," she replied and stepped around him. Another man moved into her path. She refused to let him stare her down and met his gaze. "Move!"

"Sorry, girlie, but I'm not movin' anywhere." He reached out with his dirty hand to touch her braided hair, and she smacked his hand away. Instead of deterring him, it seemed to excite him. He licked his grimy lips and snatched her braid, tugging hard and forcing her against his paunchy, stinking body. "I like 'em with a little fight in 'em!"

She tried to break free, but she was so dizzy and weak. Feeling woozy, she sagged against her attacker. All of the hopes and dreams that had been fueling her trek evaporated.

This was it. Everything she had risked, and she was going to be gang raped and probably die on this mountain. Grimly, she hoped they killed her when they were done. She couldn't survive the life of a sex slave sold to a space brothel.

Tossed over the man's shoulder like a sack of potatoes, she closed her eyes and tried not to get sick again. The rush of blood to her head caused a pounding headache. Slowly, she lost consciousness, feeling as though she were falling into the endless chasm of a mine.

Chapter Five

C IPHER WIPED THE purple dust and black soot from his face with a wet disposable cloth from the pack he kept in his tactical vest. Working in the mine for the last six hours had been hot, miserable work. All of the intel had to be inventoried, placed in the chain of custody and stored away in the lock boxes for transport back to the *Valiant*. Everything in the mine was now covered with a thick coating of grimy, oily dust, and the ventilation system was completely blocked so the air flow was practically nonexistent.

Sweating and uncomfortable, he wondered how the hell the people who lived on this mountain could work like this day after day. Brook's decision to risk her life to set those explosives made much more sense to him. Her entire life had been spent underground, toiling in the darkness and breathing in the irritating dust. Of course, she wanted to escape. Of course, she wanted a new life above ground with clean air and warm sunlight.

"That the last of it?" Pierce asked as he mopped at his neck.

"Last box," Cipher confirmed. "What's the plan when we're done?"

"Big boom." Pierce mimicked an explosion with his hand. "We'll seal this up tight." He glanced around the mostly empty room. "We probably should have kept the asset around for the final bang. She's damn good at what she does."

"She's probably on her way to the colonies by now." He grunted and picked up the last heavy box of intel. "Her rendezvous window has already come and gone."

"She might have decided to come to the *Valiant*."

"I sure as fuck hope not," he grumbled and hefted the box out of the room.

"So, it is true," Pierce said while following him out of the mine. "You *are* hot for the asset."

"Can we not do this right now?" He glared over his shoulder. "It doesn't matter if I'm hot or cold. She's gone. She's safe. It's done."

"You know there's nothing wrong with feeling attraction to the girl, right?" Pierce caught up and fell into step beside him. "She's an adult."

"Barely," he remarked with a grunt.

"Oh, spare me," Pierce replied testily. "That woman has proven herself. She's not a child. She's not a child. She's brave and smart. She adapts to high-stress situations. She's resourceful. This isn't some sheltered girl from Prime. This is a woman who has stood on her own two feet and survived. She doesn't deserve to be discounted just because she doesn't have enough months on a calendar."

Cipher suspected Pierce's rant was about more than his reluctance to chase after Brook. He had heard rumors about Ella and Dizzy's friend who lived in the tunnels under The City. She had gone missing after a raid and hadn't been seen or heard from since. She had saved Pierce at least once, and he seemed to have decided he owed her a debt.

Or, maybe, he wanted to pay her back with a collar and his care.

He started to ask if that's what this was about, but Pierce stepped away to answer a message coming through his earpiece. Cipher continued on his way, stowing the final box on the cargo transport loader and signing off on the chain of custody with the load master and the forensics tech. When it was done, he stepped toward the medic station for a cold bottle of water and ice packs for his neck.

"You need a ride back with us?" the medic asked and indicated their craft idling nearby. "Saw the rest of the SRU team head back with Torment."

"I might," Cipher said, wondering if Pierce needed him on scene much longer. He had done what he came to do and was looking forward to a shower, a meal and collapsing into his bunk.

Pierce strode toward him, his usual arrogant swagger gone, and his face a mask of worry. Cipher's gut clenched, and he asked, "What happened?"

"Look," Pierce sighed, "there's no easy way to say it. The girl? The asset?"

"Yeah?"

"She never made it to the rendezvous point."

His heart skipped a beat. Refusing to panic, he tried to

think logically. "Did they check the cabin?"

Pierce nodded. "The fixer scoped it out. It's locked up, and there's no sign of our girl anywhere."

He turned his gaze toward the mountain. All manner of possibilities flashed before him, some better than others. She might have gotten hurt while traipsing back up the mountain to the rendezvous point. She might have been attacked by wildlife. She might have been caught by a Splinter lookout after she placed the explosives. She might have been abducted by moonshiners or the skin traders she mentioned.

His gaze flitted back to the mine, and he grimaced. She might have been caught in the ventilation shaft before the explosions. The thought of her mangled and crushed threatened to drop him, but it was the possibility that she may have been taken that worried him most.

"If she was in the mine, we would have found her when the techs did their radar sweep," Pierce reasoned, as if reading his mind. "If she was taken by the Splinters, she would have been brought out when they fled the explosions."

"Your guys had drones onsite?"

"We did."

Cipher rushed to the command ship and ran up the ramp through the cargo deck to the logistics unit. He shoved a tech out of the way and sat down in front of his console. Tapping at the touchscreen, he activated his access to the highest level of security clearance with a swipe of his wrist over the chip reader.

Once he was inside the logs, he pulled up the recorded feed from before the explosion. There wasn't a clear shot of the ventilation shaft access point she had used, but there was enough of it in the wide shot that he was able to zoom. The images were fuzzy, and he silently cursed the shithead tech who had configured the camera on the drone.

"Is that a fucking bear?" Pierce asked, leaning over his shoulder for a closer look at the grainy image.

"Yes." He swallowed down the very real fear that he was about to watch that gigantic creature maul Brook to death.

"Fuck me," Pierce murmured in awe, his gaze glued on the screen and the sight of the massive bear jumping and clawing at the grate covering the ventilation shaft. "If that thing gets through the grate—"

"I know," he ground out, not wanting to even go there.

"Wait. Look!" Pierce pointed out the bear lifting up on its hind legs to sniff the air. "It's found something that smells better."

Cipher exhaled a ragged breath as the bear lumbered into the woods and disappeared. Despite the blurriness of the image, he could tell it was Brook who crawled out of the shaft, replaced the grate and then staggered off into the woods behind the bear. He had no idea where she was headed, but it was likely a higher vantage point, somewhere she could see the operation at the mine and use backup detonation triggers if necessary.

"You'll lose her after this," Pierce said, following her movement into the forest with his fingertip. "But, if we know she went into the woods, she went missing somewhere between here and the rendezvous point. Where was that?"

Cipher swiped the screen and pulled up a map of the terrain. He inputted the rendezvous point coordinates that were in her asset file and plotted them onto the mountain map. "Here."

"Shit," Pierce cursed. "That's a long way on foot. She didn't seem wounded," he added. "She must have been in fairly good condition when she set out to meet her pickup."

"Maybe," Cipher agreed uncertainly. His brain raced as he tried to come up with a way to find her. He could send drones out to search for heat signatures, but there were a lot of animals on the mountain. It would take time to sort out human and animal signatures. He could use drones to search for her clothing colors, but she was wearing drab neutral tones that melded into the forest like the most perfect camouflage.

What else could he try? *Think. Think.*

"The camera and the comm device," he shouted. "They have trackers in them. If she has them with her, I'll be able to find her."

"It's worth a try."

While he searched for the identification numbers of the equipment she had been issued, Cipher let his mind wander to the most likely possibility. She was probably hurt and bleeding somewhere on the mountain. The second mostly likely possibility was that she had been captured by someone else. If they found the gear on her, they would know she was worth something. They might take her to the Splinters, but there would be a bigger payday if she was brought to one of their outposts or ships.

He waited for the trackers on the devices to populate the map and refused to think about what would happen if she had been grabbed by skin traders. She was young, healthy and beautiful. The amount of money some sick fuck would pay to use her body was astronomical. *I have to find her.*

"There," Pierce said and tapped the screen. "Shit, she's high up that mountain."

"Which means I better start running," Cipher declared as he rose from the uncomfortable chair. "I need a rifle and some gear."

"You don't have clearance." Pierce wasn't rejecting his request. He was pointing out the facts. "You'll get dragged in front of the review board if you chase after her alone."

"Probably," he agreed, "but I'm not leaving her there."

Pierce studied him intently and then nodded. "I'll get you some gear and try to retroactively get permission for your side mission."

"But?"

"You'll have to bring her back to the ship and collar her," Pierce stated. "They'll forgive you for going after a bride."

Cipher nodded, fully aware that was the one option to keep his ass out of the clink. He logged out of the system and followed Pierce to the armory of the command ship. Once Pierce unlocked the door, he grabbed the requested gear and handed it over. "Rifle. Side arm. Survival pack."

Cipher made quick work of strapping on his gear. As he set up his watch to track the equipment Brook had, he asked, "If I need a quick exfil?"

"I'll make sure you have one," Pierce promised. "You can use one of our secure channels. How about five?"

"Five it is." Cipher adjusted the setting on his headgear and pressed his earbud into place. "I'll keep you updated."

"Don't get killed," Pierce ordered, trailing him out of the armory. "If you do, Raze will kill me. Torment will have to kill Raze. Venom will kill Torment. Terror will kill Venom. It will be a shit show of death. Stay alive and bring back your girl."

"I'll do my best."

Quick on his feet, Cipher ran into the woods. He wasn't the fastest man on the SRU, but he wasn't the slowest either. He had always been better at long distances and endurance races. Running up a damn mountain fit both of those criteria. Even so, he reminded himself that he was no good to Brook if he arrived worn out and unable to defend or carry her.

Slowing his pace, he worked his way through the trees and brush. The thinner air was hard on his lungs, but he remembered his training and kept his breaths deliberate and measured. Up and up, he climbed, checking his watch and staying on the straightest path to where the equipment was. He could only hope the camera and comm device were still with her.

She's five hours ahead of me. At least. What the fuck has

she been through in that time?

The terrible answers to that question conjured spurred him forward. He kept a steady pace as he cut his way up the mountain. He scanned his surroundings as he moved, trying to maintain situational awareness. The last thing he needed was to stumble onto a predator like that bear that had tried to snatch Brook out of the ventilation shaft.

A smell that didn't belong in the forest caught his attention. He stopped moving and closed his eyes, breathing in deep. It was a smell any human would recognize: vomit. Not the least bit squeamish, he followed the scent to a tree a few yards away and crouched down to examine the drying splatter. He recognized the rations in the slurry. He had thrown them up enough times during the more excruciating physical training at the academy to identify them.

Why was she sick? Was it overexertion? Or an illness?

He stood and glanced around the area. His gaze fell on the trampled grass. He took a few steps and crouched down to study the bent and crushed blades. The tips of his gloved fingertips moved over the depression in the shape of a boot. A man's boot. A heavyset man, by the looks of the track.

He walked the perimeter of the crushed grass and found three more tracks belonging to men and one set of very small boots that belonged to Brook. He noticed the way her tracks ended right near a convergence of the men's boots.

They picked her up and carried her out of here.
Shit.

He followed the tracks of the men out of the clearing and into a nearby camp. He recoiled at the horrible stench of blood and offal. Disgusting sounds—crunching and licking and wet growls—met his ears. Raising his rifle, he stepped forward carefully. His footfalls were as quiet as he could make them, and he managed to sneak up on a pack of ravenous wolves tearing apart the carcass of a bear.

He couldn't be sure, but it looked like the same bear from the ventilation shaft. Had it smelled the scent of the men cooking at their camp? Followed the scent of bacon or sausage all the way up here looking for a meal? Whatever the reason, the bear had made a big mistake.

Looking at the kill, he could tell the men had packed out some of the meat. With four men, they should have been able to take even more than they had left behind. The hide would have been worth a lot of money with fur traders, and the claws would have been a novelty some rich asshole in The City would have loved to own. So, what had sent them on their way before finishing the job?

Brook.

They must have heard her getting sick. They probably decided she was worth more than any bear hide or trophies. So—where did they take her?

Not turning his back on the wolves, he crept backwards toward the campsite. He spotted a red miner's helmet in the brush on the edge of the site. He knelt down and picked it up, turning it over and seeing her name scrawled inside. Tucked inside the headband was a folded piece of sweat stained fabric. He pulled it free and opened it to find beautifully embroidered words.

Bless My Heart. Keep Safe My Soul. Give Me Clean Air Down In The Devil's Hole

The piece was obviously precious to her, and he stowed it away in a pocket of his vest for safekeeping. He clipped the helmet to the back of his pack, but not before running his fingers over the divots and scratches. How many times had she been close to death in the mines? How many near misses had she survived? After all of that, he couldn't let her life end this way. He had to find her and save her.

With renewed purpose, he followed the human boot prints away from the campsite to another set of tracks. They belonged to some sort of vehicle with rugged wheels. The tracks would be easier to follow, but the vehicles meant she would be farther away from him. He couldn't hope to run nearly as fast as the vehicles could move, but he had to try to catch up. Surely, they would have to make camp before sunset. He could close the distance and find her if they camped for the night.

Only stopping for water and to relieve himself, Cipher followed the blinking dots showing the location of the equipment. It was still moving, but he kept an eye on the horizon, certain that the movement would stop as sunset approached. One foot in front of the other, he trekked up the mountain with a single thought in his head: Brook.

The air grew cool and damp against his skin. He eyed the sky, wondering if there might be rain. He hadn't spent enough time in the outdoors to understand how to read the weather like some of his fellow soldiers. The pilots were much better at taking one look at the sky and predicting what awaited them. What he wouldn't give to have a pilot at his disposal right now.

He passed through a haze of cool mist. The rain he worried about never manifested, but the mist made it hard to see his surroundings. He slipped twice, his boots sliding in mud and dead leaves. He managed not to fall too far and clambered back to his feet. Running through the mist, he wiped at his face, clearing the sweat and water from his eyes. Ahead, the sun started to set and he lost the pale gray light. He grabbed a headlamp from his gear bag and fixed it into place.

Just as he was about to start jogging again, his watch vibrated. He glanced down and noticed the dots tracking the devices had stopped moving. With a groan of thanks, he marched forward into the hazy twilight. Soon, the twilight deepened to full night. He kept walking, letting the beam of his headlight illuminate a slim path in front of him. He checked his watch to make sure he was on track, not wanting to get off course in the confusing darkness.

The mist finally stopped more than an hour later. Overhead, the clouds cleared away, and the three moons orbiting the planet filled the woods with enough light that he could turn off his headlamp. He was getting close now, so close he could smell the campfire. A short while later, he spotted the orange glow of it.

With every cautious step, he drew nearer and nearer to the campsite Brook's kidnappers had chosen. The rowdy voices of the men echoed off the trees. From the sound of it, they had been drinking. Heavily. Probably that moonshine Brook had told him was made up here. Four drunk men and one captive woman were bad odds for her. Very, very bad odds.

Hiding behind a massive tree, he glanced around the trunk and took in the scene. Four men, two of them grossly out of shape, one wiry and lean and one strong and muscled, stood around a campfire. The fattest one tended chunks of meat suspended over the lowest part of the fire. The others traded a jar of moonshine between themselves, sloshing the alcohol into their mouths and laughing like madmen.

When his gaze finally found Brook, he had to bite back the roar of indignation that threatened to erupt from his chest. She had been stripped naked and had both wrists tied above her dangling head. She slumped forward, the poorly tied and anchored ropes failing to support her body weight. The joints in her arms and shoulders were hyperextended, and it wouldn't be long before she dislocated something.

Her breasts and belly were coated in a slick sheen of saliva and vomit. Her skin seemed unnaturally red, and he realized she was very sick. She likely had a fever and dehydration. How much longer would she last without medical care?

"I don't much care how much she stinks right now," the fat blond announced to his friends. "I've fucked worse!"

The fattest of them, the man who seemed to be their

leader, pointed at the blond with the wickedly sharp knife he was using to poke at the cooking meat. "You leave her alone, Ted. We'll get three times as much for her if that tight little pussy of hers ain't been poked yet."

"She's got two other holes I can use just fine," Ted leered and advanced on her.

"Are you deaf or just dumb?" the leader shouted. "I meant what I said. Leave her be."

"She might be contagious," the wiry one commented before taking a long swig of moonshine. "Whatever she's got, I don't want."

"It's a water fever," the brute interjected matter-of-factly. "I seen it a dozen times when I was a kid. She drank some bad water, and now she's poorly."

"She gonna die?" the leader asked. "She's useless to us dead."

"Depends," the brute replied with a shrug. "Most of them die, but if she makes it through the night, she'll be fine."

"Should we give her something? Water? Moonshine?"

"No shine," the brute said with a shake of his head. "Clean water will help."

"What about those sky warrior rations she had? We could fix her up one of those."

"Hell no," Ted refused. "We can get good money for those! Let her have some water out of the canteen. If she dies, she dies."

Cipher had heard absolutely enough of their bullshit. Although he wanted to kill each man slowly and with his own hands, he understood the situation. He was outnumbered, and she was at risk of being hurt if he tried to fight them. Instead, he took up a firing position against the tree, bracing himself to stay steady, and lifted the rifle to his shoulder. He sighted each man down the scope, deciding which one would get a bullet first and then the order of the others.

Once his decisions had been made, he didn't hesitate. He fired four rapid shots, striking each man in the head. They crumpled and dropped right where they stood, their wounds soaking the ground around them with blood. Adrenaline spiking, Cipher flicked on the safety and returned his rifle to his back. He hurried into the campsite, sparing a glance at each man to be sure they were good and dead.

When he reached Brook, she had found the strength to lift her head. Her eyes were glassy, but she smiled when she saw him. "Cipher," she said, her sweet voice reduced to little more than a croak. "You came for me."

"Of course, I came for you." He wrapped one arm around her body to support her slight weight and reached up with the other to slash away the ropes with the knife he'd yanked from his belt sheath. Her arms flopped forward, and she sagged against him. Not caring one bit about the mess on her skin or the smell that clung to her, he embraced her tightly to his chest. "You're my girl, Brook. I'll always find you and keep you safe."

She didn't reply. She had gone completely unconscious, her poor body pushed beyond what it could handle. He lowered her to the ground and started to strip out of his gear. As he cleaned her with the disposable wipes in his pack, he called in and requested an exfil. With that done, he pulled off his vest and peeled out of his uniform shirt. He gently maneuvered her into the shirt, granting her what modesty he could, and then wrapped her in an emergency blanket, the thin foil-like material crinkling and glinting in the firelight.

Certain she was safe, he gathered up her backpack and the equipment that belonged to the Shadow Force. He searched the bodies for any useful intel and crammed what he found into the pockets of his tactical pants. He left the fire burning for now but planned to douse it once their transport arrived. The flames would keep predators away from the fresh kills and served as a beacon for the ship.

With his back against the nearest tree, he hauled Brook into his lap and tucked the blanket around her legs. He held her close and hoped his body heat was enough to keep her warm. Even with her fever, she trembled from the chill of the mist on her bare skin and the cool night air. His gaze moved to the sky, and he silently urged the ship to fly faster.

He finally had the mate he had always wanted, and he couldn't bear the thought of losing her now.

Chapter Six

O F ALL THE ways she had expected her kidnapping to end, it definitely hadn't been cradled in Cipher's strong arms as he carried her onto a spaceship. The strange metallic sheet he had wrapped around her crinkled as he hefted her through the cargo bay and into the main cabin. Medics ran toward them and started barking questions. So weak and confused, she barely understood them.

"I think she's been infected with bacteria or a parasite from contaminated water," Cipher said as he placed her on a gurney. "She was in the same mine as Terror. She busted open an old fire suppression system line. I'm not sure how long that water was stagnant."

"If she was with Terror, she has the same thing they're treating him for on the *Valiant*," one of the medics remarked. "Let me reach out to Risk. He'll tell us how to get her stabilized."

The entire ship started to vibrate, and she blindly flailed for support, grasping onto Cipher's gloved hand. He leaned over her, pulling off his glove, and stroked her face with his bare fingers. "Look at me," he commanded. "You're okay. We're taking off. It will be a little rough for a few minutes while we ascend and then we'll level off. The gurney is locked in place, and you have a harness keeping you on it."

"Stay," she said weakly. "Please."

He ran his thumb along her chin and smiled encouragingly. "I'm right here with you."

A medic reached up over the gurney and snapped a carabiner similar to the one on her climbing harness to an overhead mount. It allowed him to work without sliding around as the ship tilted sharply up towards the sky. Cipher slid a few inches but held onto the gurney with his free hand to anchor himself in place. He had taken his promise to stay with her seriously.

She watched his handsome face, marveling at the way he had come for her. When the skin traders had nabbed her, she had been sure that was it. No one ever escaped them. No one ever saw the girls and boys and young women who went missing ever again. Sick and unable to fight back, she had accepted she was either going to die on that mountain from whatever horrible disease had taken hold, or she would slit her own throat before letting a stranger rape her.

But here she was, on her way to space, safe with Cipher. He had tracked her down and saved her, and she would never be able to repay him.

Looking up at him through her bleary vision, she sensed he didn't expect any sort of payment. He wasn't that sort of man. His worried expression and reassuring caresses convinced her that he had come for her because he felt the same pull she did. Their gazes clashed, and she knew in that moment that she had been wrong about what happened between them at the cabin. He wanted her as much as she wanted him.

Overwhelmed but feeling secure with Cipher at her side, she stopped fighting against her exhaustion and let go. She drifted away to the sound of Cipher's voice, certain she would wake up to him at her side. Just as she expected, he was right there next to her when she came to in a brightly lit room.

"Brook, my name is Risk. I'm the physician who will be treating you tonight." Like the other sky warriors she had met, he towered over her and had wide shoulders and muscular forearms. He wore a different type of uniform, a utilitarian sort of top and pants.

Cipher ran his thumb along the back of her hand, drawing her attention. "Risk is the best. He'll take very good care of you, Brook."

Overheated and cramping, she nodded. Before she could ask if anyone else saw the thin snakes crawling out of the ceiling, Risk asked, "Have you claimed her?"

Cipher brushed damp strands of hair from her eyes and forehead. His tender gaze helped her ignore the slithering snakes for a moment. "She's mine."

"Do I have your authorization to treat her?"

"Yes."

Risk unlooped a strange device dangling around his neck and stuck two ends in his ears. As he leaned toward her, he said, "When she's better, we can arrange to put her through the bride protocol."

Not liking the sound of that but much more concerned about the spiders now crawling on the ceiling, she blinked rapidly. When they didn't disappear, she managed to speak, her voice rough and dry. "Can we move to a room without snakes and spiders?"

Risk's expression changed from relaxed to alert. He leaned closer and examined her eyes with a light so bright it hurt. He pressed the back of his hand to her forehead, his skin covered in a strange glove made from thin material like rubber. "We need to get her fever down. She's hallucinating. Much more of this and she'll seize."

Cipher was suddenly pushed away from her side, and her hand grasped futilely for him. More medical personnel crowded around her bed, and she closed her eyes to avoid seeing the writhing mass of snakes and spiders on the ceiling. Her sick brain was losing its grip on reality, and she couldn't bear to look.

Something cold and stinging rushed through the vein on her arm, and she gasped in shock. Almost as quickly as the pain registered, sleep claimed her. She fell into a bizarre world of fever dreams she couldn't escape, like a trapped miner in a cave-in. Desperate and terrified, she struggled through a black void of pain and heat.

In her delusional mind, she crawled through a maze of small and dark tunnels before dropping into a pit of snakes and spiders. Her body slid down through the pile of creepy things, and she dropped out of the bottom, falling and screaming and flailing until she hit a deep pool of filthy water. She fought her way to the edge of the pool and climbed out of the water onto a ledge of sharp rock that cut her hands and knees.

Stumbling forward into another tunnel, she emerged into a room filled with shiny canisters. The scent of hay and grass overwhelmed her, and she staggered forward, desperately searching for a way out of the room. When she found it, she tripped into the next space and landed at the bloated feet of a corpse. She scrambled away from it and out through the open door opposite.

In the shadows, a man held out his hand. He was trying to help her, but she couldn't reach him. He started to ascend, lifted by a harness toward a light in the sky, and she screamed for him to wait, to not leave her behind. In the last glint of light before he disappeared, his scarred face came into view. The one-eyed man waved at her before disappearing.

With an agonized shout, Brook bolted upright. She panted, clutching at her chest and trying to make sense of her surroundings. *Sick. Hospital. Spaceship.*

"Easy," Cipher urged in that commanding yet gentle way of his. She glanced to her left where he sat in an uncomfortable looking chair and held her other hand. "You're safe."

"Cipher," she croaked, her throat raw. "Sir."

His eyes closed briefly and then he was moving, sliding into the bed beside her. He shifted her so easily, lifting and arranging all the tubes attached to her arms and tucked into her nostrils. As if they had been cuddling together every day of their lives, he cradled her close and pressed her ear to his chest, letting her hear the soothing thud of his heartbeat. Ever so carefully, he brushed his hand along the tangled strands of her hair. "You gave me a terrible scare."

"I'm sorry, sir." She breathed in the clean, fresh scent of him, wondering whether it was his soap or aftershave that made him smell so good. "I didn't mean to drink that awful water or get kidnapped."

"Hush," he admonished gently. "None of that was your fault." He shocked her by pressing a fleeting kiss to her forehead. "You're a hero now. Everyone on the ship wants to meet the miner who saved Terror."

"I'm not a hero." She swallowed nervously at the thought of anyone thinking she was special like that. "You're a hero. The men who fight beside you are heroes."

"You can't argue your way out of this one." He swept his fingers down her cheek. "You're a hero. Accept it."

She didn't know how to accept that sort of praise. Uncomfortable, she changed the subject. "His name is Terror?"

He pulled away enough to meet her curious gaze. "They didn't tell you when you took the job?"

"No."

"Oh. Well—yes. His name is Terror. He's arguably the greatest Shadow Force operative in this lifetime. He's also the best friend of the general of this ship, of our commanding officer. Vicious would have done anything to get him back."

"He must be very special," she decided. "Terror, I mean."

"He is," Cipher agreed. After a few heartbeats of silence, he said, "But he's in a lot of pain right now."

She understood Cipher wasn't talking about the physical sort of pain that was easily deadened with the miracle medicine they had on their ship. It was something else, something deeper and impossible to cure. After what she had seen happen to him, she couldn't imagine him rebuilding his life with the memories of surviving that hellhole forever reminding him of what he had endured.

Next to her, Cipher relaxed, his muscles losing all tension, and his breaths deepened. She slowly tilted her head back so she could see his face. Smiling at the sight of him fast asleep with his arms around her, she studied him for a moment. He looked absolutely haggard, with dark circles under his eyes and stubble on his cheeks and jaw. He had obviously had a shower since she had seen him last, but she doubted he had done more than eat a quick meal before returning to her side.

To keep his promise to me.

Too tired to think, she snuggled in closer and closed her eyes, falling asleep to the steady rhythm of his heartbeat. This time her dreams were peaceful and familiar. When she woke to Cipher's sudden movement a long time later, she instinctively clutched at his side, grabbing his shirt and holding him close. His hand covered hers and rubbed along the length of her arm. Sounding reluctant, he said, "Baby, I have to get up."

She flushed at the endearment and let go. "Sorry."

"Don't be." He kissed her temple. "I'll be right back."

She sat up as he slid off the hospital bed and crossed the room to a frosted door. It slid to the side, disappearing into the wall as he approached and slid back out to close behind him. She deduced it must have been the bathroom.

When he emerged, he returned to her bedside and helped her stand. The thin gown puddled around her feet and was so oversized that Cipher had to wrap the excess around her waist and hold it. He moved the tubes coming out of her arms and nose with his other hand before unhooking a box mounted on the wall. All of the tubes were plugged into it.

"The med box can be carried or put on a rolling pole," he explained. "I'll hold it for you, but if I'm not here and you need to move around, you can ask a medic to put it on a pole."

Uncertain about the tubes, she asked, "How do I move?"

"Slowly," he said with a smile. "Carefully."

She rolled her eyes and huffed. "Obviously."

He seemed impressed. "I had no idea you had a sassy streak in you."

"You barely know me," she remarked without thinking.

He didn't take offense to that. "We have all the time in the world to learn everything about each other."

Remembering what he told Risk, she asked, "Did you mean it? Have you really claimed me?"

"Yes." He answered without hesitation. Then, as if worried he had overstepped, he said, "I should have asked you first."

"Ask me now," she replied boldly.

"May I keep you?"

She arched her brow. "Like a pet?"

He grimaced and amended his question. "May I keep you as my mate?"

She grinned. "Yes."

Her stomach swooped as he smiled brightly down at her. It was the first time any man had ever looked at her with so much joy. As he led her to the bathroom and placed the box on the counter next to the sink, she suspected he seemed so happy because he finally had someone that was his. Like her, he was alone. She understood the longing in his eyes. She understood what it was like to want someone to share the burdens and triumphs of life.

When the door closed behind her, she took a few moments to explore the bathroom. It wasn't very big, but it was the nicest one she had ever seen. There was a shower on one side and a toilet and sink on the other. As she handled her business, she marveled all the wonderful luxuries now available to her. Only briefly, while working at one of the bigger mines as a teenager, had she been able to regularly visit a real, honest-to-goodness bathroom with plumbing and hot water. Those seven months on the job had been like paradise.

Back at the cabin, she had to haul water from the well and heat it over the wood burning stove for a shallow bath in their old metal tub. Needing to pee in the middle of the night meant using and then emptying a chamber pot or braving the darkness with a lantern or flashlight, if she had the batteries, to visit the outhouse. She would be able to shower whenever she wanted, brush her teeth without having to haul water or fight off bugs and critters to pee at three in the morning.

Her initial excitement at having access to an indoor bathroom faded quickly when she realized how very poor she was compared to Cipher. As she washed her hands under the motion activated faucet and watched the soap foam on her skin, she felt deep shame. On the mountain, when a man and woman decided to live together, there were expectations of a financial nature. The man had to prove he could provide and care for his woman, and the woman needed to bring money, land or something else valuable like livestock.

I don't have anything to give him.

As she washed her face and cleaned her teeth with the provided toiletries, she tried to remember everything she had ever heard about the sky warriors and their marriage customs. Beyond the salacious sex rumors, she had only heard that they chased and claimed their brides with collars and preferred fertile virgins. She couldn't remember ever hearing anything about their dowry customs.

What if Cipher expected her to have something to offer? Would it insult him if she brought nothing, not even a set of dishes or embroidered linens?

"What's wrong?" Cipher asked when she emerged after a few minutes. "Are you in pain?"

"No." She shook her head and tried to hide her embarrassment. "It's nothing."

"It's not nothing." He grabbed the box, swept her up in his arms and carried her back to the bed. After he arranged all of the tubes, he sat on the bed facing her and tipped her chin with his thick fingers. He forced her gaze to his. "Tell me."

When he used that tone of voice, she was powerless to refuse him. "I'm poor."

He frowned. "I don't understand what that—"

"I've never had running water or an indoor bathroom," she interrupted. In a rush, she said, "I grew up without electricity. I had to chop wood and keep a fire to stay warm. Almost everything I own is used or mended or handed down from someone else. The last new thing I was ever given was the dress my mother made for me before she died. I wore it until the seams gave. I didn't go to school. All I have in the whole world is what's in my pack. I don't…" She glanced away as another wave of shame hit. "I don't have anything to give you."

His fingers gently tilted her chin again until she met his stern gaze. "You don't have to give me anything, Brook."

"I do," she insisted. "If I'm going to be your wife, I have to bring something with me. If we were back on the mountain, I would have my cabin and my land, but I don't have anything worthy of you—"

He silenced her with a very unexpected kiss. It was her first kiss—and what a kiss it was! Butterflies swarmed her belly, and the machine tracking her heartbeat sounded an alarm as Cipher's lips moved against hers. They were both smiling when they separated, but she was breathless and trembling. Her flushed face must have given her away because he asked, "Was that your first kiss?"

Shyly, she nodded and started to tell him it was incredible, but the door to the room opened and Risk stepped inside with a frown on his face. "Can you wait to give my patient a heart attack until after my shift ends? Let Stinger handle the long reports this time!"

Abashed, Cipher grumbled, "Sorry, Doc."

"Since you're already awake, let's get your morning checkup out of the way." Risk placed his hands under a wall dispenser that shot a blob of green foam onto his open palm. He rubbed his hands together, and the biting, artificially clean scent filled the air. "How are you feeling?"

"Much better," she said, fascinated as she watched him tap a glossy panel on the wall by her bed. It was some sort of data screen that had all of her medical information. He swiped his fingers over test results and the record of her vitals and adjusted the flow of her medications and fluids. "That is amazing."

Risk grinned at her. "Wait until you get to your new quarters and see the entertainment console."

"Entertainment console?" she glanced at Cipher.

"It's a screen similar to that but larger. You'll be able to watch all sorts of programs, attend classes, chat with friends. Things like that."

"You're lucky you picked Cipher," Risk said as he clicked on a small flashlight and checked her pupils. "He gets first dibs on all new tech that comes on this ship. You'll get to play with all the fun stuff before anyone else."

Catching Cipher's gaze, she said, "I'm very lucky," and meant it.

"So," Risk said and adjusted the ticklish tubes sitting in her nose, "we have you on supplemental air because your oxygen saturation levels are lower than they should be. While you were asleep, we did some testing. We scanned your lungs."

She swallowed anxiously. "Do I have it?"

"It?"

"Purple lung?"

"No," Risk assured her quickly. "You have some minor damage from years of working in those mines. We have some treatments that will help purge your lung tissues of the pollutants, but the scarring will always cause problems."

She processed that information for a few seconds. "My dad died from pneumonia. He coughed all the time and got sick every winter. That last time he got sick, he couldn't catch his breath. He gurgled and spit up pink froth." She closed her eyes as the terrible memories assailed her. "It was awful to watch him drown right there in his bed. There wasn't anything we could do."

"No, there wasn't," Risk agreed.

"Am I...?" she faltered, and Cipher gripped her hand. "Is that how I'm going to die?"

Risk shook his head. "No. You'll have issues with coughing in certain situations and catching a cold or other virus that causes congestion will make you miserable for a bit. We can treat all of those things, and we can give you medications and treatments to prevent them as well. Tomorrow morning, we'll send you to the respiratory techs for some testing on your lungs. When we get the results, we'll be able to create a regimen of breathing treatments to help clear your lungs."

"Okay."

Risk glanced at Cipher and said, "I'd like to send her over to the *Mercy* so they can put her in the tube a few times a month."

"The tube?" she asked, eyes wide. "What is that?"

"It's not as bad as it sounds," Cipher hurriedly reassured her. "It's a chamber where your body can receive oxygen and other therapies in a pressurized environment."

"We have one here, but it's malfunctioning. Until we get it replaced, we're sending those patients to the *Mercy*."

"Is that far away from here?" She didn't like the idea of being away from Cipher. This world was so new and intimidating.

"It's an hour away," Cipher explained. "*Mercy* orbits a little higher than we do. It's the main hospital ship for the sector." He squeezed her hand. "I'll be with you."

Her fears eased, she listened as Risk continued a rundown of her initial blood testing and told her about the vaccines she would need. She couldn't meet either man's gaze when Risk asked questions about her period. It made her incredibly uncomfortable to talk about something so private. Her father hadn't been able to bring himself to explain it all to her. He had sent her down the mountain to Miss Kay for supplies and answers. Having two men questioning her about her body functions was absolutely mortifying.

Clearly sensing her discomfort, Risk let the issue drop after establishing that she had an irregular cycle and had never been sexually intimate. "Your weight concerns me," he said, changing the subject. "You're very lean. Too lean," he added. "It's why your cycle is irregular. We'll get a nutrition plan arranged to help."

"I've always been small," she said. "Even when we had a lot to eat, I was smaller than everyone else my age."

"How big were your parents?"

"Not very big," she said, trying to recall her mother's size. "Mama was a little taller than me and only a little heavier. Daddy was short enough to walk upright in most of the tunnels." She eyed Cipher and tried to gauge her father against him. "The top of his head might have reached you right about here."

"Genetics, then," Risk decided and tapped something into screen where all of her medical information was displayed. When he was done, he reached into the pocket on the front of his shirt and retrieved a small metallic card in a clear, shiny sleeve. He waved it in front of the screen and Cipher's information popped up on it. "Cipher filled out the forms last night so you're officially his mate. This is your ID chip."

She took the card from him and turned it over in her hand. The protective film made it a little difficult to read to all of the numbers stamped into the surface of it. In the very center of the card, there was the tiniest little sliver of metal. It wasn't any bigger than a grain of rice. "This thing holds information?"

"It does." Risk pulled a metal tray on wheels over to the bed and then walked to the dispenser for more foam to clean his hands. After he pulled on a pair of those strange gloves again, he waved his hand in front of a drawer, opening it and taking out a sealed package. He placed the package on the tray and tore it open along the perforated edges. It unfolded like a blossoming flower, draping the tray with bright blue cloths and exposing a set of medical tools. "This looks like it will be painful, but I promise it's nothing more than a pinch."

"What kind of a pinch?" She shifted away from the tray and eyed the menacing tools. "Because Gertie Bluestone pinched me one time at a summer picnic and gave me a bruise bigger than a plum."

"Not that kind of pinch," Risk promised. He held out his hand for the card, and she gave it to him. He made quick work of removing the chip from the sealed card, loading it into a syringe and cleaning her wrist with a small wipe that left her skin feeling numb. "Okay. On three," he said, holding the syringe above her skin. "One. Two."

She scowled at him as he pushed the needle into her skin before three. Grudgingly, she admitted he was right. It was only a tiny pinch, and it was done.

"Okay?" Cipher asked, rubbing her back as he stood at her other side and held her hand.

"Yes." She smiled up at him. Her stomach growled, and both men laughed. "Sorry."

"Your breakfast tray should be here soon. You'll have to hit the mess hall," Risk told Cipher. "We'll keep an eye on her for you."

Cipher seemed hesitant to leave her. She intertwined their fingers. "I'll be fine. You should go eat. If you need to work, I'll be okay here."

Reluctantly, he admitted, "I need to debrief again and meet up with Raze. I've also got to meet with logistics to get our new quarters sorted."

"Go," she urged. "I'll be here when you get back."

He wavered but finally nodded. After a quick kiss, he trailed Risk out of the room. Not long after both men were gone, another medic knocked and entered the room with a breakfast tray in hand. "Good morning, ma'am. I'm Chance. I'm one of the medics who will be treating you today."

"Good morning, Chance."

He placed the tray on the rolling table next to the bed. "Do you need help with anything?"

"No, I—"

The clatter of metal interrupted her. A second later, a man erupted in anger and shouted, "Fuck off, Risk. And you, too, Vee. Get the fuck out. Go. GO! And take your fucking sedatives with you."

The crash of shattering glass startled Brook. She stared wide-eyed at her open door and then glanced at Chance who had taken a protective position in front of her bed, putting himself between her and any danger. There was more bellowing, this time from a deep and even angrier voice, and then another clang of metal. A door slammed, and she jumped, fisting the sheets in her hands as she waited for something else to happen.

When it stayed silent, Chance relaxed and turned back to her. Apologetically, he said, "I'm sorry, ma'am. There's a patient on the floor who isn't feeling so well. He's a bit difficult. You're safe, though. He wouldn't hurt you, not after what you—" He stopped suddenly as if realizing he had said too much.

"Is it the man from the mine? Terror?" she asked softly.

Chance glanced over his shoulder to make sure they were still alone. "Yes, ma'am."

"Can I visit him later?" She wanted to apologize for leaving him behind.

Chance furiously shook his head. "No, ma'am. You absolutely cannot leave this room. You're a new bride, and there are men on this ship who will try to steal you away from Cipher."

"What do you mean? Anyone can steal me?"

"Until you're in a permanent collar? Yes."

She scooted back on the bed, eying him warily, and he held up a hand. "I'm not going to steal you, ma'am. I have a mate waiting for me back on Prime. Our parents arranged it."

"That's a thing?" she asked, curious about this new culture.

"For those of who have pure bloodlines, yes."

"What's a pure bloodline?"

"You know the men you see around here with pale

hair? Almost white?" He gestured to his own head. "This is what our ancestors on Prime looked like. Some of us belong to very old families that took mates only from Prime, not from any of the new planets we conquered. It used to matter," he explained, "but the old ways are dying out and only the older generations care about that kind of thing now."

"Like your parents?"

"Like my parents," he echoed. "But, thankfully, my chosen mate is a girl I've known most of my life." He tapped the face of his watch and held it out for her to inspect. On the small screen, there was a photo of Chance and a beautiful blonde woman. "Nika," he said. "This was taken at my father's retirement party a few months ago."

"She's gorgeous. You look very happy together."

He nodded and drew back his arm. "Her brother and I are friends. We all grew up together so I kept in touch with her. One thing led to another, and now we're engaged."

"That's sweet." Brook smiled at him. "When will you two get married? I mean—mated?"

"Five weeks," he said, grinning. "I get our new quarters assignment a few days before she arrives."

"Maybe we'll be neighbors," she suggested.

"Not likely, ma'am."

"Why not?"

"Your man is a highly ranked officer with connections to the SRU and Shadow Force. You'll be allotted one of the best apartments available. Nika and I will have a starter home in one of the lower levels of the mated housing section."

"Is that how everything is doled out here? By rank?"

Chance nodded. "Rank and valor points."

She wasn't sure if that was fair or not. She didn't know enough about Cipher's world to understand how points were amassed and ranks were earned.

"I have other patients to tend, but I'll be back later to pull those lines if your labs come back within the ranges Risk wanted. If you need anything, tap this button right here."

After he left, she shifted the tray of food closer and lifted the lid. She recognized the thin porridge, but everything else on the tray looked weird and inedible. There was a cube of something bright red and wiggly in one compartment of the tray. She poked it, and it watched it jiggle back and forth. There was a cold packet with a picture of a fruit she had never seen. When she picked it up, the contents were mushy, and she hurriedly put it down, making a face and wondering what the hell it was.

The bottle of water seemed safe enough, but the carton of juice held her attention. The image on the front was the same fruit from the cold packet she had just picked up and dropped. Curious, she bravely poked a straw through the foil seal on the top and brought it to her lips. She hesitated before tasting a sip.

"Oh!" It was delicious. Sweet with a slight tang, it exploded on her taste buds. Wondering if the cold packet of mushy stuff tasted the same, the ripped along the designated line and squeezed some of it into her mouth. Her eyes closed in utter happiness as the same flavor melted on her tongue. It was the juice but slightly frozen and creamy.

As she enjoyed her first breakfast in space, her thoughts turned to Terror. The fever dream flashed through her mind. The guilt of leaving him there to suffer darkened her mood. He might yell at her or throw things, but she had to apologize. She had to let him know that he did matter and that she would never forgive herself for leaving him with those monstrous captors.

She just had to figure out how to sneak out of this room first…

Chapter Seven

"**Y**OU FINALLY DID it!"

Cipher jerked forward as Venom slapped him across the back in congratulations. "Yes."

"Good for you, Ci." Venom squeezed his shoulder. "Dizzy and I can't wait to meet her."

"Brook," Cipher said. "Her name is Brook, and I'm sure she'll be thrilled to make new friends on the ship."

"Brook," Venom repeated. "I like that. It's…natural."

"That's one way to describe her," Cipher agreed as he knocked on Raze's office door. "Boss?"

"Come in," Raze bellowed from inside. "Figured it would be you," he said, gesturing to the open chair in front of his desk. "Sit down. You've got a shitload of forms to complete."

Cipher dropped into the chair and took the tablet from Raze. Venom sat next to him and stretched out his long legs. "You already debrief?" the sniper asked.

"Just got finished with it." Cipher logged into the tablet screen and groaned at the sheer number of forms waiting for him. "Are they serious with this? Three hundred and four pages?"

"That's at least eighty more than when I claimed Dizzy," Venom remarked as he leaned over to look at the screen.

"About two hundred less than when I claimed Ella," Raze chimed in with a wry smile.

"Stole," Venom corrected. "When you assaulted a pilot and stole her, you mean."

Raze threw a stylus at him. Venom caught and whipped it right back. Raze snatched it just before it whacked him in the face. He frowned at Venom. "Easy, man, or you'll have to deal with Ella."

Venom grimaced. "The last thing I need is Ella and Dizzy ganging up on me because I gave you a black eye."

"How is Dizzy feeling?" Cipher asked while scanning the next page. Venom's mate was expecting their first baby and had been having a rough couple of weeks.

"So much better." Venom grinned and looked happier than Cipher had ever seen him. "It was like someone flipped a switch. She hit fourteen weeks, and the sickness stopped overnight. She was sewing this morning when I left."

At the mention of Dizzy making clothing, he glanced at Venom. "I may need to commission some things for Brook. She's going to have problems with the standard clothing sizes offered. She's very small."

"Like Hallie small?" Raze asked.

"About," Cipher confirmed.

Raze made a face. "Underfed her whole life, I guess."

With a solemn nod, Cipher said, "She's had a hard life down there."

"Most of them do." Venom tapped at his watch. "It's painful to see some of them at the Grabs. They're so thin and pale."

"We think we know what it's like to suffer and sacrifice, but some of these brides?" Raze shook his head. "It's a fucking travesty. That planet is overflowing with resources, but they're all starving down there."

"Their government is garbage," Cipher said as he initialed another box.

"Was," Raze corrected. "Election results were in this morning."

Cipher glanced up from the tablet. "I take it Ella's outreach worked?"

Raze smiled. "Every candidate she supported and canvassed for won their races. It's a brand-new day down there."

"It'll get worse before it gets better," Venom insisted. "The people in power are not going to be happy about losing it."

"No," Raze agreed. Then, soberly, he said, "That's why they brought in Rage and his crew."

Cipher exchanged a knowing look with Venom. Rage and his small band of specialists everyone called the Mad Lads had a reputation for suppressing rebellion and forcing the governments of planets they planned to annex to accept the terms offered to them. Rage was a hard man, much like the Vicious and Terror who had graduated from his same year at the academy. Rage would get Calyx under control—or the planet would never be the same again.

"Did you get your quarters assignment yet?" Raze asked, changing the subject to one less tense.

"That's where I'm headed after this." Cipher swiped to the next page.

Venom leaned back and scratched his shaved head. "There are two units open on our floor. They're way down at the end of the hall, but Brook would have Dizzy and Ella nearby."

"Naya, too," Raze added. "She might get along well with Naya. They had the same hardscrabble upbringing."

It was an option Cipher hadn't considered. "I'll ask Menace if they want to meet her."

"Let me talk to Ella. She loves throwing parties. I bet I could convince her to host dinner for the two of you. Let Brook meet new people in an organic way, you know?"

Cipher nodded. "That sounds nice."

"Great."

All three of their watches started to vibrate, and they groaned in unison. Raze answered the alert by tapping his shoulder mic. "SRU Alpha Command."

"Raze, Orion here. Bring Venom and Cipher to SFHQ."

The admiral's stern voice had them all exchanging worried glances. Orion and Shadow Force had a history, especially after Terror's stunt with Menace's mate. If he was calling the three senior officers of SRU down there, it wasn't good.

"Copy that, sir." Raze gave them a look. "You heard the admiral."

"SRU B Team," Venom called his crew as he stood and exited the office. "Mal, you're up as team…"

As Venom handled his crew, Raze issued orders to the A squad. Cipher locked the tablet and placed it on the desk before following Raze out of the office and joining up with Venom. They traversed the ship to the Shadow Force unit and cleared security to find Pierce waiting for them.

He led them into the logistics room where Torment, Vicious, Orion and a tired-looking Risk stood around the large table in the center. Savage, the operative that had been sent to take Terror's place while he had been missing, leaned over a holographic image, his head close together with Keen, the best detective the academy had ever produced. In a corner, arms crossed and dark eyes narrowed, Grim, the deadliest assassin in Shadow Force history, and his protégé Lethal watched silently.

"Raze," Orion greeted gruffly and extended his hand. He nodded at Cipher and Venom before gesturing to the table. "We have a problem."

"That's the understatement of the century," Keen interjected in his gravelly voice.

"When your mate sent her intel and recon," Savage addressed Cipher, "we focused mostly on the information that would help us rescue Terror. We set aside everything else until we had him in our hands."

"And?" Ciphered stepped up to the table where the image of a canister had been amplified and digitally enhanced.

"She captured these images and video of Splinter forces moving crates filled with these canisters. They aren't marked, but she said something in her report that caught my attention," Savage continued.

Torment swiped his fingers through the air over the table and tossed a video file to the screen on the opposite wall. Brook's face appeared, her skin smudged with grime from the mine and her hair still damp from the filthy water in the broken pipes. The file began to play, and Cipher smiled at the sound of her voice.

"There was something strange about that room with the canisters. It smelled wrong—like a barn, like hay—and I felt woozy going over the grate there."

Cipher's gaze instantly snapped to Torment. "Nerve gas?"

Torment nodded. "A shipment of canisters from the Factory that were on their way to incineration were hijacked."

"Splinters?" Raze asked.

"An independent outfit of arms dealers," Keen clarified.

"They've been on Shadow Force's wider radar for a while now," Savage added. "They don't operate in this sector so they aren't a running concern for us. When they arranged to sell their cargo to a cell here, that changed."

"When?" Cipher asked.

"7 weeks ago," Keen answered and inclined his head toward Grim.

The assassin was rarely seen aboard the *Valiant* even though it was his home base. When he was seen, Grim was usually staring stonily from some shadowy corner. There were rumors that he was born mute or had lost his tongue in an early mission gone bad. Cipher didn't believe either one. He thought Grim just didn't have much to say.

Without uncrossing his arms or moving away from the wall, Grim growled, "Our man on the inside alerted us to the deal. We were able to intercept the two ships outside the Gamma-6 moon base. We recovered most of the stolen cargo, but the Splinters managed to offload seven crates before we arrived." His gaze settled on Cipher. "Your mate found them down in that mine."

"If she smelled hay, that's got to be NA-4," Cipher reasoned. "It's deadly, but we have antidotes."

"Not enough," Risk stated as he rubbed his jaw. "Not nearly enough."

"How fast can we get the amount we need?" Orion asked.

"I don't know that we can," Risk admitted. "After the public campaigns against bio weapons, they phased out those older gases. Whatever antidote we have in central stockpile is all we have. Gathering up the antidote in circulation will be a logistical nightmare."

"The antidote isn't our problem," Grim insisted. "There was a mistake at the factory when they were loading up the old gas to be destroyed. A canister of NA-9X made it into the crates. It wasn't in the recovered canisters."

Fear rippled down Cipher's spine. He met Risk's shocked gaze. The doc looked ready to puke as he exclaimed, "Are you fucking kidding me?" He glanced around the room. "You guys didn't think to lead with that part of the story? The part where our enemies have a canister of the deadliest gas our scientists ever created? A colorless, odorless killing machine with no antidote?"

From the grave looks on Vicious and Orion's faces, they hadn't been apprised of that fact either. Vicious finally asked, "How deadly is it?"

"A drop would kill everyone in this room," Risk explained. "Worse than that, it sticks around. Literally. The residue clings to anything it touches. It's just as deadly administered through the skin as through the nose."

"So anyone who touches a victim or tries to render aid will also die," Vicious muttered.

"Not just die," Risk said insistently. "They will suffer a horrible, agonizing death. You come in contact with NA-9X? You choke. You bleed out of your eyes and mouth. You lose control of your bowels and bladder. Your stomach will violently erupt. You seize and drown in your own blood and mucus and vomit."

The room went silent as every man imagined such an end.

"That's why they never made the gas in any useable quantity," Savage said. "The scientist who discovered it did so on accident and killed his entire lab. The war council had the R&D sector try to replicate the discovery. They killed more than seven hundred workers at that lab when the gas was made and escaped the vapor locks. They finally managed it on the third try, but Shadow Force decided it was too dangerous and ordered them to seal away the small quantity they had."

"Then it's no mistake the canister was in the crates marked for destruction," Orion decided. "Somebody on the inside wanted that gas to get to the Splinters."

"Well," Vicious sighed, "now they have it. We have to figure out what they plan to do with it."

"I would take it home to Prime," Torment said. "Use it to make a statement."

"Using it on a ship filled with families is a statement," Orion grumbled. "Do we have any way of detecting the NA-9X?"

Cipher felt all eyes on him. Realizing they expected him to come up with a solution on the fly, he suggested the first thing that came to mind. "We have sensors on the probes for dirty bombs. NA-9X isn't one on the list of compounds it recognizes, but if we can get the chemical signature, I can manually add it to the program. If we can get more sensors programmed, we can work with the ship's environmental crew to place them throughout the ship for early detection."

Orion turned to Vicious. "I'm ordering a stop to all incoming cargo and transport ships. Nothing gets close to this ship without a thorough search. That goes for luggage and personal items, too."

"We'll need an emergency action plan," Vicious replied. "We can modify the shelter in place and abandon ship drills?"

Orion agreed with that idea and added, "Let's prioritize mates and offspring and figure out a way to shut down ventilation in the family areas to protect them in the event of a gas attack."

Vicious nodded and looked to Raze. "You need to get the SRU teams ready to deal with a gas attack. Whatever equipment you need, I'll make sure you get."

"On it, sir," Raze promised.

"Cipher, Risk, you stay here and work with Shadow Force," Orion ordered. "I want preliminary plans on my desk from Shadow Force, SRU and Medical by the end of shift today. Understood?"

After a round of nods and yes sirs, Orion, Vicious, Raze and Venom left. Risk rubbed his tired eyes and sighed before dropping down in the first available chair. "We should get Reckless over here and read him in on the situation."

Torment scoffed. "Not a fucking chance that Orion gives that asshole clearance to board his ship."

"Who is Reckless?" Keen hadn't been on the *Valiant* long enough to learn all the names of the personnel serving on this ship and the others in the fleet.

"He's the head of pulmonology on the *Mercy*," Risk explained. "He's one of the few guys in the medical corps who has first-hand experience with mass casualty gas deaths." He made a face. "He was fresh out of med school and stationed at the R&D lab working on NA-9X. The experience was so bad he asked to be sent to the front lines." He scratched the back of his head and sighed again. "Reckless is an irritating asshole, but he's an expert."

"Does he have clearance?" Keen asked.

Torment groaned and rubbed his face as Savage pointedly ignored him and confirmed the doctor did.

"Then let's get him over here," Keen urged. "Pierce?"

Pierce, who had been quietly watching from his guard positioning the door hesitated. He shared a glance with Torment as if to question the wisdom of bringing Reckless aboard the ship.

Savage noticed it and growled, "Do we need to review the chain of command?"

"No, sir," Pierce said. "I'll be back with Reckless."

Glad that Raze had fostered a much more cooperative and friendly environment within SRU, Cipher moved to a console and logged into the air traffic control data for the day Brook had been in the mine. He scanned the data starting from that day to this one and then went back a week before her trip into the mine. "There are no unauthorized ships coming into or out of the planet's airspace."

"Anything from the colonies? Something we might have rubber stamped through traffic control without boarding and checking?" Torment moved to the console and leaned down to read the air traffic reports.

"The usual cargo transports from the colonies," Cipher said, scrolling through the logs. "Everything going out the last forty-eight hours went through The City departure vector. Those are all scanned and logged." He pointed to the manifest scans attached to each ship's log. "Everything was tagged and scanned clean."

"What's that entry?" Torment indicated red stripe.

"Looks like it's the cargo ship from the skyport that crashed," Cipher replied. He checked the manifest. "It was all building supplies. They were destroyed when they hit the atmosphere."

"This is our medical ship?" Torment gestured to the next line.

"Yes. It took all survivors to the *Mercy*."

"If the gas is still on the planet," Torment said, straightening up, "we might be able to intercept and retrieve it."

"It would be a hell of a lot safer to attempt a retrieval in the wide-open spaces down there than in the tight quarters of a ship," Grim commented.

"Do we have anyone still inside the cell on Calyx?" Keen asked, his focus moving to Savage who shook his head.

"Devious was our last link to the cell on the planet," Savage answered.

"Maybe not," Torment chimed in, snapping his fingers. "Devious had assets on the ground. If we can find them, we might be able to work them."

"What about the Splinter shithead we captured?" Grim asked. "Has he said anything yet?"

"He's a bit tied up at the moment," Torment replied impassively. Everyone in the room knew exactly what that meant. "He may be more willing to talk when I visit him later."

"Who was Devious's handler?" Keen asked.

"Terror," Savage said and grimaced. "He's not exactly in a cooperative mood at the moment."

"That's a fucking understatement," Risk grumbled

from his seat. "He took a swing at the general and threw a rolling cart through a window. I seriously considered having Venom come down to the infirmary to shoot him with a tranquilizer."

"So, asking Terror is out," Keen muttered. "He kept files, right?"

Torment shook his head and interjected his opinion. "His files are all in code, and he never put down the names of assets. Ever. If he knows the names of the assets, they're up here." He tapped his temple. "And you're going to have to ask nicely to get them."

Cipher stayed quiet and kept his gaze on the screen in front of him. He wanted absolutely no part of dealing with Terror or trying to find lost assets. Technically, he was on modified duty while Brook was in the hospital. He fully intended to keep his ass right here on the ship, safe with his new mate. After all this time waiting for the right one, he had no desire to risk his life hunting down assets who didn't want to be found.

"Here," Torment said, suddenly appearing next to him. He placed four plump, firm oranges on the desk. "For your mate."

Cipher had heard the story about the muckraker down in The City sending Torment a box of the expensive fruit along with photo evidence of Terror. For Torment to share such a personal gift with Brook was a statement that Cipher understood loud and clear. Torment approved of her and considered her someone worth protecting.

"Thank you, Tor."

"She needs all the calories and vitamins she can get," Torment gruffly replied, downplaying his concern.

Thinking of Brook and the way she had been so embarrassed about not having anything to give him, he asked, "Do you think I could ask Danny for a favor?"

"You can ask, but it won't be cheap. He charges inflated prices when he deals with personal favors."

"I wanted to get Brook's belongings from her cabin. She only had a backpack with her. When I was at the cabin, I saw all of the important things her father and mother had left behind. I'd like her to have them."

Torment's brow arched. "I never took you for a romantic."

"Yeah, well, let's try not to spread that around," he grumbled. "Pierce already busted my balls."

Torment laughed and then turned his attention back to the computer screen. "Let's get a look at the ventilation systems."

Cipher pulled up the ship schematics and began studying the ventilation, heating and cooling systems. Like most ships of this class, they were extensive and difficult to reach, some of the points so narrow only robotic probes could reach them. It was going to be a headache to access and place sensors, but it would have to be done to keep everyone on the ship safe.

But especially my mate.

Mate.

I have a mate.

Mine.

She's all mine.

He had fought, bled and suffered to earn the right to a mate and the privilege of passing on his superior genes to a new generation. Brook represented his future, and he was determined to make that future with her a bright and happy one.

Chapter Eight

A FTER HOURS OF boredom and loneliness, the door to her hospital room finally opened. When Cipher stepped inside, holding a duffel bag in one hand and a gift bag in the other, Brook sat up so quickly she yanked her nasal cannula right off her face and out of the box supplying her oxygen. "Ow!"

"Brook!" Cipher snorted with amusement and quickly crossed the room to plug the tubes back into their ports. He tucked the lines behind her ears and back into her nose. "Careful, sweetheart."

"Sorry, sir." Feeling suddenly bashful, she glanced down at her hands. "I'm just excited to see you. Other than Chance and Stinger coming in here to check up on me, I haven't had much interaction."

"I'm sorry for being gone the whole day and most of the evening." He brushed his fingers down her cheek before leaning down to kiss her. It was a gentle, chaste kiss that left her wanting more, so much more. "I was called in for work, and it took longer than anticipated."

She studied his face and noticed the tight line of his jaw. "Something bad happened?"

He seemed a bit surprised she had read him so easily.

"Not yet, but it might."

"Is there anything I can do to help?" She hated to see him stressed.

His expression softened. "You're doing it right now."

Confused, she asked, "How?"

"You're being my friend and my partner," he explained. "You're letting me know that you care."

"I do care." She gripped his hand. "I know we're new to all of this, but I do care about you, Cipher. Anything I can do to help, I will."

"I know." He kissed her again, this time letting his lips linger on hers. He stroked her hair, feeling the dampness. "You took a shower?"

"Yes." She lifted her arms and bent them to show she had free range of motion. "They pulled out those awful tubes. As long as I keep drinking all the fluids they bring and my vital signs are stable, I don't need them."

"Did you have any problems with the shower controls?"

"Chance showed me how they worked."

Cipher's eyes narrowed. "He went into the bathroom with you? Alone?"

She rolled her eyes at his jealousy. "He was a perfect gentleman."

Cipher didn't seem convinced. She had a feeling he would have words with Chance in the morning. He let the issue drop and presented the gift bag to her. "This is for you."

"Thank you." She had noticed the bag when he entered

the room and excitedly opened it to see what he had brought her. Her eyes darted to the bright orange fruit on top, and she gasped, "Where did you get these?"

"Torment," he said, bending down to unzip the sides of his boots. He toed out of them and left them next to the door. "He wanted you to have them."

"Why?" She had only tasted an orange once before as a child. She and her parents had shared one at a company picnic. They had been given out to each family as a gift for the year's record-breaking production of minerals. Even now, all these years later, she could remember the taste of it bursting on her tongue.

"Because you saved Terror," he said, taking off his belt and gear and placing it on the counter near the door. He lined each piece up in an order he had obviously used for years. "You're lucky to have someone like Torment in your corner. He's the kind of friend everyone needs when shit gets real."

"I can see that," she murmured, watching as he unbuttoned his uniform shirt and folded it loosely. He wore a dark undershirt that clung to his muscular chest and arms. She swallowed hard, wondering what it would be like to run her hands over his skin and feel all that power beneath her fingertips. Her face flushed at the thought of having his strong, heavy body on top of hers, pressing her into a mattress. Her gaze drifted lower and settled on the taut curve of his bottom.

Unbidden, the image of him between her legs, thrusting into her while she gripped his behind, appeared in her mind. She could practically feel his panting breaths on her neck and smell the scent of him surrounding her as he made her his wife. She squeezed her thighs together as the pulse of heat there throbbed almost painfully.

The machine tracking her heartbeat betrayed her thoughts, chiming loudly as her heart raced. Not wanting to get caught leering, she glanced away as he turned and busied herself with unpacking the contents of the bag. If he suspected she had been fantasizing about him making love to her, he didn't say it. Instead, he lowered the safety rail on the bed and gestured for her to scoot over to make room. She happily did so and welcomed him into her space.

"The book and pamphlets are given to all new brides," he explained and draped his arm around her shoulders. She didn't even try to hide the smile that tugged at her mouth when he pulled her in close to cuddle against him. "They explain everything you need to know about living on the ship and your rights as a bride and mate."

She thumbed through the guidebook. "I'll read through it tomorrow, sir."

His lips brushed her temple. "Take your time. There's no rush or test."

"Speaking of tests," she muttered, "they made me blow into this huge straw earlier to see how well my lungs work. It was awful."

"I'm sorry." He rubbed her arm. "I should have been here."

"No, you were where you needed to be. I'm just whining a bit."

"That's okay. You're allowed to be upset and irritated about things. Especially right now," he added. "You're in a whole new world. You have strangers asking you to take uncomfortable tests. I would whine, too."

She eyed him with disbelief. "I don't think your people have that emotion."

He snorted. "You haven't met all of us yet. Eventually, you'll cross a soldier or pilot who will change your mind."

"I guess." She reached into the bag and withdrew a tablet device. Holding it in her hand, she was surprised by how light it felt and how easy it was to handle. She glanced at him in shock. "Is this mine?"

"All yours," he confirmed. "I've already set it up for you. Would you like to me show you how it works?"

"Yes, sir."

Not for the first time, she noticed the way his eyes seemed to flare when she called him sir. He seemed pleased to be shown respect, and she was happy to give it to him. He had more than earned her respect with his actions toward her.

"It's all touchscreen," he explained, taking her small hand in his larger one and showing her how to swipe the screen. Icons appeared on a pale grey background. "You can change this background to anything you'd like. A photo, a painting, your own design, a solid color," he said, pointing out the icon to tap to change the settings for the tablet. "These icons take you to different applications. Library, entertainment, messaging, vid-calls, navigation, education, shopping, cooking, medical care," he listed the options while pointing them out to her. "Try it."

She took the tablet back from him and tapped on the icons, exploring all the options available to her. She marveled at the technology and wondered how it worked. As if reading her mind, Cipher said, "I can teach you how to code and make your own programs."

"Really?"

"Yes." He kissed her. "Really."

Not wanting him to move away so quickly, she reached out and cupped his face, gently holding him in place. He understood what she wanted and turned slightly. The tablet was forgotten on her lap as Cipher let her take control of their kiss. She clung to his broad shoulders and moved her lips against his. Her hands trembled as the excitement of being so close to Cipher overwhelmed her. Feeling brazen, she flicked the tip of her tongue against the seam of his mouth. He groaned low in his throat and tangled his fingers in her long hair, gripping the back of her head as he swung his leg over hers.

Trapped beneath him, she let out a shuddery breath and kissed him again, clawing at his shoulders and silently begging him to stay on top of her. She pressed her thighs together, aching and needy in a way she had never experienced. He seemed to know what she was feeling because he rocked against her, sliding his strong thigh between hers and nudging it against the place no man had ever touched. She gasped, her eyes wide at the incredible sensation of his leg between hers, and pumped her hips to chase the feeling again.

"Fuck," Cipher growled. His hand flew to her hip, his long fingers gripping her tightly and holding her still. She whimpered and tried to rub herself against him again, but he was too strong. "No," he said sternly. "Not here."

"Please, sir," she begged, her voice so needy and desperate that it shocked her. "Please."

"No." He kissed her slowly, taking his time as he plundered her mouth and held her right where he wanted her. "I don't want to share this with anyone. You are mine. *Mine.* And no one else will ever see or hear what you share with me."

Part of her wanted to defy him and fight for the stimulation she wanted to feel again. Most of her wanted to follow his command, to submit and accept his decision. Something told her that she would be rewarded for her obedience. She craved his praise and found it easy to nod and say, "Yes, sir."

As if understanding how hard it was for her to ignore the demands of her body, he nuzzled her neck. "I promise it will be worth the wait."

So far, he had proven himself to be a man of his word. She couldn't wait to find out how he would make it worth her while.

Cipher untangled their legs and sat up, taking his arm from her shoulders. It wasn't done in a punishing way but for practicality. He picked up one of the oranges and began to methodically peel it. She watched his hands, seeing the way his deft fingers moved so elegantly. It was a strange way to describe a man as big and strong as Cipher, but it was the only word she could think of as he peeled away the thick orange rind without tearing the fruit or spilling a drop of juice.

In her aroused state, it wasn't hard to translate the movements of his fingers on the fruit to the way they would touch her body. She hadn't ever made love, but she wasn't an innocent child. She knew what people did together in their bedrooms. Working in the mines around so many men, she had heard more than her fair share of filthy stories and jokes while toiling away in the shadows, forgotten and unseen. She had heard other women complaining about their men when using the locker rooms at the mines. Looking at Cipher, she didn't think she would have many complaints about him.

Her gaze traveled the long length of his legs to the top of one of his socks. It had rolled down a bit, probably when she rubbed against him. Feeling playful, she used her thin, nimble toes to grasp the thick, soft fabric. She began to tug down his sock, making sure to stroke his calf with her toes, and he shot her a warning look. "Keep that up, and I'm going to tie you to the bed."

Heat flared low in her belly at the thought of being restrained beneath him. She had heard the stories of the naughty things the sky warriors did with their mates. The image of Cipher skimming his skilled hands over her naked body while she strained against her bonds left her breathless and eager. "Promise?"

"Brook." There was hard edge to his voice, but the warmth in his gaze tempered the sternness of it. "You're going to be a handful, aren't you?"

She nodded and grinned mischievously. "I hope you're up for it."

He didn't miss the cheeky way her gaze fell to his zipper. "Eyes up here, mate."

She reluctantly dragged her gaze to his face. "Yes, sir."

Shaking his head, he opened the orange with his thumbs, spreading out the wedges of fruit like the petals of a blossoming flower. He plucked one of the wedges free and brought it to her mouth. When he dragged it across her lower lip, she blushed and followed his silent command to open her lips and take the fruit. It tasted just as delightful as she remembered, and she closed her eyes, savoring the flavor.

When she tried to feed him a piece, he shook his head. "This is for you."

"I know." She brought it closer to his mouth. "I want to share it with you."

He let her feed him, and she smiled at her little victory. They shared the rest of the orange with silent, tender smiles. It was late by the time they finished, and Cipher yawned despite his valiant attempt to hold it back. Taking his hand, she said, "I'll be perfectly fine here if you want to go back to your quarters and get a proper night's rest."

"I won't be perfectly fine," he replied. "I feel calmer with you. I need to know you're safe." His gaze hardened, and she wondered if it had something to do with the work that had kept him away from her all day and most of the evening. "It's not up for discussion."

She arched an eyebrow at that. She enjoyed the way he took command when they were doing things that were intimate, but she wasn't so sure about him being so dominant in all areas of their life. He must have seen the unease on her face because he hastily apologized and explained, "There's a threat to the ship, Brook. I need to be close to you."

"I want you to be close to me, but I don't want to be told things aren't up for discussion. I'm not a child, and you're not my father."

Duly chastised, Cipher nodded. "You're right. You're not a child, and I'm not your father."

She grasped his wrist and drew his gaze. "I know you're under a lot of stress. I can tell you're worried about keeping me safe."

"I am," he admitted, his shoulders relaxing. "That's not an excuse, though."

"No, but it's an explanation."

Hesitantly, he asked, "Can I stay?"

"Yes." She wanted him with her, especially now that she knew there was a possibility something terrible might happen. She would need Cipher's help to navigate the massive ship if they had to evacuate. More than that, she wanted him next to her in bed. She wanted to feel safe and secure. She wanted to get used to sharing a bed with this man who was now, for all intents and purposes, her husband.

"I'm going to shower." He got off the bed and walked to the counter to pick up his duffel bag. "I won't be long."

"Take as much time as you need."

While he was in the bathroom taking care of his nightly routine, she decided to make the bed as comfortable as possible for him. She adjusted the bed using the buttons Chance had demonstrated during his second visit to her room. She carried the bag of gifts to the counter and placed it next to his gear. She thumbed through the guidebook for new mates and opened the pamphlets explaining all the services and resources available to brides and families. Interested in trying out some of the educational options, she tucked the pamphlets into the book for later.

She was arranging the three remaining oranges on top of the book when Terror's voice shattered the quiet peace of the infirmary. His angry shouting ricocheted around the hospital unit, escalating as he snarled at the unfortunate person who had dared to bother him. The bathroom door opened suddenly and Cipher emerged, dripping suds and water and hastily securing a towel around his waist. "Get away from the window, Brook."

She reacted immediately, moving closer to the bed. "It's just Terror."

"I know." Cipher approached the door with a predatory grace that fascinated her. His gaze darted to the counter where his gear was waiting if he needed it. He turned the lock on the door, securing them inside and tapped the window to activate the frosted glass. "He's the most dangerous man you'll ever meet, and if he's not in the right state of mind, he could kill everyone on this floor before SRU could get a team together."

"I don't doubt that, but I don't think he wants to kill anyone."

"With a man like Terror, it's not about wanting to kill. It's instinct. It's as easy as breathing."

Cipher remained tense until a door slammed and Terror's voice faded to nothing. Standing there, naked except for a towel, he held her full attention. His body was *incredible*. She hadn't realized there were so many muscles in the human body. She could see every sinew, his body rippling with raw power when he moved. His right shoulder and upper arm were tattooed with lines of numbers and letters and strange symbols.

"It's the story of my time as a soldier in the alpha-numerical language we use to program our technology." He had caught her staring. "We mark the right sides of our bodies with our military exploits, our successes and victories. The left side is for you."

"For me?" she asked, taken aback.

"For us, our family," he explained. "You'll go here." He touched the area above his heart. "Our children will branch out from you. I'll carry you on my body until I die."

She swallowed hard at the depth of emotion in his voice. He had wholly committed himself to her the moment he had taken her from the forest. He was ready to permanently fix her name to him and to honor her in the same way he had his victories as a soldier. It was a heady moment, realizing that Cipher was all-in with her.

"Do I get one?" She touched her chest. "Can I put your name on my body?"

He seemed pleased by the idea. "Some mates do. It's your decision."

Outwardly bold but trembling with nervousness inside, she closed the distance between them and slowly extended her hand toward his tattooed arm. She traced the markings on his skin, fascinated by the secret story they told. She wanted to learn this coding language so she could read his tale and understand him on a deeper level.

Cipher's breathing shifted as she moved her fingers over his wet skin, her fingertips gliding in the water and soap still clinging to him. She kept her eyes on his chest and arm, but she could feel the rise in the front of his towel as he grew aroused by her. It would be so easy to tug on his towel and finally see what he looked like, to discover what he felt like if she stroked the length of his manhood. She glanced up at him, seeing the tension in his jaw and the fire in his eyes. Remembering how he had shut her down earlier, she pulled her hand away and stepped back. "You should finish your shower before the soap dries."

His nostrils flared, and he inhaled a ragged breath. For a moment, he wavered. She could see indecision warring in his eyes. He wanted to pick her up and throw her on the bed, ruck up her hospital gown and bury himself inside her. She wanted it just as much as he did.

But he didn't.

He nodded stiffly and retreated to the bathroom to finish his shower. Feeling both frustrated and amused, she cleaned up the water he had dripped all over the floor and climbed into the bed to wait for him, rolling onto her side in a comfortable position. He wasn't gone long, and when he returned, freshly showered and wearing only a pair of shorts, he turned down the lights and slid into bed behind her. Her heart stuttered wildly in her chest as she waited for him to make a move.

Finally, he draped his arm over her waist and hauled her back against his body. He nuzzled her neck and kissed her cheek. She relaxed into him, relishing the heat he shared and feeling secure and protected. He must have felt the same way because his breaths deepened, and soon, he was asleep.

Rest didn't come as easily for her. She couldn't stop thinking about Terror. His angry shouts echoed in her mind. The urge to talk to him couldn't be ignored. Until she saw him, she wouldn't be able to sleep.

Years of living in the woods, hunting and tracking, helped her ease out of bed without waking Cipher. He looked so relaxed in bed, and she wanted to get back to him as quickly as possible. Barefoot, she moved quietly to the smaller box of oxygen that Chance had switched her over to during his last visit before the end of his shift. It was light and easy to carry.

After taking one of the oranges and tucking it away in a pocket of her too-big gown, she pressed her ear to the door and listened carefully. Fairly confident the hallway was clear, she unlocked and opened the door slowly, holding her breath and hoping it wouldn't squeak. She slipped through the small gap and into the hallway. The medic station was empty. She guessed the medics were doing their rounds and wondered how much time she had until someone noticed she was missing. Not long, she supposed, and hurried off to find Terror.

Uncertain where he was, she tried to pinpoint the area where the shouting originated. Choosing a hallway that seemed darker than the others, she crept along, staying close to the wall. None of the rooms she passed were occupied. Their doors were open and their interiors dark. She paused outside one empty room, noting the missing glass in the window and the door hanging from its hinges. Certain she was getting closed, she kept going.

At the very end of the hall, there was a faint glow of blue-white light through a frosted window. She couldn't see inside, but she strongly suspected this was Terror's room. Hoping he wouldn't go berserk, she rapped her knuckles against his door before opening it. When she stepped inside, she found him sitting in a chair in the far corner, his face hidden in the shadows. True to his name, he struck fear in her heart as he leaned forward and revealed his scarred face and body in the shaft of light beaming down from above his bed.

"You shouldn't be here," he rasped, his single eye trained on her.

"I know," she admitted softly and closed the door behind her. "But I am."

Treating him like a wounded animal, she moved very deliberately, her steps slow and her arms at her sides. His gaze moved to the oxygen box she carried, and he frowned. "You're wounded?"

She shook her head. "The mines have wrecked my lungs."

A flash of sympathy crossed his face. "You never should have been in those mines."

"But I was," she replied simply. "It was the only life available to me." Hesitating, she looked around the room for a place to sit. Finally deciding that the easiest way to talk to him would be to give him a sense of control, she folded her legs and sat on the floor in front of him, making herself small and unthreatening.

He stared down at her as if he couldn't make sense of her. "Why are you here?"

"I wanted to apologize for leaving you behind."

Obviously taken aback, he asked harshly, "What?"

"When I was in the duct," she explained, "I should have found a way to get you out of there. I shouldn't have left you there for another night of their torture."

He stared unnervingly. "You did the right thing. You aren't a covert operative."

"It doesn't feel like I did the right thing."

"That's how you know it was right," he replied matter-of-factly. "Doing the right thing is never easy. It's always painful. It will always make you second-guess yourself."

She tilted her head and studied him. "You must feel a lot of pain then."

"I do." He avoided her gaze and admitted, "My whole life has been nothing but pain."

Without thinking, she reached out and grabbed his hand. He stiffened but didn't tug free. He let her hold his hand and seemed fascinated by the sight of her paler skin on his. "I'm sorry, sir."

In disbelief, he asked, "Where the fuck did they find a girl like you?"

"In a cabin in the woods without running water or electricity," she answered with a small smile. She let go of his hand and reached into her pocket to retrieve the orange. She presented it to him. "It's not much, but it's like a taste of sunshine in the dark."

He stared at the orange as if it had jogged some bitter-sweet memory. His hand trembled slightly as he took it. He brought the ripe fruit to his nose and inhaled the scent, his eye closing briefly as emotion overwhelmed him. His mouth twitched with what might have been the beginnings of a smile or maybe even a grimace. "Thank you."

"You're welcome, sir." Certain she had stayed about as long as he could handle, she rose to her feet and picked up the box. "If you need anything, I'm down the other hall, right across from the medic station. I can listen if you have something to say, or we can sit quietly together."

He didn't say anything. His one eye remained focused on the orange he held. Accepting that as her dismissal, she murmured, "Good night, sir."

"Did you see anyone else in the mine?" he asked, his voice rough and raw.

"Only the other soldier," she said. "The one who died."

"Devious."

"Yes. Him."

He turned the orange around in his hands. "You didn't

see a woman? Young like you. Quiet. Silent. Deaf."

"No." Whoever this woman was, she seemed important to him. "Someone like that wouldn't be hard to find on the mountain. People who are different are easy to remember. I could ask Miss Kay."

"Who is Miss Kay?"

"She's with the Red Feather. She's the one who asked me if I wanted to work with your forces. She knows everyone and everything. If there's a deaf woman on the mountain, she'll know how to find her."

He shook his head. "Leave it be."

She nodded and left his room, wondering who the mystery woman was. Someone who had helped him? Someone he owed a debt? Thinking about the skin traders on the mountain, Brook had a bad feeling the woman may have ended up in the same situation she had been in before Cipher rescued her.

When she turned away from the door, she gasped sharply and froze. The biggest man she had ever seen stood a few feet away from her. He had the shocking white hair of the pureblooded sky warriors and wore a uniform different than Cipher's. He looked important with all of the colorful bars and metallic adornments on his shirt. She noticed the wedding band glittering on his finger.

"My mate, Hallie, is from your planet." He lifted his hand to show her the ring. "We married in the way of your people." He lowered his hand. "Cipher will do the same for you if you ask him. He's one of the best men on this ship. Loyal, honorable, respectful. He'll be a good mate to you."

"Yes, he will," she agreed. She glanced back at the door to Terror's room. "Am I in trouble, sir?"

The corner of his mouth lifted with a smile. "I think you *are* trouble. Cipher is going to have his hands full with you."

Worried she had done something to put Cipher in jeopardy, she asked, "Is Cipher in trouble because of me?"

"No." His gaze shifted to the door, and he frowned. "Terror is my best friend. We've known each other since we were children. He spoke more to words to you, a stranger, than he has to me since we rescued him."

"Sometimes, it's easier to tell things to a stranger," she reasoned. Thinking of Terror's haunted face, she added, "Everyone who knew him before he was taken walks in there expecting the old version of him, but that man doesn't exist anymore. The man in there? The one I talked to? He's a new man. Maybe he hasn't even quite figured out how much he's changed yet. Maybe he needs space. Away from familiar faces that are putting pressure on him to be someone he can't be anymore."

When he stared at her, silent and impassive, she worried she had massively overstepped. "I'm sorry. I shouldn't have—"

"No, you definitely should have," he assured her. "You've got a big heart, Brook." His expression turned tender and warm. "Hallie will absolutely love you." He gestured to the hallway. "Come on. Let's get you to back to Cipher before he wakes up and realizes you've escaped."

She frowned. "I didn't escape. I went for a walk."

He chuckled at her response. When they turned the corner, she spotted Cipher hurrying out of the hospital room. His shirt was untucked from his pants, and he was hopping into his boots. His panicked expression changed to one of irritation as soon as he saw her being escorted back to the room.

Quickly straightening, he saluted the man now standing still next to her. "General."

Oh, no. Oh, shit. What have I done?

"At ease, Cipher." With amusement in his voice, the General said, "I think I found something that belongs to you."

"Apologies, sir. It won't happen again." He pinned her in place with a look that made her squirm like a naughty child.

"I'm sure it will," the General replied with a laugh. "This one has the same mischievous gleam in her eyes as Hallie. Get a collar on her, soldier."

"Yes, sir."

The general nodded at her before pivoting on his heel and returning to Terror's room. She avoided Cipher's intense stare as long as possible. When she did finally meet his gaze, she was surprised to see that he wasn't angry with her. If anything, he looked relieved. He held out his hand, and she clasped it, letting him take her back into the hospital room.

As soon as the door was closed, he boxed her in against it, his hands on either side of her head, and leaned down to capture her mouth. She mewled as he kissed her, his tongue stabbing insistently against hers. When he broke away, he said, "I thought another man had taken you."

Regret and guilt soured her belly. "I'm so sorry! I didn't mean to make you worry."

He narrowed his eyes. "Did you go see Terror?"

She nodded.

He sighed heavily. "I warned you that he was unstable."

"He wasn't unstable with me. We talked, and it was nice."

"Just talked?"

"I gave him an orange?"

"An orange?"

"They're tasty," she defended herself. "I thought it might give him a few moments of enjoyment."

"Brook," he whispered and then kissed her again. "You sweet, sweet girl."

She bit her lower lip. "Are you mad at me?"

"No." He dragged her lip away from her teeth with his thumb. "I was scared, not angry. I'm frustrated that you left like that, but I trust that you won't do something like this again."

"I won't," she promised. "I won't leave without telling you first."

"Good." He cupped the back of her neck and drew her in for a hug. With a smile in his voice, he added, "Maybe I should have tied you down after all."

She giggled and wrapped her arms around his waist. "The night's still young."

He groaned low. "Risk had better discharge you soon."

Her heart raced at the thought of being alone with Cipher. She couldn't get out of this hospital fast enough.

Chapter Nine

S WINGING HER LEGS back and forth from her perch on the edge of the hospital bed, Brook kept her hopeful gaze on the door of her hospital room. This morning, Risk had finally decided she was healthy enough to be discharged into her mate's care.

She smiled giddily at the thought of finally seeing her new home. She had so many questions. What did home look like on a spaceship? So far, everything she had seen was bright, clean and sterile with lots of gleaming metal and shiny plastic.

Surely, their quarters weren't so plain. How big would they be? Smaller than her cabin? Larger? And what kind of technology would there be?

She had already explored all the technology available in her hospital room. The tablet had been a revelation. She had never in her life had that many books at her fingertips. All the books she had read before now had been heavily used copies with soot-stained pages passed around the mine camps until they were falling apart. Most of them had been texts on mining or farming or survival, but there had been a handful of adventure stories and even once a romance. She had never dreamed of being able to visit a library. Now, she could hold an entire library in her hands and read whatever she wanted whenever she wanted.

Movement outside her room caught her attention. She straightened up and stopped swinging her legs when she realized it was Cipher. Unable to stop smiling, she greeted him a bit shyly when he stepped into her hospital room. "Hi."

He grinned. "Hi."

"You come here to break me out finally?"

"The warden has decided you've done your time, but he warned me you were anything but a model prisoner."

"Sorry," she said, blushing at the thought of the trouble she had caused two mornings ago when she had tried to figure out how the stickers on her chest relayed her heartbeat to the machine on the wall. "I didn't mean to cause such a ruckus with their Code Blue or whatever it was."

"I know you didn't," he said gently and crossed the distance between them. He dwarfed her even as she sat on the tall bed. Up here, in his world, she felt impossibly small. As if reading her mind, he said, "Risk has given you a nutritional plan to follow. He wants you to gain at least ten percent of your current body weight before—" He stopped abruptly and swallowed. "Well, let's focus on the ten percent."

"Before what?"

Cipher slowly lifted his hand until he cupped her face. His touch elicited a flutter of excitement in her belly. Her time in the infirmary had been somewhat akin to torture.

The obvious desire between them burned brighter with each passing day. Their restrained kisses and curious touches left them both aching for more. Today—finally—they were going to have the privacy Cipher demanded they have the first time they were together.

"Before we try to have a baby," he explained. His gaze searched her face as if trying to read her response. "If you want to have a baby," he added. "We haven't talked about that or what it means for our relationship but—"

She interrupted him by turning her face and kissing his palm. He inhaled sharply, and she smiled up at him. "I want to have a family. Someday," she added. "With you."

"Good," he said roughly. "That's what I want with you. If you decide to stay," he amended. "You don't have to stay. You can go. If you want. I won't keep you against your will."

Amused by his rambling, she gripped his big wrist in both her smaller hands. "I want to stay."

"If you change your mind…" He hesitated. "It's okay if you want to change your mind. It happens sometimes. There's no pressure from me for you to stay. If you realize in a few weeks that you want to go to the colonies and live free and experience more of life, I'll let you go. I won't fight it."

She had never imagined Cipher to be uncertain about anything. She sensed that what he wanted more than anything was for her to stay with him, to build a future and a family together. Yet, he seemed afraid to project those desires on her or to take away her ability to choose.

"I'm here because I want to be here, Cipher." She hoped to reassure him. "If I change my mind, I promise you'll be the first to know."

He exhaled a long, steady breath and nodded. "Good." When she let go of his wrist, he ran his fingers down her bare arm. "You look beautiful in this dress."

She blushed and spread her hands over the sunny fabric dotted with white flowers. "Thank you."

"I tried to find something more similar to what you normally wear, but Naya didn't have anything in her shop in the correct sizes. Dizzy offered to have you come by her studio sometime this week for measurements so she can make things for you."

She hadn't met the other wives yet, but Cipher had told her about them. She was eager to make new friends and hoped they would like her. "I like the dress. I haven't worn one in a long time. It's nice to have something pretty and new."

"You can have all the pretty, new things you want," Cipher assured her. "After you've had time to adjust to life on the ship, I'll have Dizzy or Naya take you down to the women's only sector. You can shop and buy all the things you need."

"I don't need much," she insisted. "I can make do."

"I know you can." He stroked her face. "You don't have to make do anymore. I'll take care of you now."

She had to swallow down the emotion that welled up inside her. Wanting to be always honest with him, she admitted, "I've wanted someone to take care of me for so long. I'm so tired of being strong and alone. I know I can take care of myself, but the thought of having someone else take care of me is like a dream."

"You'll be safe here with me, Brook," he promised. "I'll provide for you and any children we have. I'll make sure you have what you need and more. I'll take care of you—in every way."

She met his dark gaze and understood he meant in *every way*. The idea of being stripped naked by him, tumbled into bed and shown what real pleasure was made her almost dizzy with excitement. She had heard enough rumors to know what happened in the bedrooms of the sky warriors. They did things. Naughty things. Decadent things. Dangerous things.

And she wanted to know *all* those things.

"I have something else I want you to wear." Cipher reached into the pocket of his pants and retrieved a stark white collar with a shiny buckle. "May I?"

She had read the pamphlets and welcome guide for new brides. She knew exactly what the collar meant and why it was so important that she wear it for him. She supposed some women fought against it, maybe even hated it, but she couldn't wait to feel it on her skin. She wanted to belong to him. She wanted everyone to know she was under his protection.

Wordlessly, she slid off the tall bed until the leather soles of her new slipper like shoes touched the cold floor. She presented her back to him and swept her long braid off of her neck and over her shoulder. Cipher stepped closer, and his body heat penetrated her back and made her want to lean into him. He draped the opened collar around her neck, placing it low enough that it wouldn't irritate and buckled it with enough room for him to slide his finger under it.

His heavy hands rested on her shoulders, and he bent down, his breath tickling her skin before he placed tender kisses above and below the collar. "I will never harm you. I will never force you. I will never leave you behind. I will take care of you for the rest of our lives."

His words were spoken like vows. He didn't love her, and she didn't love him—*yet*—but he was giving her the promises a man gave to his wife. He meant every word, and she wanted him to know she was taking this as seriously as he was.

Turning to face him, she gazed up at the towering giant of a man who had rescued and claimed her. She took a moment to consider her words. "I will never take you for granted. I will honor you. I will make your life interesting and probably a little frustrating." His lips twitched with a smile at that. "I will support you and care for you."

Cipher's expression softened, and he clasped the back of her neck, tilting her head back to give him access. He was so tall that he had to practically bend in half to capture her mouth, but he didn't seem to mind. He was tender at first, his lips just brushing against hers, but when she gripped the front of his uniform shirt, he let go of that control. He kissed her as if he had been waiting a lifetime to make those promises to her.

When she whimpered and tried to deepen the kiss, he pulled back and kissed her forehead. "Not here, little one."

"Yes, sir," she whispered and licked her lips.

Cipher actually groaned. "You're going to kill me with that."

She stared up at him with confusion. "With what?"

"Sir," he said simply.

"Oh." She hadn't considered it was wrong. All her life, she had been taught to show respect to older men. "Should I stop?"

"Hell no," he said hurriedly. "You have no idea what it does to me." His gaze darkened, and she trembled with excitement. "But you will soon."

Taking her hand, Cipher grabbed her small bag of belongings from the hospital bed and tugged her along until she fell into step beside him. She may have imagined it, but she thought some of the medics looked relieve to see her go. In the hallway outside the hospital unit, he led her to the elevator. It was nothing like the rickety, squealing rust buckets that were in some of the deeper mines. She marveled when Cipher used the chip implanted in her wrist to activate the elevator.

"So, what happens now?" She leaned back against the wall of the elevator and smiled up at him.

"We settle into our new quarters and get to know each other a little better."

"Only a little?" she asked, feeling bold now that they were alone and on their way to their new home.

"Maybe a lot," he said, moving closer.

The elevator slowed and came to a halt on a floor that wasn't their own. The doors opened to reveal four hulking men with the strange pilot haircuts. The stripes shaved into the side of their heads was a way of showing their rank, but she hadn't been that interested in the pilot part of the bride's guide so she had skipped over it. Uncertain whether these men outranked Cipher or not, she glanced up at him to see how he would react.

He nodded stiffly before dropping her hand and sliding his arm around her shoulders. His forearm rested just below her collar, and he pulled her into his body, her back flush with his front. The men avoided looking at her, keeping their gazes averted, and filed into the elevator. Each one gave Cipher a short, "Sir," before focusing straight ahead on the closing doors.

The awkward elevator ride ended a few floors later. The men stepped out onto a floor that seemed very busy, and Cipher leaned forward to slap at the touchscreen console, tapping the close button until the doors slid together. He finally relaxed when the elevator started to move again.

As if realizing he had manhandled her, he quickly let go. "I'm sorry."

"It's okay." She missed the feel of his arm around her, holding her close and safe. Wanting to show him that didn't mind, she took his hand and lifted his arm back into place. "I liked it."

He groaned as if in pain, and his arm tightened around her. "The things that come out of your mouth, Brook."

"Are they good?" she asked uncertainly.

"Yes," he said, leaning down to kiss the top of her head. "So very, very good."

Happy to have pleased him, she leaned into his warm body and enjoyed the closeness for the rest of their elevator ride. When they reached their floor, he reluctantly let her go and took her hand. They stepped out of the elevator and into a hallway lined with doors. Some of them had wreaths or welcome mats, making the hallway joyful and inviting.

"This is us," he announced. "Go on."

Nervous but excited to see her new home, she placed her wrist near the scanner and waited for the chirp and green light. Once it was unlocked, she opened the door and stepped inside an entryway. Immediately, lights flicked on and a friendly female voice welcomed them before giving a rundown of the temperature, humidity and important notifications from their message system. She glanced back at Cipher in awe, and he smiled encouragingly, gesturing for her to keep exploring.

The entryway of their quarters opened into a large living area with more furniture than she had ever seen. A small couch, a large couch, a comfy chair, tables and lamps. The entertainment center looked exactly like the one shown in the guidebook. Right now, it displayed a lifelike image of a fireplace with a roaring fire and all the sounds she would expect, right down to the occasional pop.

Off the living area, there was a kitchen filled with gleaming appliances she couldn't wait to try. A small round table sat off to the side with just two chairs. The guidebook had mentioned that many of the tables had extra leaves and chairs that were stowed away in a hidden storage compartment along the wall. The idea of hosting a dinner for Cipher's friends started to come together. She wanted him to be proud of her and her homemaking skills.

As she turned back to face the living area, something familiar and unexpected caught her eye. She hadn't seen the built-in shelves along the left side of the room on her first look. Seeing them now, she hurriedly crossed the room and gasped. "My things!"

"I called in a favor." Cipher placed the hospital bag on the chair and crossed his arms over his broad chest. "I wanted this to feel like your home as much as it is mine."

She lovingly ran her hands over the things she had left behind in her cabin. A lantern, her father's old mining helmet, faded family photos and mementos. He had arranged them on the shelves like curios in a museum, melding his treasured things with hers.

"I put the maps here." He crouched down and tugged open a wide, deep drawer filled with rolled maps. "I thought we might pick some of the important ones to frame. They'll be interesting to have on the walls."

She started to cry and wiped at her face, embarrassed to show so much emotion over a few old maps. Overwhelmed by his gesture, she wandered away from the shelves and into the room adjacent to the living area. It was a spacious bedroom. *Our bedroom.* Her gaze drifted to an obscenely big bed and lingered on the metal rings attached to the headboard. Even as inexperienced as she was, she had no trouble imagining how they were used.

But it was the neatly folded quilt draped over the foot of the bed that broke her composure. Her mother had sewn the quilt from scraps late in the evenings after working backbreaking day shifts in the mine. Brook could still remember sitting at her mother's feet while her mother sang and sewed, her nimble fingers working long strings of thread through the fabric and batting. It had broken her heart to leave it behind, but Cipher had just put the pieces back together for her.

Sobbing now, she felt Cipher approach from the door behind her. She pivoted toward him and threw her arms around his waist, burying her face against his hard chest and crying. He stroked his hand down her braid and rubbed her back with the other. She clung to him, so incredibly grateful he had come into her life.

"I'm so sorry, Brook. I thought you would be happy about the surprise."

She reared back and stared up at him through the tears. Realizing he thought she was upset, she rolled her eyes and huffed. "No, you big idiot! I'm overwhelmed at how wonderful you are! How romantic this is!"

"Oh." Clearly relieved, he used his impressive strength to haul her right off the floor and into his arms. He walked them to the bed and sat on the edge of it, placing her on his lap with her legs draped over his. He pressed his lips to her temple and then her cheek before turning her face for a gentle kiss. "I'm glad you're happy about it, but I'm sorry I made you cry."

"It's okay," she said, sniffling and wiping at her face. "It was a good cry."

His callused thumbs raked over her cheeks, swiping away the last of her tears. He kissed her forehead and held her close, soothing her with the caress of his hand along her side. A while later, when she was still and relaxed, he said, "I'm letting the idiot remark slide for now, but next time, you'll have to face the consequences."

She lifted her head from his shoulder and gazed into his dark eyes. "Such as?"

He shifted her on his lap, drawing her left leg up and around his waist. The other followed naturally, and she found herself scandalously wrapped around him, only her thin panties and his pants separating their private parts. As if amused to have her off-kilter, he smirked playfully and pulled her even tighter against him, rubbing her along the hard length of him that she was staggeringly aware of now.

"Such as this," he murmured low and then smacked her bottom.

She squealed with shock and indignation, but the hand that had just whacked her smoothed over her stinging bottom. *His hand is under my skirt. His hand is on my ass. Oh my…*

Overheated and nervous, she asked, "Do you really want to spank me?"

"Yes." He captured her mouth again, this time shocking her by flicking his tongue insistently between her lips until she surrendered. His tongue swept hers, and she felt so lightheaded she clutched at his shoulders, desperate not to fall.

"Why?" she asked, feeling completely out of control as his hand stroked her bare thigh. No man had ever touched her like this. No man had ever kissed her like this. Gazing at Cipher, she was so glad he would be her teacher.

"Did you read the pamphlet about pain and pleasure?" He dragged his mouth along the curve of her neck, and she started to shake.

"Yes."

"It's the way I'm built, Brook. It's the way I'm wired." He nipped at her throat, and she whimpered. "I want to be in control. I want to dominate you. I want to own you."

Trying to keep a level head, she pulled away enough to stare into his eyes. A quiver of fear made her suddenly serious. He was so much bigger and stronger. If he did some of the things she had read about in the guidebook, he could seriously injure her. "Do you want to hurt me?"

"A little," he admitted, never taking his eyes off her face. "Not in anger and never enough to harm you. Only enough to highlight the extreme pleasure you're capable of feeling."

Satisfied with his answer but also afraid of the unknown, she asked, "Do you want to hurt me right now?"

"No," he answered without hesitation. The hand on her bottom dragged her closer, and he kissed her so sweetly. "Right now, I want to teach you all the things about your body that you don't know yet."

Thinking of his hands and mouth on her body, touching all the places she rarely dared, showing her the kind of pleasure she had only imagined, she decided it was time for courage. Knowing what would make him go absolutely feral with desire, she leaned closer. "I'm a very good student, sir."

Whatever doubts he may have harbored seemed to flee in that moment. Wrapping her braid around his fist, he tugged her head back and licked a slow line up the center of her neck before claiming her mouth in a kiss that left her breathless and aching. With her hair tight in his hand, he had complete control over her movement—and she liked it.

"There it is," he murmured against her skin. "There's that submissive spark I want."

"What else do you want from me, sir?"

"Everything you have to give." He skimmed his lips along her jaw and squeezed her bottom in his big hand. "I want it all."

"Take it," she pleaded, her entire body on fire. "Take me, Cipher."

He groaned with need and tilted her head until they were eye-to-eye. "Remember you asked for this."

Chapter Ten

G ENTLE. CAREFUL. SLOW. Gentle. Careful. Slow.

Cipher silently repeated his mantra as he moved Brook into a standing position and rose from the bed. Taking her hand, he led her toward the door she hadn't asked about yet. He had considered easing her into the things he liked, but her natural curiosity and bravery had him reconsidering that plan. Trusting that she would tell him if things were too uncomfortable or intimidating, he unlocked the door and tugged her along behind him.

The lights immediately turned on at the setting he had chosen when configuring the space, a perfect medium between too bright or dim. He left the door open behind them, making sure Brook had a quick exit. When she stepped in front of him, he suspected the open door was a moot point. With a look of wonder, she glanced around the space as if cataloguing everything. He wished he could hear her thoughts. Was she curious? Afraid? Nervous?

"May I touch your things, sir?"

"Our things," he corrected. "This is our room to enjoy. You can touch anything in here."

With a coquettish smile, she asked, "Even you?"

"Definitely me," he agreed, crossing his arms as she

began to explore. He held himself back, giving her time to get comfortable in their space.

"Do all the quarters have these rooms?" She ran her hand along the metal countertop lining one wall. "Or just officers?"

"All quarters in the mated sector have them. The higher your rank, the bigger your space. Each man is allowed to furnish the space however he pleases. Some couples convert them to extra bedroom space if they have more children than their quarters can comfortably house."

"I'd imagine the couples who spend a lot of time in these rooms have that problem," she remarked playfully.

"That's probably true." He watched as she moved to the swing mounted to the ceiling. She touched the black leather seat and gave it a little push. Her hand slid along the seat to one of the chains. "If you want to try something, you can. With your clothes on," he added quickly. "We don't have to do anything in here until you're ready."

"I'm ready." She held his gaze and spoke clearly and steadily. "I want you to teach me everything you know."

"That might take a while," he said, taking a step toward her and uncrossing his arms.

"Then I guess it's a good thing that I'm currently unemployed and have nothing but time to fill."

For now, he decided to ignore the currently unemployed part of her statement. He was more interested in starting her first lesson. Looking around the room he had spent the last few days arranging, he decided the lounge chair facing the floor to ceiling mirror was the perfect place to begin her lessons. It had a curved shape, almost like a sideways S, that allowed a couple to use it in a variety of different and interesting ways.

He closed the distance between them and held out his hand. She bit her lower lip with anticipation and then smiled as she placed her small hand on his. When they reached the chair, he maneuvered her in front of it and sat down on the steel gray leather. He leaned forward and slipped off her shoes before he tugged at the tie holding her wrap dress closed. His cock throbbed almost painfully in his pants, and he knew that just a few strokes of her soft hand on his shaft would send him over the edge embarrassingly fast.

This isn't about you. It's about her.

Ever since she had eagerly taken his collar, he had been aching for her. His entire body hummed with desire and the need to touch and taste her. He had seen her naked body that night in the forest, but his gaze had been more clinical and less appreciative. Today, he planned to take his time and study ever last inch of her. He wanted to learn all the places that made her sigh or gasp.

She wore no bra under the dress, and her breasts were flushed, the nipples taut and begging to be licked. So he did. When she cried out in surprise, he smiled and did it again. "You're so sensitive."

"I'm sorry."

"Don't be," he said, using his thumb and forefinger to massage the now slick tip. She whimpered, and he moved his mouth to the other side. Her hands flew to his head, and her short nails scratched through his hair. It was as if she couldn't decide whether she wanted to push him away or hold him in place. When he pulled free, he flicked his tongue against the little peak and enjoyed her moan. "Sensitive is very good."

"Oh," she replied breathlessly.

He dragged the dress the rest of the way down her body and flung it behind him. Her panties were the simplest style carried on the ship. Someday, he might want to see her in wildly erotic strips of fabric, but for now, she would be most comfortable in familiar and modest things. Gripping the sides of them, he pulled them down her slim hips and lean thighs to reveal a sparse thatch of dark hair.

She pressed her knees together, displaying her anxiety at being naked in front of him. Wanting to set her at ease, he caressed her waist and settled his hands on her hips. "You are incredible, Brook."

She seemed uncertain as she asked, "Are you sure? I know I'm not very big in the right places."

Hating that she felt unattractive because her body didn't look a certain way, he placed his palm against her cheek. "I chose you because I like you exactly as you are."

She seemed to think that over for a few seconds before relaxing. "You're sure you don't mind that these aren't bigger?"

Cipher's cock throbbed at the sight of her cupping her own breasts. "They're perfect." He leaned forward and kissed between them. "You're perfect."

She giggled as his mouth moved lower, and he smiled,

wondering just how ticklish she was. He grazed his finger-tips along her rib cage, and she erupted in a fit of laughter. Loving the sound of her laugh, he dragged his fingernails along her belly. She lost it, laughing so hard she fell forward onto him. He wrapped his arms around her as they dropped back onto the lounger. His heart hammered in his chest as he reveled in the feel of her body on his. He had waited so long for a mate, but it had been worth it.

She was worth it.

Brook sat up, her hands on his chest as she straddled his waist. Flushed and glassy-eyed with lust, she smiled down at him, and he knew in that moment he was a goner. Somehow, some way, he had found her. The one. The only one. He had never been the type to believe in fate but he had to wonder now. What were the odds that he would be the soldier sent to meet her?

"May I undress you?" she asked softly. "I want to see you."

He nodded and sat up, his hands drifting lower to her bare bottom. She breathed harder as he caressed her curves. The urge to flip her over, spread her legs and bury his face in her pussy nearly overwhelmed him.

Still straddling him, she grasped the bottom of his shirt and pulled it free from his pants. Her nimble fingers moved along the row of buttons lining his shirt before she pushed it off his shoulders and dragged it down his arms. She pulled off his undershirt next and tossed it aside. Her eyes widened with appreciation at the sight of his bare chest. Her smaller hands were so warm and soft as they glided over his skin. She traced his battle scars, her face darkening with sympathy as she ran her fingers over each ridge and bump. "These must have hurt."

"They did." He gave in to the desire to feel her hair. Taking the end of her loose braid in hand, he uncurled the tie holding it together and let it fall to the floor. He unwound the long strands of her dark hair until they were free and hanging in waves around her shoulders and back. He brushed his fingers through them, enjoying the silky feel on his skin. "Will you wear this down for me?"

Her hands moved to his shoulders, and she leaned forward until her lips nearly touched his. "Yes."

His mouth curved to a smile as she pressed her lush lips to his. Unpracticed and uncertain, she kissed him lightly at first. She grew bolder and flicked her tongue in a way that had him instantly opening to her, welcoming her exploration. She moaned into his mouth when her nipples touched his chest, and he gripped her waist, desperate to keep her right there.

"Cipher," she whispered and rocked her body against his. His stiff cock tented the front of his pants and gave her something to rub against. He could already smell her arousal, could feel the heat of her through his pants. The thought of having her slick cunt gliding over his shaft left him dizzy with lust.

When her hands fumbled with his belt, he reached down to help her. She smiled shyly as their hands worked together to rid him of his pants only to have them get caught on his boots. He cursed under his breath, and she giggled, the sound so pure and sweet that his frustration fled. She shimmied down his body and off the chair. "Let me help."

Leaning on his elbows, he watched as she knelt at his feet and unzipped his boots. She tugged them off and set them aside before peeling away his socks and placing them inside his boots. Taking hold of his pants, she pulled them the rest of the way off his legs. She folded and placed them on the floor next to his boots. Her tremulous gaze met his heated one as she grasped the waistband of his boxer-briefs and began to lower them.

She gasped when his cock sprang free. In a shocked and breathless rush, she asked, "Are they all this big?"

He snorted at her reaction. "Up here? On this ship? Yes."

She stared at his penis for a moment before turning doubtful. "I don't think this is going to work, sir. I mean...look."

He bit back a groan as she measured his shaft with her hands and then placed them against her own body, showing him just how deep the length of him would be once he was inside her. "It will work," he assured her. "We'll take it easy."

She remained unconvinced but nodded nonetheless. Taking hold of his underwear, she dragged them down his thighs and off his legs, placing them on top of his pants. She sat back on her heels, her palms naturally resting on her knees in a submissive pose that made his heart race. She smiled shyly up at him, and he didn't even try to hold back.

"You're utterly fucking perfect." He wanted her to know how special she was to him. "Absolutely perfect."

Blushing, she lowered her gaze. "Sir…"

He silenced her protest with a stroke of his fingers down her cheek. "Believe what I tell you, Brook. I won't ever lie to you. In here, especially, we have to trust each other. We have to be honest. Can you promise me that?"

"Yes, sir."

"Good girl. Now, stand up and turn around for me."

She did as he asked, rising gracefully from the floor and pivoting away from him to face the mirror. He placed his hands on her waist and gently guided her back toward the chair. She placed her trust in him as he lowered her down onto his lap and draped her legs over his thighs. He shifted and moved his cock between their bodies, pressed against her bottom and lower back, keeping it out of the way so he could concentrate only on her.

He could feel her breathing faster, shallower. She met his gaze in the mirror directly in front of them. Her skin had flushed a dark shade of pink at the realization that he could see all of her secret places. She leaned back against him, turning her head to look up at him, and he lowered his face until their lips met in a sensual kiss. He let his hands roam her body, caressing up her belly and chest to cup her breasts. "Have you ever been this far with another man?"

"No," she answered breathlessly.

"If I do something that makes you uncomfortable, I

want you to tell me." He held her gaze in the mirror to make sure she understood. "It won't upset me in any way if you tell me to stop."

She placed her smaller hands over his. "What if I ask you not to stop?"

"Then I definitely won't," he murmured against her lips. She met his seeking kiss with a grin that made him want her even more. He brushed his thumbs over her nipples and asked, "Do you touch yourself? Make yourself come?"

"Sir!" she gasped against his mouth as her face turned bright red.

"It's not shameful, Brook. It's a normal, healthy thing to do." He slid his hands down her ribcage and then her lower belly. "We're supposed to enjoy our bodies." He moved his hands to her thighs, stroking down toward her knees before sweeping back up toward her belly. "If you can show me how you like to be touched, we can enjoy our bodies together."

As if overcome with embarrassment, she buried her face in his neck. He stroked her soft skin until she finally admitted, "I try sometimes, but it doesn't ever happen."

"It? You mean an orgasm?"

She nodded against his neck. "It feels good, but I think I'm doing it wrong."

He had a feeling she was too wound up to let go. "Show me."

Still keeping her face shielded, she shook her head. "I can't."

"How about I touch you, and you tell me what feels good and what doesn't?" He kept his hands on her upper thighs. "Is that okay?"

"Yes."

Wanting to set her at ease, he caressed her thighs and placed light kisses along her neck. She sighed and nuzzled into him, her plump lips grazing against the pulsing vein in his throat. He let his hands glide higher, sweeping up to her belly and breasts and then back down to her thighs. He turned them as traveled back up her body, letting his fingers run along the curve of her inner thighs. She inhaled a shaky breath as he drew closer to her pussy, but he switched the motion at the last second and moved his hands toward the tops of her thighs and back up to her belly and breasts. He repeated the motion a few times, enjoying the trembling breaths that tickled his neck as he drew closer and closer to her sex.

Finally, he let his hands move right where they both wanted them. She sucked in a sharp breath as he started to stroke her labia and trace the seam of her cunt. He caught her watching them in the mirror and gently spread her outer lips, showing her what she looked like. "Have you ever seen yourself like this?"

She swallowed hard. "No, sir."

"Look," he commanded. "Look at how pretty your pussy is, Brook. Pink and wet and soft." He swirled a finger around her opening. With his fingertip now slick, he eased his way back to her clit and traced a half circle along the top and sides. He kept up the simple motion, gliding over the hood and letting her get used to the sensation. She clutched at his legs, anchoring herself to his thighs with her hands. He took that as a good sign and kept stroking her clit.

With one hand moving between her breasts and belly, he used the other to tease her with light circles. She watched him in the mirror, her eyes dark with desire. The heady scent of her arousal filled the air, and he could feel her growing wetter and wetter under his fingertips. Her breathing shifted, and she rocked her hips. Reading her reactions, he changed the movement of his fingertip to a side-to-side motion. Trembling, she gasped and curled her toes against his calves. "Cipher!"

"Let go," he urged.

"I can't."

"You can." He nuzzled her neck. "Close your eyes and let go, baby girl."

She did exactly as he commanded. As she cried out her joy, he grazed his teeth along her neck. She was so beautiful as she came, rocking and shuddering on his lap. He watched the flush creep along her skin and pinched her nipples to give her a bite of pain with the pleasure. When she whimpered and tried to pull away from his hand, he cupped her sex and placed soft kisses on her shoulder.

Before he could ask her if she was okay, she turned quickly, straddling him and dripping her slick heat all over his throbbing cock. She crashed her mouth to his and wrapped her arms around him, pressing her body to his. Her unsteady and unpracticed kisses were sweeter than any he had ever received, and he let her take control. His hands settled on her bottom as their tongues dueled, and he let his fingers brush between her cheeks, touching her in a place that she likely considered taboo. She shuddered and pressed into his hand, silently showing him that she wasn't afraid of trying new things.

Her hand slid down between their bodies, and she grasped his cock. The feeling rocked him to the core, and he dropped back on the curved sofa, dragging her right along with him. She wiggled her hips and trapped his shaft between the puffy lips of her cunt. He growled, and she grew emboldened, wiggling her hips even more. She reacted with the same enthusiasm as she realized how good it felt to rub herself along his erection.

"Fuck," he groaned as she moved back and forth. Her slick heat glided along the underside of his shaft, and she swiveled her hips, grinding her clit against the head of his cock. It felt incredible for him, and judging by the look on her face, it was even better for her. He wanted to slide her forward a little higher and thrust into her, but she was enjoying herself too much. He wanted to watch her come apart on top of him. "Brook. *Fuck.* Don't stop. Keep going, baby. Make yourself come on my cock."

"Cipher," she whimpered and scratched at his chest. She held his gaze as she moved faster, using him to chase her climax. She was so wet and making a mess of them both as she rocked and swiveled, grinding and smashing until they were both grunting. Her legs started to shake on either side of his hips, and she clutched one of his hands, bringing it to her chest and holding so tight her knuckles turned white. "Cipher!"

Hearing her call out his name as she orgasmed sent him reeling over the edge. He thrust up against her pussy and painted her lower belly with his seed. He groaned as he pumped out his pleasure in long pent-up waves. She held his gaze and his hand as she moved slowly, swiveling until they were both panting and spent.

She fell forward on top of him, nestling her head in the crook of his shoulder. Neither cared about the mess between them. He stroked her back and combed his fingers through her hair as she fought to catch her breath and come down from the high of her back-to-back climaxes. When she finally roused, lifting her head and catching his gaze, she had a mischievous grin on her face. "Can we do that again?"

He laughed and dragged her mouth to his, claiming it with a sensual kiss that promised more. "Give me fifteen minutes and a water break."

Chapter Eleven

BROOK WAITED IMPATIENTLY for Cipher to return to the bedroom. After tidying up their hastily discarded clothing, she had ducked into the bathroom to clean up while he left for the water break he had negotiated. Her entire body vibrated with excitement as she knelt on the bed, hands on her knees as she watched the door with mounting anticipation. She had known that it would feel good to have an orgasm, but she hadn't realized it would feel like that.

It was like free falling, like being weightless and bathed in sunshine. She wanted to feel it again and again. She wanted to share that feeling with Cipher over and over until they were boneless and exhausted. She wanted to experience the stretch and burn of his huge cock sliding into her and come with him closer than any other person had ever been to her.

When he finally appeared in the doorway, an almost empty glass of water in his hand, she perked up and grinned. "I think that was more than fifteen minutes."

"I'll make it up to you," he promised before downing the water and setting the glass on the bedside table built into the wall. In the next instant, he was on the bed and crawling toward her. She giggled as he gave her a little shove, sending her onto her back, and grasped her ankle, tugging her right into the middle of the bed where he wanted her.

When his hands disappeared under the pillows, she didn't think much of it, but then she felt something against her wrists and jerked her head away from his to see what he was doing. She spotted the lined leather cuff a heartbeat before it was locked around her wrist and then secured to one of the rings on the headboard. Showing his skill at apprehending terrorists, he quickly secured the other one. She swallowed nervously. "Sir?"

"If you don't like it, just ask me to stop and I'll unlock them," he promised. He ran his hands along her sides and admitted, "I've wanted to cuff you to my bed since the night I met you."

She melted at his admission. Knowing he would never hurt her, she said, "I trust you."

"I will never do anything to break that trust." He sealed his vow with a scorching kiss. She instinctively wrapped her legs around his waist as they kissed. She shivered as his skillful fingers ran down her ribcage. Trapped under his bigger, harder body, she reveled in the way he made her feel so small and protected. Life on the mountain had always been so uncertain, and for the first time since her father's death, she felt calm and safe. No matter what the future brought, Cipher would take care of her.

And—*oh, hell*—he was really taking care of her right now.

His talented mouth skimmed her throat and danced between her breasts. She gasped at the feel of his mouth on her nipples. He licked and suckled and then teethed the peaks until she panted with need. His mouth moved lower, trailing ticklish kisses down the slope of her belly, around her navel and then on the crest of each hip. When he slid even lower, she raised her head to watch him. She had heard people talk about using their mouths down there, but it had always seemed strange and uncomfortable to her.

Now, it seemed like the most natural and wonderful thing in the world. She didn't fight Cipher as he pushed her thighs apart and stared hungrily at her. He groaned low in his throat and said, "I'm going to eat your pussy until you scream."

She blushed hotly, wondering if she would ever get used to hearing him say such filthy things. He pressed her thighs even farther apart with his broad shoulders and used his fingers to spread her open. The first swipe of his firm tongue had her crying out in shock. It felt incredible. It was like nothing she had ever experienced or imagined. His tongue was firm and warm as he lapped at the little nub that gave her so much pleasure. It was a completely different feeling than his fingers, and she couldn't decide which she liked better.

His tongue traveled from her clitoris to her opening, darting inside and tasting her in a way that made her squeal. Cipher laughed against her pussy, the vibrations making everything feel even better in the most delicious way. He used his tongue the way she imagined he would soon use his cock, thrusting in and out until her thighs were shaking and her feet were arched off the bed. Just when she thought she couldn't take anymore, he moved away his tongue back up to her clit.

"Sir!" It seemed so easy and right to call him that as he mastered her body. He fluttered his tongue over the pink pearl that had already given her so much pleasure, and she inhaled a ragged breath. Her entire body thrummed with anticipation. Deep in her belly, an invisible wire coiled tight, like the trigger mechanism for a timed explosion. She didn't try to fight the overwhelming sensation Cipher created with his tongue. She gave into it, surrendering to him and everything he had to offer.

Her climax knocked the air right out of her lungs. Her hips lifted from the bed, pressing her sex against this wonderful mouth, and she tugged at her bonds, simultaneously loving and hating the restraints. Held in place with the cuffs, she couldn't escape as he changed his tactic and sucked her clit. The sensation overwhelmed her, but she was brought right back into her body when he slid a finger into her soaking channel.

It was the first time she had ever had anything inside her. It felt strange at first but coupled with his flicking tongue, it began to feel very, very good. She moaned as he did wicked things with his mouth and worked his thick finger in and out of her. She lifted her head and watched as he pleasured her with his tongue and hand. Even restrained in cuffs, she felt powerful. This incredibly strong man was on his belly with his face buried between her legs and giving her pleasure. She knew, deep down inside, that with one word, she could stop him. She could have her orgasm and then ask him to leave her be—and he would. There was power in her submission, and it made her feel safe.

When he added a second finger, she lost it. Head thrown back, she closed her eyes and focused only on the feel of his mouth and fingers working her closer and closer to the edge. That flutter of euphoria began to quiver in her belly, and she chased after it, surrendering to Cipher until she screamed. His name echoed off the walls of their room, and she strained against the cuffs, rocking her hips while the waves of pleasure rolled through her body.

When it was over, she sagged against the bed, her legs limp and open, her hands curled loosely and dangling from the cuffs. Cipher kissed her inner thighs and petted her abdomen as she came down from the best high of her life. He finally moved to a kneeling position and reached across her body to the bedside table. He grabbed something from the drawer and sat back on his heels. He flipped the cap on the tube and squeezed a dollop of something clear onto his palm.

"What is that?"

"Lubricant," he explained and tossed the tube aside. He slathered the gel on his ruddy shaft and then pressed the excess into her. She gasped at the sensation of the cool gel coating her inner walls and squirmed when his fingers withdrew. "It will make this easier for you."

Fascinated, she watched him stroke his cock and then take it in hand. He dragged the tip through her folds, swirling it around her ultra-sensitive clit before sliding it down to her opening. She drew in a breath as he breached her entrance, the thick head of his shaft filling her in a way that she had never known was possible. Keeping her eyes glued to his, she let her legs fall apart as he pressed deeper inside of her.

There was none of the pain she had been told to expect. It was different and strange, but good. So very good. He was so big she felt impaled on his cock. It was obscene to think about how deep he had reached inside her. As if sharing her thought, he put his huge hand on her lower belly to feel the movement of their now joined bodies. He groaned as he bottomed out inside her, reaching as far as he could go, and she mewled, her inner muscles squeezing him and drawing another groan from his throat. "Your little cunt is going to kill me."

The dirty words left her lightheaded and aching. He started to thrust into her, using steady strokes to ease her into the new experience of being fucked. She hooked her ankles behind his backside, anchoring herself to him. Cipher leaned down to kiss her, claiming her mouth in a way that mimicked what he was doing with his cock. His tongue thrusted against hers, and she whimpered at he overwhelming sensuality of the moment.

"You feel so good, Brook." He kissed her cheek and then her jaw. "You're so hot and wet." He punctuated his words with a harder thrust, and she cried out, shocked by the sensations he evoked. "Do you like that? Do you want me to fuck you? Hard? Fast?"

"Yes," she answered breathlessly. "Yes. Please."

"Please what?" He nipped at her neck and soothed the bite with his tongue. "Beg me, Brook."

"Please, sir," she pleaded, her gaze clashing with his. "Please fuck me, sir."

He growled and gripped the front of her collar. With her hands restrained overhead and his hand on her collar, she was trapped right where he wanted her—and that was exactly where she wanted to be. It felt perfect. It felt right to be completely at his mercy as he thrust into her again and again, driving them both toward the promise of a climax that would leave them dizzy.

His other hand moved between their bodies, and the first flick of his fingers on her clit had her screaming. Stretched around his cock, her pussy was on fire. She felt sensations in places she hadn't known existed until that moment, places she committed to memory because she wanted to feel them again and again.

"I'm going to come, sir." The words tumbled out of her mouth unbidden. She clenched her thighs around his waist as he picked up the pace, pounding her into the bed.

"Let me feel it," he urged, still gripping the front of her collar. "Let me feel your tight little pussy milking me for every last drop."

His deep, rumbling voice pushed her over the edge. She cried out with pure joy as her climax exploded from her core. What she had experienced earlier was nothing compared to the utter elation of being filled and stretched as she orgasmed. It was another level of pleasure, and it rocked her whole world.

"Brook," he groaned. "Brook. Brook. Brook." He slid deep, knocking the air from her lungs, and his hips stuttered. She could feel him throbbing inside her, could feel the heat of him filling her. She kept her legs around his waist, holding him inside her as he rocked and shuddered.

When he was spent, he unfurled the fingers holding her collar and captured her mouth. His kisses were gentle but passionate. He rode the aftershocks with her, reaching up to release her wrists while they exchanged slow and easy kisses. He wrapped his arms around her, rolling onto his back and bringing her with him. He stayed buried inside her as he cradled her to his chest and combed his fingers through her hair.

Closing her eyes, she snuggled in closer. There was so much she wanted to discuss with him, but she was so totally overwhelmed by what she had experienced she needed to rest. He didn't seem to mind. In fact, he seemed to need exactly what she did. Safe in his arms, she drifted off to sleep.

Hours later, she woke to the smell of something delicious and the ticklish sensation of Cipher's fingertips gliding up and down her spine. She had rolled onto her belly at some point during her nap, and now he was behind her, kissing her neck and shoulders and waking her with soft caresses. She mewled and wiggled back against him, feeling the heat of his bare chest and the stiff fabric of his pants. "Is it late?"

"Almost dinner time," he said, tracing the shell of her

ear with his fingertip.

"I don't know how you can tell time up here," she lamented with a sigh. "There is no sunlight. It's the one thing I miss about life down there."

"We have engineered sunlight," he reminded her. "The ship's lighting mimics a day and night cycle. The climate does the same. We can adjust the screens on the windows so you have a similar view to what you had in your cabin. It will help you adjust."

"Do you ever miss it? Real sunshine and fresh air and the smells of nature?"

He shook his head. "I've been in ships so much of my life that I start to miss the comfort of climate control when I'm on the surface."

"I can see that. Having cool air all the time is nice. It sure beats sweating through a sticky, hot night in my cabin."

"Well," he nuzzled her cheek, "you'll probably still have plenty of hot, sticky nights here in these quarters."

She giggled and hid her face. "You're terrible."

"You didn't think so earlier." He nibbled her ear lobe. "You have enough time for a bath before dinner is ready."

A hot soak sounded really good. Wondering how sore she was after making love to Cipher, she tested the situation by moving her legs. Surprisingly, she felt only a slight ache. It was more of a throbbing feeling, similar to the way her hands sometimes felt after a long day of working in the mines.

"Are you in pain?" He gently rolled her over and studied her face. "There are pills you can take or creams to apply."

"I'm a little sore, but it's not bad." She drew her finger along the outline of one of his tattoos. Her earlier shyness had all but vanished. After the way Cipher had enjoyed her body, she no longer felt embarrassed by her slim figure and small breasts. More importantly, now that she had gotten a taste of how good sex felt, she wanted more of it.

"Later," he said as if reading her mind. "Bath first and then some food." He nuzzled her cheek. "Then we can play."

She nodded in acceptance of his schedule and let him help her out of the bed. Her hand in his, she followed him into the adjacent bathroom. Like the rest of their quarters, it was done in muted grays and whites. He sat on the edge of the tub and activated the faucet with a wave of his hand. As he tested the temperature of the water, a thought struck her. "How do you get freshwater up here?"

Cipher looked at her and smiled. "I wondered how long it would take you to ask questions like that." He hesitated. "Are you sure you want to know?"

"Yes."

"It's manufactured and recycled. Mostly," he added and reached for a bottle on a small built-in shelf. As he twisted off the lid and poured some of liquid inside into the bath water, he explained, "The ships are loaded with freshwater when they set out on their maiden voyages. Every drop used on the ship goes through a series of filtration systems that cleans and reclaims it. Our environmental systems extract water vapor from the air to keep the humidity on the ship at the correct value. The extracted water is condensed, cleaned and reclaimed."

As she watched the pink bubbles form in the water, she wrinkled her nose at the idea of drinking reclaimed bath water but then decided it was no different than drinking water filtered through layers of rock and sand. It was likely cleaner and safer to drink reclaimed water than to sip straight out of her well back home.

"The sewage too?" She suspected it was also reclaimed and filtered.

"Yes."

She made a face but not for the reason he was likely thinking. "I would hate to have that job!"

Cipher laughed. "It's mostly automated. Engineers keep an eye on the processes. It's rare that plumbing engineers have to get their hands dirty."

"But what happens as you lose water in the cleaning system? Wouldn't the levels eventually drop so low that you wouldn't be able to sustain the loop?"

"Yes. We receive shipments of water to replenish what can't be cleaned or reclaimed. It's only a fraction of what we recycle, though."

"The weight of all that water must be an incredible burden on the ship's engines," she murmured, thinking of how hard it was to carry a bucket or two from the well to her house.

"The physics of all that is something we can talk about later," he offered. "I can show you the models and systems."

"I'd like that." Others might find it boring, but she was excited by the prospect of learning something new from Cipher.

"Come here."

She stepped between his legs, and he gently turned her around to face the sink and mirror. He combed his fingers through her unruly hair and separated it into three sections. Surprising her with his skill, he braided her hair and then coiled it into a bun at the back of her head. He secured it with clips he pulled from the pocket of his pants.

"I'm impressed." She glanced over her shoulder at him. "Where did you learn that?"

"My older sister," he said quietly. "She got hurt as a young kid and had problems with her hands, even after surgery. I helped her with things like her hair when I was on leave from school."

It hadn't even occurred to her that he had family somewhere. Feeling terrible for not asking before, she turned to face him. "I'm so sorry I didn't ask about your family. I just…well…I sort of assumed you didn't have anyone."

"You weren't wrong." His hands settled on her hips. "My dad died in battle when i was eleven. My mother and sister were killed in a Splinter attack on our home planet seven years ago."

"Cipher," she whispered sympathetically. Cupping his jaw in her small hands, she said, "I'm sorry about your family."

"Thank you." He kissed her palm and sent a frisson of heat through her arm. "My family would have loved you. My mother was from a planet where women were equal to men and worked outside the home. She was a mechanical engineer. That's how she met my dad. My sister studied mathematics at a university on our planet." He traced her collarbone. "Someday, I'll take you to my home world. You'll love it."

"I've never traveled anywhere." She glanced around the bathroom and shrugged. "This is the farthest I've ever been from home."

"We can go anywhere you want, Brook. I have months of saved leave. I'd like to travel the universe with you."

She grinned. "That sounds incredible."

"Doesn't it?"

She nodded and then worried her bottom lip. "What does your future look like? Our future, I mean. Do you serve in the military forever? Do you retire?"

"I can do either. I'll have enough points to retire in a few years. If I choose to separate from service, I'll be strongly encouraged to remain here and settle on Calyx. We intend to colonize your planet."

She perked up at that revelation. "I own a chunk of land on the mountain. Not just the cabin," she explained. "I own the twenty-one acres around it. I have the deed in my pack. We could build a bigger, nicer cabin someday."

His eyes brightened at that thought. "I think I'd like that."

"Yeah?"

"Yeah." He rubbed circles on her hipbones. "We can look at some plans later. Daydream a little."

She grinned. "I haven't daydreamed like that since I was little."

"Me either, but maybe it's time we let ourselves dream of a different future."

She leaned in to kiss him. "Together?"

"Together."

Their lingering kiss filled her with so much hope. She wasn't foolish enough to think it would always be this easy and simple. At some point, they would butt heads and argue, but she was determined to try to make it work with him. This wasn't the way she had envisioned her life, being claimed by an alien sky warrior she barely knew, but it felt so *right.*

"Let me help you in," he said, standing and guiding her over the ledge and into the rectangular tub. It was clearly designed for a big man like him, and she could practically swim in it.

"Do you want to join me?" She waved her hand through the hot water, scooping up the pink bubbles and watching them slide between her fingers.

He wavered, his gaze darting from her to the open door. "Let me take dinner out of the oven."

While he was gone, she enjoyed the luxurious feel of the water and the delightful sugary sweet scent of the bubbles. She closed her eyes and inhaled and felt as is she were standing in a bakery crammed with the most delicious cakes and pastries. She had only been in a bakery once, on a trip to Connor's Run with her father. He had let her buy a cupcake, and they had shared it under the shade of a nearby tree. It had been so sweet that it gave her a tummy ache, but it was still one of her fondest memories.

"You okay?" Cipher frowned with concern as he shucked his pants, revealing he wore nothing underneath them.

"Just reliving a memory," she said, smiling up at him from her nest of bubbles.

"A good one?"

"Very good," she confirmed and scooted forward to make room for him. He stepped in and lowered himself behind her. When his strong arms embraced her, she leaned back into him and sighed with utter contentment. It felt so good to be held by him. The last few days with Cipher had forced her to acknowledge that she had been starving for companionship and touch. The way he seemed to always want to be close to her, to sleep next to her in the hospital bed and hold her hand, convinced her he felt the same way.

The unexpected blare of an alarm startled her, and she yelped, sloshing water out of the tub and onto the floor. "What is that?"

"Easy," Cipher said, hugging her close. "It's a drill." He shifted her forward a few inches. "We need to get out."

The shockingly loud klaxon made her head hurt. She scrambled out of the tub as a stern male voice ordered them to evacuate the ship. She grabbed the towel Cipher thrust at her and hurriedly dried her body. Had this been a real situation and not a drill, she would have left their quarters soaking wet. As it was, she was still damp when Cipher tossed her yellow dress at her and a clean pair of underwear he grabbed from a drawer.

"Shoes," he said, fastening his belt and gathering his gear. Dazed by how quickly he had gotten dressed, she hurried to comply with his order. He snatched her hand and tugged her close. "Stay right next to me. Pay attention to the route we take. Someday, this drill will save your life."

Not might. Will.

As she scurried along behind Cipher, she had a sinking feeling her life in space was about to get very, very scary.

Chapter Twelve

F *UCKING DRILLS.* IT was normal to have a series of drills after a Grab. Orion wanted all of the new brides to understand how to navigate the ship and evacuate in the event of an emergency. There were regular drills between Grabs, most of them simple and routine fire or evacuation exercises. This one, however, was different. There wasn't a Grab scheduled for another month, and there was nothing routine about what awaited them in their pods.

As he held tight to Brook's hand and guided her along the pathway illuminated with blinking green lights, he wondered how many of the other men guiding their mates to escape pods were aware of the true threat. The gas still hadn't been located on the planet's surface, and there was no indication that it had ever made it to space. Until Shadow Force was able to find the gas and secure it, life on the *Valiant* was under serious threat. One drop of gas, and thousands would die.

While Brook had been recovering in the infirmary, he had been busy at work with the environmental engineers and Pierce to put together a network of modified sensors. They were being deployed as quickly as possible, but the robots required to place most of them in tight quarters were impeding the workflow. Orion had maintained his decision that the family sectors be protected first, then critical sectors like the bridge, engineering and medical. The other portions of the ship would have to wait which left a huge chunk of enlisted and unmated men vulnerable.

Rounding the corner to the evacuation staging area, Cipher pulled Brook in front of him and slid his arm around her shoulders, mirroring the stance of many of his fellow officers. He spotted Menace and Raze in the crowd first. Dizzy and Venom caught his eye next. His friends kept their wives close as he did, ready to defend and protect them.

The pod doors opened and the automated system ordered them to file into their places. They moved quickly but calmly into their assigned pods and into their specific seats. He and Brook were at the very end of the first row. Raze and Ella were next to him with Dizzy and Venom on the other side of them. Menace and Naya capped off the front row, and he stood at the doorway, counting and recounting as the rest of their floor took their seats. When they were all buckled in, Menace shut the door and activated the launch sequence. Instead of the usual simulated launch on the communication screen at the front of the pod, they were greeted with a recorded message delivered by the admiral.

"As the captain of this great ship, I am charged with maintaining the safety of each and every person living on it. The lives of the airmen, soldiers and families aboard the *Valiant* are paramount in all decisions I make. Tonight, it falls on me to inform you that we are facing a new threat to our safety here on this ship," Orion explained. "Intelligence missions have gathered information that leads us to believe the Splinter cell in our sector has acquired and plans to use nerve agents in a coordinated attack."

While Orion paused on screen, allowing his words to sink in, Cipher glanced around the pod. It was clear which men had been apprised of the threat earlier in briefings and which were just now learning the details. Dizzy seemed unnaturally pale as she clung to Venom's arm. Naya, always brave and headstrong, reached for her husband's hand as if to tell him they were in this together. Ella looped her ankle around Raze's, tucking herself in closer and holding his steady gaze.

Next to him, Brook swallowed hard. They shared a look that spoke volumes. She had uncovered the threat. It was because of her that everyone on the ship had advance warning and a chance to prepare for the worst. If she hadn't risked her life to save Terror, the Splinter cell would have been able catch them off-guard with a devastating attack.

On screen, Orion explained that each and every person on the ship would be fitted with a gas mask and drilled on the proper way to protect themselves in the event of an attack. Cipher had already heard the spiel earlier that morning while attending a classified combined SRU and Shadow Force meeting. He interlaced his fingers with Brook's as she stared with rapt attention at the screen. If she was terrified, she was hiding it well and seemed to be intent on memorizing every word the admiral had to say.

After Orion ended his speech, the screen automatically began playing a short film on the proper shelter-in-place and evacuation steps in the event of a gas attack. They were instructed to seek shelter in the bathroom in their quarters, put on their masks and seal the door until a second alarm cleared the way for an immediate evacuation. Once the second alarm sounded, the evacuation would proceed as usual.

When the film was finished, the screen instructed them to exit the pod single file and receive their masks for fitting. He tucked Brook in front of him, one hand on her hip and the other on her shoulder as they moved toward the exit. Out in the hallway, there were two lines—one for the men and one for the women. There weren't any babies or children on their floor yet, but Cipher had seen the tiny pediatric masks earlier that morning. The sight of them had twisted his stomach and made him more determined to do whatever he could to help Shadow Force locate and neutralize the missing gas canisters.

Showing no hesitation, Brook joined the women's line and waited for her turn. She clearly recognized the medic at the front, a younger man Cipher had met in passing at the infirmary. She smiled warmly at Chance and chatted with him as he showed her how to place the mask and tighten the straps to form a proper seal. Cipher looked away just long enough to get his mask and demonstrate he could attain the correct fit.

By the time he looked back, Brook had already moved

ahead to wait for him. Her mask dangled from her hand, and she seemed strangely unbothered by the whole experience. He reached for as he drew near, and she happily slid close, matching his strides as they returned to their quarters. Once they were safely inside, he trailed her to the kitchen where she placed her mask on the table and then leveled a stare his way. "How bad is it?"

"Bad," he said, wishing he could tell her everything. "We wouldn't even know about the threat if it wasn't for you, Brook."

She frowned. "I'm sure you would have learned about the canisters eventually."

"Too late," he replied, certain that would have been the outcome had she not gone into the mine to recon.

"Is there anything I can do to help?" She wrung her hands. "Maybe I could go back to the mountain? Ask around and see if anyone noticed a truck leaving that area?"

"No." The word came out harsher than he had intended. Taking a step toward her, he cupped the back of her head. "You've done more than enough."

"But if there's a chance I could help…?"

"You'll be asked," he assured her. "Shadow Force won't waste an asset."

"I would be careful," she promised.

"I know you would." He kissed the top of her head. "I just don't want you in that position ever again. I want you here, safe, with me."

"Are we safe?" She placed her hands on his chest and gazed up at him. "Will those masks actually work?" Before he could answer, she said, "Suffocation and fires caused by gas were daily worries for me down in the mines. A mask is only as good as the seal and filtration, but if the gas burns skin, they're useless." She glanced at the mask she had tossed onto the table. "Will that do enough to protect us?"

He wanted to lie to her. He wanted to hold her tight and tell her that everything would be fine, that the masks were rated for all levels of nerve agents and would save her life. He wanted to—but he didn't.

"It depends on the gas used."

"I thought so," she murmured. "What happens if it's the worst gas?"

"We die. All of us," he said reluctantly. "They have a canister of extremely deadly gas that can kill when it touches our skin. If that gets released on this ship, we're all dead. Within minutes," he added. "And it won't be an easy death."

"Of course not," she said. "The Splinters want to hurt you. Giving you and your families easy deaths isn't their way."

"I'm sorry, Brook." He brushed his knuckles along her cheek. "I brought you straight into danger."

"I'd rather be here with you, facing the scary shit together, than down there alone on the mountain or starting over in a strange place in the colonies."

She meant every word. He could see it in her honest expression. "I'll do everything in my power to protect you, Brook."

"I know you will." She rose on tiptoes and sought his

mouth. He met her halfway and enjoyed the plump heat of her lips. When she pulled back, she asked, "So, what's for dinner?"

Happy to leave thoughts of death by nerve gas behind, Cipher retrieved their dinner from the oven and gave her a quick tour of the cabinets and drawers. She put away their gas masks, stowing them in the bedroom, and rejoined him in the kitchen, grabbing silverware and setting the table. Instead of sitting across from him, she moved her chair to the right of his. It was more intimate that way, and he heartily approved of her change.

After they finished dinner, he showed her how the various pieces of equipment worked. He stood back as she sorted their table scraps into the slots for compostable and non-compostable items. He walked her through the types of trash that would go into the recycling and incineration chutes and taught her how to use the dishwasher.

"How do you ration water up here?" Crouching down, she had her head in the dishwasher as she examined the nozzles. "If you have to reclaim every drop, surely it's a waste to clean your dishes this way."

"These machines are very efficient. They use a mix of water and ultrasonic vibrations with specially formulated detergents to clean the dishes. The cycles are calibrated to use tiny amounts of water. As far as rationing goes," he said as she rose and closed the door on the machine, "it depends on rank and family size."

She frowned. "Why does rank matter?"

"It's the way our world runs," he answered matter-of-factly. "The higher you climb, the more perks you and your family earn. It goes the same with valor points. Almost every man on this ship is here because we are the best of the best. We survived some of the worst battles of the war. We have more valor points than most soldiers or airmen could even dream of earning. It's why the mated section has such spacious quarters and full amenities like water in the bathrooms."

"As opposed to?"

"Ships without families have non-water bathing. Instead of water, you are cleaned with sonic vibrations and an ultra-fine powder."

She grimaced. "Gross."

He shrugged. "It's actually not that bad."

"Hard pass," she insisted and pointed her thumb down. "I'd rather go back to hauling buckets of water from my well than take the human equivalent of a bird's dust bath."

"Thankfully, that's not a choice you have to make. We'll always have better quarters than most," he assured her. "Even if we transfer to a different ship in the fleet, we'll have a large space and the best amenities."

"And if we decided to move back to the planet? To build a real house? How do we pay for the construction? How do we fund our lives?"

"I have a pension," he explained. "I'm fully vested. The longer I serve, the more I'll earn." He hesitated before adding, "If I die while in service, you get the full pension plus all the benefits of being a mate such as healthcare for life."

Her expression turned serious, and she took a step toward him, grabbing hold of his shirt and commanding his gaze. "I don't want a pension or benefits. I want you."

"Good," he murmured, lowering his face toward hers, "because I don't intend to die anytime soon."

He claimed her lips, and she wound her arms around his waist. She was so short that standing to kiss like this wasn't comfortable for very long. He had plenty of ideas how to make it more comfortable, but there were things they needed to take care of first. Reluctantly pulling away, he said, "Let's get your breathing treatment out of the way."

She made a face. "Do I have to?"

"Yes." He kissed the tip of her nose as she pouted.

"It tastes so gross," she protested. "It makes me cough and shake."

"I know it does." He hated that she had to endure the treatments. "I wish you didn't have to do them."

She sighed unhappily. "Well, let's get it over with."

"The pharmacy delivered your medicine and equipment yesterday." He took her hand and led her into the bedroom. She sat in the oversized reading chair in the corner while he opened a cabinet to show her where he had stowed her medical things. He had observed her treatments while she was in the hospital so he knew how to put together the nebulizer and insert the medication cartridge.

Pulling out the ottoman, he sat on it in front of her and handed over the nebulizer mask. She grumpily slipped the mask into place over her mouth and nose and began breathing in the medicated mist. She started to cough after a few seconds, and he reached for her hand. The coughing ended a short while later, and she breathed deeper and easier. By the time she reached the end of the treatment, her hands were shaking from the burst of adrenaline caused by the medication that dilated the vessels and cells in her lungs.

When the treatment was finished, she removed the mask and closed her eyes. She drew her short legs up onto the chair, hugging her knees to her chest and dropping her head back as she inhaled slow breaths. He stood up and kissed the top of her head before gathering up the nebulizer and taking it to the bathroom to clean it. After it was dry, he returned it to the cabinet and then segued to the kitchen to get her a box of juice. She was currently obsessed with the blue drink made from a variety of different fruits and vegetables and sweetened with outrageous amounts of sugar. With her orders to gain weight, he had happily picked up two cases of it from the commissary.

"Here you go." He handed over the box of juice and sat on the ottoman.

"Thank you." She slipped the thin straw into her mouth and sipped the juice.

He placed his hands on her calves and rubbed lazy circles on her skin. "You okay?"

She nodded. "Just feeling jittery and awake."

With a mischievous smile, he teased, "I think I know of a way to calm you down again."

The corners of her lush mouth lifted with amusement. "That so?"

"If you're up to it," he said, studying her carefully. "If you'd rather rest, we can do that instead."

"I'd rather rest after you show me your method of calming me down." She lowered her legs and leaned forward, smiling coyly around the straw as she sipped more of the juice. The sight of the straw between her lips had him thinking of something else he'd like to see in her mouth.

Standing, he held out his hand and tugged her off the chair. She trailed close behind, still sipping her juice as he led her into their playroom. He left the door open again, wanting to set her at ease. Her gaze roamed the room as she drank the last of her juice. When the box was empty, he took it from her and set it aside. "Is there something in here that looks interesting to you? Maybe something you want to try tonight?"

She didn't even hesitate and walked straight to the swing. "This."

"Good choice," he remarked, joining her. "Do you want to try it in a simple way, or do you want to get a little wild?"

"Wild," she said hurriedly.

Amused by her enthusiasm, he grinned as he moved to the nearest set of drawers. "Why don't you pick out something from this drawer and this one?"

Always curious, she made her way to the drawers he had opened and looked at the items inside. "Is this a blindfold?"

"It is." He took the long length of red silk from her hand. "Sensory deprivation can be an interesting way to amp up your pleasure centers."

"Ear plugs?"

He nodded and picked them up. "Blocking out hearing and vision puts you in a vulnerable and excited state."

She bit her lower lip. "I want to try the blindfold, but I'm not ready for the ear plugs yet. Your voice makes me feel safe," she admitted shyly.

Hearing her say that did crazy things to his heart. He cupped the back of her head and drew her in for a little kiss. "Blindfold it is."

Smiling, she moved to the second drawer and frowned. "Are these pieces of jewelry?"

"In a sense," he said, picking up the one she seemed most fascinated by. "They're clamps."

"For?"

"Your nipples."

"My what?" Eyes wide, she stared at him as if he had three heads. "Why would anyone want their nipples clamped?"

"Because it feels good."

She narrowed her eyes. "Says who?"

"Says everyone who uses them."

She seemed unconvinced. "Doesn't it hurt?"

He shook his head. "They can be uncomfortable if they're too tight or pulled on, but sometimes that discomfort makes the pleasure feel even better."

She took the clamps from his hand and looked them over for a few seconds. Keeping her eyes downcast, she said, "I don't think my nipples will be much fun for you to play with, Cipher. They're awfully flat and plain."

He tipped her chin with his fingers and held her gaze. "There's nothing about you that is plain, Brook. Especially not your perfect tits," he added, being deliberately crude to make her blush. "I'll show you exactly what I mean."

She swallowed hard and nodded. "If you say so, sir."

"I do."

She turned back to the drawers and opened a third. He hadn't intended to show her anything in there for a few weeks. Although she seemed keen to explore her sexuality, he wasn't sure that interest extended to her bottom. Watching her with interest, he held his breath as she picked up the biggest anal plug in the drawer. The shiny black toy looked absolutely obscene in her small hand, and he realized it would likely never be one they could use.

"What is this?"

"It's an anal plug."

"A what?" Her eyes were huge as she glanced from his face to the suddenly offending object in her hand. "You put this...*where*?"

"In your bottom."

"I don't think so!" She dropped the toy as if it were burning her hand, and it bounced inside the shallow drawer.

"Not that one," he clarified quickly. "That is way, way too big for you. I wouldn't ever pick that toy out of the drawer to use on you."

She seemed mollified by that. As if trying to understand, she asked, "Why would you put that in *there*?"

"It feels good."

"For whom?"

"You."

"I doubt it." She dubiously eyed the offending toy. "How do you even get it in there?"

"With a lot of patience and lubrication," he stated, enjoying this back and forth with her.

"And then what? You just leave it in there?"

"You can," he said. "Or you can use it to help you prepare for a nice, long ass fuck."

"A *what*?" she spluttered. Suddenly turning, she pressed her backside against the counter as if to protect it from a sneak penis attack. "You want to put your…your…*you know what* in my butt?"

"Eventually, yes," he said, taking a step toward her. "If you don't like it after the first time we try it, we'll never do it again."

"But…why? Why would you want to put it in there?"

"The same reason I enjoyed putting it in your pussy," he answered. "It feels good to be inside you. It feels good to be squeezed by your heat." Boxing her in against the counter, he dipped his head. "Because I like hearing your scream when you come." He kissed her left cheek. "Because I want to make you come so hard you think you're going to pass out." He kissed her right cheek. "Because I want to own you." He kissed her on the mouth. "All of you."

Her breaths had quickened, and she gazed up at him with wonder and uncertainty. "Does it hurt?"

"It can if it's done incorrectly, but I won't hurt you. I'll take my time, and you'll be begging for my cock in your ass when I'm done with you."

Her face had gone bright red. Even her ears were pink and hot. "Is that what you want, sir? For me to beg you to fuck me like that?"

Now he was the one breathing faster. "Yes."

Her eyes flashed with excitement. Finally, she said, "Okay."

"Okay?"

"You can show me what it feels like to have something in my bottom."

He hadn't been expecting that at all. Worried he had pressured her, he hurriedly said, "Brook, you don't have to—"

"I want to," she assured him. "But nothing big and scary. Please," she added with in a small voice.

"I wouldn't dare," he promised. Looking at the drawer, he picked up the slimmest, smallest plug that was only barely thicker than his middle finger. "What about this one?"

She looked at it for a few seconds and nodded. "Okay."

With a raging hard-on tenting the front of his pants, he carried the toys she had selected to end of the counter where they would be within arm's reach of the swing. He took a towel, a medical grade glove and some lubricant from another cabinet. With everything in place, he held out his hand. "Ready to play?"

Chapter Thirteen

"**O**H, YES." HER heart raced as she let Cipher tug her close. She surrendered as he wrapped his strong arms around her and captured her mouth in a punishing kiss. Even though some of the things in the playroom scared her, she trusted Cipher not to harm her. She trusted him to teach and lead her through this new and wonderful world of sensual delights.

His tongue darted against hers, and she whimpered at the sudden invasion. Clinging to his shoulders, she happily wrapped her legs around his waist when he lifted her in his powerful arms. He made her feel so small and delicate—and protected. Earlier, faced with the very real threat of a gas attack, she hadn't been nearly as afraid as she should have been. With Cipher at her side, she could face any threat.

His hand reached up under her skirt, and he grasped the waistband of her panties. He jerked them down her hips, moving her away from his body just long enough to drag them free from her legs. He took hold of the side tie of the wrap dress and gave it one good tug. Just as quickly as he divested her of her underwear, he yanked away the dress.

Naked, she giggled with excitement when he plopped her down on the swing. It swayed back and forth as he guided one ankle and then the next into the padded stirrups. She felt wickedly exposed with her legs splayed like this. He stared at her with such desire in her eyes that she shivered. He made her feel so beautiful.

"If I do something that you don't like or if something becomes uncomfortable, you have to tell me, Brook." His callused palm ran along her leg and thigh, leaving a trail of gooseflesh. "This is about your enjoyment as much as it is mine."

"I know."

He reached over and grabbed the length of red silk. "I'm going to blindfold you first. Is that okay?"

"Yes, sir." She closed her eyes in anticipation of the cloth touching her face. He was careful as he tied the strip at the back of her head and managed not to snag any of her hair. He took her left hand and then the right, guiding them to the leather straps of the swing that functioned as handholds.

"Do you want me to restrain your hands?"

Excitement fluttered in her belly. "Yes."

Unable to see him, she felt more intensely aware of his body heat and scent. Under the fluffy sweetness of the bubble bath smell that clung to his skin was the natural scent she had come to recognize as his. He radiated heat as he secured one wrist and then the other with the built-in cuffs. She gave them experimental yanks, just hard enough to assure her that she couldn't break free easily. Something about that realization made her sex throb.

She liked being out of control. She liked being at his mercy. It was a heady truth to acknowledge, but there it was. When he had talked of owning every part of her, she had nearly swooned. The thought of being his completely—of letting him have the parts of her no other man had even seen—filled her with the greatest sense of rightness. She belonged here. She belonged with him—to him.

She heard the soft clang of metal before she felt it gliding along her lower belly and up toward her chest. She swallowed nervously as Cipher swirled his finger around her nipples, drawing them into tight peaks. He brushed his fingers over the sensitive tips, and she curled her toes. In all her life, she had never experienced the kind of sensations he evoked. How many times had she bathed herself, cleaning her breasts and rubbing her hands over them, yet never feeling this wild ache that he had awoken?

When his mouth touched her left breast, she cried out and bucked, sending the swing into motion. Cipher chuckled darkly against her skin and suckled her. He flicked his tongue over the peak just as he had her clitoris earlier, and it brought to mind all the things she desperately wanted to feel again. She wanted his mouth between her legs more than anything.

Cipher pinched her nipple, not hard, and then she felt the firm bite of the clamp. She hissed in shock but held still, terrified to pull back and hurt herself. As if reading her mind, he soothingly petted her belly. "You're okay. It's not tight enough to cause damage."

"Yes, sir," she replied shakily.

"Do you want me to remove it?"

"No." *Yes? Maybe?* "No."

His mouth was suddenly on her other breast. He did the same thing with that nipple as he had the first, using his tongue to tauten and tease it before squeezing it with the clamp. The same little bite made her gasp, but she didn't feel pain. There was a steady throb in time with her elevated heartbeat that seemed strangely reassuring.

"The chains attach to your collar," he explained, taking hold of the white bridal strap around her neck. He fixed the chains of the clamps to the small metal ring that dangled from the front of the collar. "If you lift your head too far, you'll feel a pull. Depending on where you are in your arousal state, that might feel good or not so good."

She gave her chin an experimental lift and experienced the tug on her nipples. It wasn't painful exactly, but it wasn't something she wanted to do for very long. Wondering how that sensation would change as Cipher brought her closer to a climax, she decided she would test it. But, for now, she was anchored in the feeling of his hands gliding along her sides and down her thighs.

She heard something scrape against the floor—probably the low stool she had seen earlier—and then Cipher's hands were on her inner thighs. His lips skimmed after his hands, tracing the same path. The ticklish kisses had her wiggling on the surprisingly comfortable swing. The rough stubble on his chin scratched over her skin, leaving a line that was sure to be red tomorrow. She found herself wanting that redness. She wanted to look at her legs tomorrow and see the evidence of what he had done to her. She wanted to wear his marks like a secret.

"Your cunt smells so good," he murmured before nuzzling between her legs.

She whimpered at his dirty remark and was very glad for the blindfold that kept her from having to look him in the face as he said it. His fingers replaced his face, and he parted her folds with them, baring her to what she imagined was his intense gaze. Did he like looking at her down there?

"I'll never get tired of seeing your pussy like this. Wet and swollen and ready for me," he said while tracing a finger along the center of her. "Are you sore?"

"A little," she admitted, her belly quaking as he dragged his finger around her entrance.

"Poor baby," he murmured. "Let's see if I can make it better."

And then his tongue was on her.

She cried out and rocked her hips. He laughed before diving in with such enthusiasm that her head started to spin. Splayed out in this position with her legs supported in the air amplified everything he did. In their bedroom, his tongue had felt incredible. Here, on the swing, it felt phenomenal.

Cipher's tongue mimicked the same motions as his cock had earlier, and for a brief moment, she thought she was legitimately going to die. She couldn't breathe as his tongue thrust in and out of her. When he licked a long, slow stripe right to the top, she moaned and shuddered. He set a methodical pace, swirling and flicking in a rhythm that soon had her clutching at the straps near her bound wrists. His hands gripped her inner thighs, keeping them wide apart as he tortured her with this tongue.

She felt the first fleeting shiver of joy and embraced it. She tensed her thighs and curled her toes, pressing herself to his mouth. His tongue moved faster now, flicking with broad strokes that made her gasp and groan. He hummed against her flesh and tugged the connected chains of the nipple clamps. With a shocked cry, she came hard and fast. "Sir!"

He groaned happily and kept lapping at her, his fingers digging into her thigh as he held her in place. The hand that had been tugging at the chain stroked down her belly and between her legs. The final waves of her climax began to slow, and she dropped her head back against the swing's support, not caring at all that the motion caused a slight pinch on her overly sensitive nipples. Cipher was right. It felt *good.*

Two of his fingers swiped along her labia and then slowly eased inside her soaking channel. The soreness from earlier had been lessened by the attention of his tongue and the euphoria of her climax. She relaxed into the invasion, keeping her eyes closed behind the blindfold and letting herself sink into the sensations. He moved his fingers in and out of her at a languid pace. The feeling was incredible, and she wondered why she hadn't thought to touch herself like this all those lonely nights in the cabin.

It wouldn't have been close to this.

Cipher's sure hands knew exactly how and where to touch her. They were confident and skilled—but why was he pulling away from her now?

"Sir?" Her voice was little more than a high-pitched whine as she lifted her hips and blindly searched for him.

"Patience, baby girl."

She strained to hear what he was doing, but he was so quiet that she barely detected anything. When he returned to her, she felt the heat of him before his hands returned to her body. One hand was bare and the other was covered in the glove he had set out earlier. She heard a small *snick* noise. The bottle of lubricant?

Her guess was confirmed when, seconds later, she felt the cold gel coating his fingers as they probed her *down there*. Having him touch her bottom was a revelation. At first, it felt wrong to have his fingertips swirling over such a secret place, but as his fingers moved with more pressure, it began to feel...*interesting*.

"Is this okay?"

"Yes," she answered breathlessly. "It's more than okay."

He laughed softly before pressing a finger into her. "How about this?"

She sucked in a shocked breath at the sensation of being breached. "Yes, sir. Good, sir."

"And how about this?" He shocked her by putting his mouth back on her clit while working that finger in and out of her bottom.

She reeled at the sudden and overwhelming sensations.

His tongue fluttered over her clitoris while his finger thrust into her. There were nerve-endings she hadn't even known existed until that moment. Strangely, she felt unbearably empty in her pussy and found herself craving more from him.

"Still good, baby?"

"Yes, sir," she all but moaned. "So good, sir."

"Do you want to come with my tongue on your cunt and my finger in your ass?"

Her entire body flushed with embarrassment at his question, but she couldn't deny him an answer. "Yes. Please," she added in a whine. "Please, sir. Make me come."

"You keep asking me nicely like that and I'll give you whatever you want," he promised before returning his mouth to her pussy. He dragged her clit between his lips, sucking it before flicking his tongue around it. She cried out and pumped her hips, causing the swing to sway back and forth in the most relaxing way.

She was so excited she could feel the wetness dripping out of her. In the back of her mind, she wondered for a moment if Cipher found that unpleasant, but the sounds he made as he licked her convinced her otherwise. He liked the way she tasted. He liked how wet she was and how she responded to him. He liked using his mouth to give her pleasure.

The fingers of his other hand moved in the slick heat of her entrance. Before she could react, he thrust two thick fingers into her pussy. Impaled on fingers in both of her most secret spots, she shouted his name and threw back her head, tugging on the nipple clamps and overwhelming her body with ecstasy. In and out, his fingers thrust into her while his tongue pushed her closer and closer to the edge.

There was no use in trying to hold it off or delay the wonderful explosion. When his fingers curved inside her, she saw stars. She screamed his name as wave after wave of sheer bliss rolled through her body. "Cipher! Sir! Oh! *Please. Please. Please.* Don't stop!"

He didn't. He kept right on, thrusting and licking until she sagged against the swing and shuddered with after-shocks. The fingers that had been in her bottom were replaced with slim plug she had chosen earlier. It felt different inside her, not as firm as his fingers or as wide and also cooler. He tugged the plug in and out of her bottom, working it shallow and then deep until she was whimpering.

The blindfold was suddenly yanked free and tossed aside along with the glove he had been wearing. In a few quick movements, he unbuckled his belt, unbuttoned and unzipped his pants and shoved down his boxer briefs. Her lusty gaze fell on his big cock. The tip was ruddy and leaking shiny fluid. She wanted to reach for him, to touch and stroke him, but her hands were still restrained over-head. Instead, she used her feet to pull him in closer.

"If it's too much, I can take out the plug," he offered as he dragged the head of his cock between her slick labia.

She didn't care if it was too much. She wanted it. All of it. With him. "I want to feel you inside me."

He gave her exactly what she wanted. He gripped her

hips and slid into her on one slow thrust. They both groaned, and she let her legs fall farther apart, glad for the ankle stirrups. Without having to support his own weight, Cipher seemed to have more range of motion. He alternated fast snaps of his hips with more deliberate and deep movements. One of his hands moved to the chains between her breasts, and he gave it a tug, drawing the chains taut and letting the clamps pull on her hard nipples.

When he started to take her faster and harder, his gaze moved to her face. He seemed to be watching her intently for any signs of pain or discomfort. It was so very strange to be filled in both places, and it seemed to amplify the slide of his cock in and out of her. Wanting him to let go, to use her for his pleasure, she said, "Don't hold back, sir."

"Fuck," he swore and changed his tactic. He stopped holding back, just as she had asked, and began to use the swing to his advantage. His incredible physique gave him the stamina he needed to really work the swing, holding onto the suspension straps and using them to rock her back and forth on his cock. She felt him so deeply inside, and the pressure on her clamped nipples seemed to translate straight to her clit.

Licking his thumb, he placed it against her nub. She didn't know how much more she could take. Maybe he didn't know either. Maybe he was trying to find her limit. Only, there was no limit today. She wanted it all.

He tugged on the nipple chain again and rolled her clit between his fingers. That was all it took. She locked eyes with him and surrendered to the rapturous bursts that exploded in her belly. He growled like a damn bear and started to snap his hips, thrusting and thrusting until he slammed deep and groaned. Like before, she could feel him pulsing and twitching inside her. She could feel the bloom of heat from his seed filling her.

Teetering on his feet, he slumped forward, his face against her collar bone. He blew out a noisy breath and then kissed her neck. "You're amazing, Brook."

"Me? You!" Giggling, she tried to hold him in place with her thighs. "I'm tingling. All over. It's like that feeling you get when you jump off a cliff into deep water."

He smiled and nuzzled into her. His mouth sought hers, and they shared a few wonderfully sweet kisses. Carefully, he unlatched her wrists and rubbed each one before pressing his lips to them. The clamps were removed next, and she hissed at the sudden rush of blood back into the compressed surfaces. He eased the discomfort with his mouth, gently laving until she mewled like a kitten. He discreetly removed the plug, wrapping it in a towel he retrieved from a drawer.

When he helped her out of the swing, she leaned heavily into him. He returned everything to its correct place and tidied up the space before sweeping her up into his arms and bridal carrying her to the bathroom. He gave her some privacy and then made her laugh when she stepped out and he picked her up again, carrying her to bed and tucking her in to wait for him.

After he finished using the bathroom, he slid in next to her. She happily wiggled closer when he opened his arms, and she rested her head on his chest, letting his heartbeat soothe and relax her. Just before she fell asleep, she whispered, "I'm so glad you came for me and brought me home with you."

"I'm glad you let me keep you."

Her eyes heavy, she stroked his chest. "Whatever happens, Cipher, I'll be right beside you."

"And I'll be right beside you," he promised. The last thing she remembered was the gentle feel of his lips brushing across her forehead as he whispered, "I'll keep you safe."

Chapter Fourteen

"**I**S IT ALWAYS this busy?"

Cipher looked up from his tablet as they waited on the Departures deck for their transport ship to the *Mercy*. A constant stream of soldiers and airmen along with wives and even small children moved along the wide corridor. "Yes."

Although she enjoyed people watching, she was more interested in what he was designing on his tablet. He used his stylus to drag circuitry blueprints around the screen. "Is this one of your freelance projects?"

He nodded. "Civilian use."

Over the last five days, he had shared so much of his work with her. Anything that wasn't classified was fair game. He had also started teaching her how to code. She was a novice and made lots of mistakes, but he was so patient and encouraging. "Maybe someday we can build something together."

He smiled at her. "I hope so."

"Flight 6A boarding. Flight 6A boarding."

"That's us," he said as the automated voice called out overhead. "Ready?"

She wasn't, but the appointment for her first time in

the hyperbaric chamber was today. Cipher had offered to reschedule when she had admitted her reticence, but she had decided it was better to face her fear. "I'm ready."

"I'll be with you the whole time." He took her hand and interlaced their fingers. "I won't leave you."

She leaned forward and pressed her forehead to his. "Thank you."

"Come on, baby." He tugged her into a standing position and led her toward the boarding ramp for their vessel. "Let's find you a window seat."

She fell into step beside him, amused when he slowed his normally fast pace and long strides. When she noticed the way he constantly scanned their surroundings, she melted a little more for him. They were probably in the safest place possible, but he still maintained a protective stance, ready to shield her at any moment.

After they scanned their wrists at the entrance to the ship, they found seats in the front row. As promised, he secured the window seat for her. Like a child surrounded by presents on Wintermorn, she practically bounced in her seat as she waited for the ship to depart. She barely remembered her first flight so her excitement was high.

"Before we dock with the *Mercy*, you'll be able to see Calyx from above and at least one moon," he explained, handing her his tablet to hold while he adjusted his safety belt. It had clearly been used by someone much smaller and thinner, probably a wife, so he had to unfurl quite a bit of extra belt. "If you enjoy the flight, we can look into a pleasure cruise. There's a line that operates out the colonies that's highly recommended. I know a few guys who have taken their mates on it."

"Where does it go?"

"It does a four-day loop around the colonies. There are shore excursions and it docks with a sky casino. It's supposed to be a lot of fun."

"I've never gambled before," she said, settling back into her seat. "There were always games running on payday at the mines, but it always seemed like a waste of money."

"It is," he agreed, "but there's nothing wrong with us doing a little frivolous spending every now and then." He swept loose strands of her hair back behind her ear. "Who knows? Maybe you'll be my lucky charm, and we'll hit it big."

She grinned at that image. Leaning closer and dropping her voice, she asked, "Are you going to rub me all over like a lucky rabbit's foot?"

His eyes flashed. "I just might."

Smiling like a fool, she glanced away and out the window as the ship began to move. The motion was smooth until it launched from the docking station when the ship bounced slightly and then veered off away from the much larger battleship. As their transport gained distance from the battleship, a giant floating construction platform came into view. "What is that?"

He looked around her to see. "It's the new skyport. It's phase one in the colonization plan. They need a skyport to dock supply and personnel ships. Once the skyport is finished, they'll be able to start working on the infrastructure for the base down on the planet's surface."

"Where?"

"They haven't made their final selection yet. There's a shortlist of sites." He gestured for her to hand over his tablet. After tapping on the screen for a few seconds, he showed her the list of sites being proposed. "This was the latest operation bulletin. Blue Shores seems like the most popular spot."

"I can see why," she murmured, looking at the beautiful images of blue sand beaches and shimmering water. "Have you ever been there?"

"Once," he said, "for Venom's wedding to Dizzy. I only had a few hours of downtime, but it was a very peaceful place. The people there are incredibly friendly."

"I've heard the food is amazing." She had seen a brochure for Blue Shores vacations years ago. It was the sort of thing that seemed like an impossible dream at the time. Mountain people didn't go on vacations, especially not to expensive seaside resorts.

"It was pretty good," he agreed. "The fish is so fresh, and they use lots of interesting spices and sauces." He brushed his fingers over the back of her hand. "You want to go?"

She glanced over at him in surprise. "What? Like…today?"

He shook his head. "You can't travel off the *Valiant* or her sister ships until you've finished the probationary period and we've signed our final agreements. But, maybe next month? If I can get the time off?"

"Are you serious? Yes! Of course!" She didn't even try to contain her excitement as she leaned over and kissed him. Glad they were alone in their row, she let her lips linger on his before reluctantly pulling away. A sudden thought struck her. "Can I have a bathing suit?"

"Yes. Definitely," he said, his voice husky. "A very small one. With ties. For easy access."

"You'll have to come shopping with me."

"Oh, I will definitely be helping you in the fitting rooms."

She blushed. "You'll get us kicked out of the shop."

"Probably," he agreed before sneaking in another kiss.

"I've never had a bathing suit," she admitted as she snuggled in close to his side. "I swam all the time as a kid, but I either did it completely naked when I was little or in old shorts and a cutoff shirt when I got older. I always wanted one, though. A red one or a green one."

"Sounds like we're buying two bathing suits," he murmured before kissing her temple. "Red and green and very skimpy."

Content to be cuddled up against him, she enjoyed the rest of the flight as he tapped away at his tablet and made design changes to the device he had imagined. As they neared the *Mercy*, he set aside his tablet and gestured for her to look out the window. When she did, she gasped at the incredible sight before her.

Calyx, her home planet, looked impossibly huge and bright. There were swirls of white obscuring some of the land masses and oceans. Never had she imagined that she would see something so incredible.

That's where I lived. That's where I was born. And now I'm up here in space.

"What do you think?" he asked gently.

"It's wonderful."

He smiled tenderly and held her hand as she stared out the window, her face pressed up close to the glass like a curious child. When one of the three moons came into view, she couldn't believe how much texture there was on its surface. Down on the mountain, looking up at the night sky, the moon seemed so smooth and white. Up here, this close, she could see deep gouges in its shockingly pink surface. It was the palest pink, lighter than any flower she had ever seen. There were valleys and hills and even mountain-like projections.

"I had no idea," she said in awe. "I had no idea the moon looked like this."

He brushed his hand down her braid, and she leaned into his touch. He never made her feel small or insignificant or ignorant when she said things like that. He only encouraged her to learn and experience all that was possible now. Her eyes stung with tears she refused to shed as she realized how lucky she was to have found Cipher.

"You okay?" he asked softly.

She nodded. "Yep."

He must have seen that she wasn't ready to talk about what she was feeling because he let the issue drop. A short time later, they docked with the hospital ship and exited their transport vessel. They were greeted by an older soldier missing both arms. The mechanical limbs attached to his body fascinated her, and she had to remind herself not to stare as Cipher checked them in for her appointment and received the directions to the floor and room where they were expected.

When they reached the pulmonary unit, they were met by a medic who directed them to a small waiting area. They had barely taken their seats when she heard a familiar voice call, "Brook?"

Surprised to see Chance standing in the open doorway of the pulmonary unit, she smiled as she rose to her feet. "I didn't expect to see you here!"

"I'm floating between ships," he explained. His gaze moved to Cipher who had risen with and now trailed her to the door. "Sorry, sir, but Reckless doesn't allow family in the treatment rooms."

Cipher frowned. "I'm her mate. I should be with her."

Chance glanced back at the hallway behind him. "I agree," he said, his voice lowered, "but Reckless has standing orders. She comes in alone—or she doesn't come in at all."

"It's okay, sir." She clasped his hand and gave it a little squeeze. "I'll be fine. Chance took very good care of me when I was in the hospital. I'm sure he'll look after me now."

Cipher seemed less than enthusiastic as he said, "Okay, but I'll be right here waiting for you." He pinned Chance in place with a glare. "If anything happens to her…"

"Understood, sir."

She rose on tiptoes and pecked his cheek. "I'll see you soon."

Falling into step with Chance, she walked at his side as they traversed the bright halls of the unit. They passed hospital rooms with patients asleep in beds, hooked up to all sorts of monitors and machines. Most of them looked very ill, and she wondered how many would never wake up again.

"They were on a cargo ship that fell out of orbit and crashed near the mine where you found Terror," Chance explained when he noticed her worried gaze. "Their escape pods malfunctioned and failed to launch. They had no pressurization or breathable air. They're basically dead," he stated matter-of-factly, "but Reckless is keeping them alive on machines to test out different lung therapies."

"That's horrible! How is that even allowed?"

"It's in our contracts," Chance explained. "When we agree to serve, we give our lives to the cause. They own us until we retire or die."

Her stomach lurched at the thought of Cipher being hooked up to machines and tormented like that. Wondering what the hell kind of doctor she was about to meet, she looked back over her shoulder at the door. How fast could she run down that hallway and back to Cipher?

"This way," Chance said, gesturing to another hallway. "We'll be all the way down at the end."

She mustered her courage and followed him into the procedure room. She stood nervously by the door and took in her new surroundings. In the very center of the room was a large tube-like structure. It was white with a hinged, clear lid and shiny blue padding in the center. "Is that where I'm going?"

Chance glanced at the tube and nodded. "After you change," he said and handed her a hospital gown. "Take off everything. Even the collar," he added. "You need to wipe your entire body down with these." He placed large sealed wipes on top of the gown. "Be thorough. The environment inside the chamber is highly flammable." He glanced at her hair. "Is there product in your hair?"

She shook her head. "I washed it yesterday."

"Wipe down your hair as well. Secure it under this cap. When you're done, come out, and we'll get started." With an anxious look at a door across the room, he stepped closer. "Listen, Reckless can be very harsh. He's just a miserable son-of-a-bitch. Whatever he says to you—don't take it personally. He's like that with everyone."

"Okay." She hesitated before walking over to the changing room he had indicated. Once inside, she peeled out of her clothing and unbuckled the collar. It felt strange to remove it, especially when it held so much meaning to the sky warriors. There was a small mirror mounted on the wall, and she flushed when she noticed the splotches on her neck where the collar had been. Cipher had taken hold of it earlier that morning while pounding her into the bed, marking her skin with his need and desire. She ran her fingers over the marks and felt a flutter of heat between her legs. Cipher was the sweetest, gentlest man, but inside the bedroom, when they were together, he could be wild and rough.

And she absolutely loved it.

Thinking of him, she cleaned her body as instructed and slipped on the gown and cap. When she stepped out of the changing room, there was another man waiting with Chance. Instantly, she recognized that Reckless was not a nice person. There was something in the air, a familiar vibe that set off her internal alarms.

"They let this little scrap of a girl pass the health inspection?" He looked at her as if she were the ugliest thing he had ever seen. "What the hell is Raze doing over there? Doesn't he know we have standards? She'll never be able to carry a baby to term with a shrunken, malnourished womb."

She went cold as his mean words washed over her. She was thin, yes, but she wasn't sickly. She had lean muscles and plenty of strength to climb and crawl and work in the mines.

He stepped toward her, and she took an instinctive step back. He glowered at her. "Get over here. Now."

She bristled at being ordered around by such a mean old man but didn't dare tell him no. She stepped in front of him and flinched when he reached out to touch her. He roughly gripped her chin, turning her face left and right. "So, you're the dirty little rat they found to crawl through the tunnels and free Terror, huh?"

"Sir," Chance cut in, offended on her behalf. "I don't think that sort of language is appropriate for a mate."

"Did I ask you for your opinion?" Reckless kept his

irritated gaze on her as he said, "Chance, your parents have the right idea, arranging your marriage to a nice, clean girl from home." He sneered down at her. "Look at this one. Uneducated. Underfed. Her parents were probably cousins or siblings. Spent her entire miserable life crawling through mine shafts like an animal." He shook his head with disgust. "Cipher is one of the smartest men in our entire force. His genes are wasted on trash like this."

"Sir!" Chance grimaced.

"Get her hooked up to the sensors," Reckless ordered before moving to the control panel on the chamber. "I want a fertility panel run on her before the next scheduled treatment. If she's as low quality as she looks, we aren't wasting more treatment resources on her."

Chance shot her an apologetic look, and she shook her head slightly, letting him know that she didn't blame him for the horrible things coming out of his superior's mouth. He applied the sensor stickers to her chest and back, keeping his eyes away from her naked skin as he shifted her gown out of place to reach the areas he needed.

"Get into the chamber, girl," the doctor said when Chance was finished. She hesitated a moment too long, and he snapped, "Are you deaf? Get in now!"

She scrambled to comply. Too afraid to ask for a stool or help, she clambered into the chamber using her climbing skills. Once she was inside, she slid down onto the blue padding and placed her arms at her side.

"Don't talk. Don't move. Breathe in and out until the treatment is done."

"Yes, sir."

He seemed marginally pleased with her reply. He shut the chamber lid and locked it in place before disappearing from view. Alone and unable to see anything but the ceiling above her, she glanced around the confined space. There were locks on the inside of the lid, probably as a fail safe if the outer locks released too early. That morning, over breakfast Cipher had explained the way the chamber worked. She understood that an uncontrolled depressurization would be catastrophic.

A hissing sound startled her, but she remained still. She felt a strange pressure pushing her down and then her ears popped. She swallowed and cleared them. Slowly, she became aware of a strange smell in the chamber. It was a sharp scent, and her lungs burned a bit when she inhaled. She tried not to panic, but bad memories from the mines overwhelmed her. How many times had she only just escaped death from methane by pulling on a respirator?

"You're okay." Chance stared down at her through the glass lid. She tried to smile, but she was sure it came out more like a wince. "The treatment may feel uncomfortable, but you're getting plenty of oxygen. Breathe as deeply as you can. I'll be right out here the entire time if you need me."

She nodded and closed her eyes again. Stuck in this tube, she was taken back to her life in the mines. Tight spaces had never bothered her. Neither had the dark. Even a hint of methane on the air did little to scare her.

But something about Reckless sure as hell did.

He clearly didn't approve of her. Was he like that with all brides? Or only the ones who looked like her? After meeting so many kind men on the *Valiant,* she couldn't understand why Reckless was so mean. Had something terrible happened to him? Was that why he was so bitter and cruel?

Not wanting to waste any more time on Reckless and his mean words, she turned her thoughts to Cipher and his offer to take her to Blue Shores. His teasing about the bathing suit gave her a pretty good idea of what they would be getting up to on their trip. As insatiable as he was, she had a feeling she wouldn't be spending much time out of their hotel room.

After what felt like an eternity, Chance tapped on the glass. "You're done. Hold tight, and I'll help you out when the cycle finishes."

When she finally was allowed out of the tube, she sat up and felt immediately woozy. Chance supported her with one hand on her back and the other gripping her hand in front. The air felt weirdly thin as she inhaled, and she started to cough violently. Chance was ready for it and pressed a paper-thin towel to her face. "Let it out," he urged. "It's part of the process."

She hacked and coughed, fighting for her breaths as her battered lungs tried to purge the impurities the treatment had loosened. In between coughs, she gagged and spit into the towel. Pink sputum tinged with black and purple pooled against the towel, and she recoiled at the sight of it.

That was inside of me. That was trying to kill me.

"Deep breaths," Chance coached. "I know it's scary, but you need to try."

She did as he instructed, and after a few minutes, the coughing eased but she started wheeze. The towel was moved away, and Chance slipped a mask over her nose and mouth. She immediately recognized the disgusting nebulizer treatment taste and made a face.

He smiled apologetically. "Sorry."

Sitting up in the tube, she held the mask to her face and finished the breathing treatment. She desperately wanted Cipher with her. He would have rubbed her back, told her sweet and encouraging things and then offered her a box of juice when she was finished. Chance stayed nearby, but he didn't offer the comfort only her mate could.

When the treatment was complete, Chance helped her back to the changing room. She slumped against the wall as the jitteriness started. Uncertain whether she could manage on her own, she opened the door just a crack. "Chance?"

"Yes, ma'am?" He avoided looking at the door but moved closer.

"Can you get Cipher, please? I need his help."

"Of course, ma'am."

She made her way to the cold metal chair and settled onto it. Her legs and arms trembled wildly as she waited for Cipher to make his way to her. In a shorter time than she expected, he jerked open the door, stepped inside and shut it behind him. Obviously worried, he knelt in front of her and cupped her face in his big, warm hands. "Are you okay, little one?"

"I am now." She leaned into his reassuring touch as fatigue overwhelmed her. "I don't think I can get dressed by myself."

"You don't have to," he said, pressing a tender kiss to her lips. He was so gentle as he helped her out of the hospital gown and back into her clothes. "Next time, I'm coming back here with you."

"I don't think that's a good idea," she said sleepily. "You'll end up punching that mean doctor in the face."

He pulled back and searched her face. "Mean doctor? Who? Reckless?" When she nodded, he scowled. "What did he say to you?"

"Nothing worth repeating," she murmured, resting her cheek against his chest. "You're so warm."

"And you're sleepy as a kitten," he replied, gently rubbing her back. "Let's get you home."

The trip back to the *Valiant* was a blur. She could barely keep her eyes open as Cipher led her through the *Mercy* to the transport ship. Once he had her buckled into her seat, he lifted the armrest between them and hauled her right up against him. She rested her tired head on his chest and drifted off to sleep.

She woke to the sensation of Cipher unbuckling her seatbelt. He caressed her sleepy face and helped her stand. She clung to his hand and arm as they navigated the Arrivals deck and waited for an elevator. As soon as they stepped onto their floor, he swept her up into his arms and carried her the rest of the way to their quarters and then into their bedroom. She didn't protest as he placed her on the bed, stripped off her shoes and tucked her under the covers. He took off his boots and belt and slid into bed beside her.

Gathering her close, he rubbed her back. "I'm sorry the treatment took so much out of you."

"It's not your fault," she murmured, still so tired. "I hope it works."

"It will," he assured her. The soothing strokes of his hand made her eyelids droop. "Later, I want you to tell me what Reckless said, Brook."

"Yes, sir." She yawned and snuggled in closer. "But you have to promise me you won't storm over there and kick his ass. I'm not cut out to be a prison wife."

He chuckled and kissed the top of her head. "Physical violence isn't my thing. There are much better ways to get revenge on someone."

Certain he had all sorts of scary ways to hurt someone, she tucked her leg between his. As she drifted off to sleep, there was a brief flash of a memory that she couldn't quite place. The Drowned Door? Why in the world was that coming to mind?

Too tired to think about it, she promised herself she would try to figure it out later. For now, she was content to nap in the warm cocoon of Cipher's arms.

Chapter Fifteen

WHILE CIPHER WATCHED Brook sleep, he couldn't stop thinking about all the horrible things Reckless might have said to her. The doctor had a terrible reputation when it came to mates who weren't from their home world. It was the main reason Orion kept him on the *Mercy* and off the *Valiant* and why Reckless was rarely sent down with the Grab teams.

Brook let out a soft whine in her sleep, and he nuzzled his face against her cheek before drawing her in a little tighter. The thought of Reckless talking shit to her and disrespecting her infuriated him. She was so good and kind, such a giving, sweet soul. His hands started to clench, and he had to consciously will them to relax. Even though he had promised her he wouldn't hit Reckless, he had a feeling that might be a promise he broke.

Wanting to keep her safe and protected from all the ugliness in the world, he closed his eyes and inhaled the sugary sweet scent of her soap and shampoo. He had been surprised when she had chosen to keep using that particular bath set. He had been sure she would gravitate toward the woodsy scented one. Not that he minded either way. Whatever she liked was just fine with him.

His watch started to vibrate, and he groaned, knowing it was surely bad news. He glanced at the screen, saw the red alert and disentangled himself from Brook. The communication console in the living area started to blare, and she sat up, groggily wiping at her eyes. "What's wrong? Another drill?"

"No, I'm being called in to SRU." He moved quickly to the cabinet where he stowed his gear and began strapping it on over his uniform. "You'll be safe here."

"I'm not worried about me," she insisted, getting out of bed to join him at the cabinet. "I'm worried about you."

"Baby, I've been doing this forever." He snatched his helmet up and then his gear bag. "I'll be fine."

If she wanted to make him promise he would come back, she fought the urge. Instead, she rose on tiptoes and sought his mouth. "Be careful."

"I will." He gave her bottom a little pat. "Get back in bed. Rest. I'll be back later."

"Should I cook dinner?"

"Absolutely not," he said, brushing his mouth against hers. "You are to stay in that bed or on the couch until I get home."

"I will." She followed his instructions and got back into bed as he rushed from the bedroom to the living area to silence the comm unit.

Hating to leave her, he left their quarters and ran into Raze at the elevator. The boss was still pulling on his boots and looked as if the call had interrupted a session of afternoon delight. Confirming Cipher's suspicion was the unmistakable smudge of deep red lipstick on Raze's neck. "Boss?"

"Yeah?" Raze hopped into the elevator on one foot while zipping up the boot on the other.

"You got a little something…" Cipher gestured to his own neck.

"Shit." Raze laughed and wiped at his skin. "I'm such a sucker for Ella in lipstick." The boss gave him a once-over as the elevator started to descend. "You look entirely too well put together for a man who is supposed to be on his honeymoon."

"Brook had her first tube session today," he explained while strapping his wrist tablet into place. "We were napping when the call came."

"Is she okay alone? You can go back to her, Ci. I'll pull someone from another backup team."

Cipher shook his head. "She's resting—and you don't have anyone else to pull. Venom's team is on the *Dauntless* and Gamma is supporting a mission in The City." He flashed his wrist tablet to show the location of their other teams. "It's me or you're a man short."

"We have our recruits. Some of them are ready for live action." He jammed his earpiece in place and tapped his throat mic. "Threat, what's the situation?"

Cipher slipped his earpiece in place in time to hear Threat say, "…an attack on the Mercy. Three men down. Suspect at large. They're on lockdown."

"Do we have a dart available?"

"Blaze is holding at missions departure. Ship is fully

loaded. It's the backup prepared by G team before they left."

"Alpha, SRU Leader," Raze addressed their entire team. "Meet at missions departure deck. Will brief en route." Clicking off the main channel, Raze glanced at him and asked, "Did you notice anything when you were over there?"

Cipher shook his head and tapped at the elevator control board to change their destination and override any stops. "It was quiet and as busy as it normally is."

"They've got that psych unit over there, right?"

"Yeah."

"Maybe one of those patients got loose and…?" He made a stabbing gesture. "Happened before when I was fresh out of the academy. A couple of seriously unwell guys broke out of their locked unit and killed eleven people before they were apprehended."

Tapping his radio, Cipher asked, "Threat, what's the info on the victims? Any suspects?"

"Attack happened in the pulmonary unit," Threat answered, breathing hard as if he were running. "Two medics went down."

"Was Chance one of them?"

"Yeah, actually, he was."

"What is it?" Raze asked as the elevator opened.

"Chance was Brook's medic during her visit." He fell into step beside Raze as they hurried toward the waiting ship. "He was her day medic while she was in the hospital, too. She's friendly with him. This is going to upset her."

"Going to upset his bride even more," Raze muttered as they boarded the ship. "He's got a girl coming from back home in a few weeks."

Cipher winced. "Let's hope his injury isn't serious."

Raze nodded and ducked into the cockpit to talk to Blaze. Cipher took his seat at the logistics station next to Threat and logged in to access the security feeds from the *Mercy*. When he reappeared, Raze did a head count on the team and then the ship was moving. Cipher braced himself on the console as the ship rocketed out of the launch bay, picking up incredible speed as it raced toward the *Mercy*. The darts were the fastest ships in the fleet and would get them to the *Mercy* in less than fifteen minutes.

"Report?" Raze asked, standing between the two benches where the team sat and holding onto an overhead cargo loop to steady himself.

"Security guard reported he was making his final rounds before the end of his shift. He found two medics and a doc down."

"Which doc?" Raze asked, gripping a second loop as the ship veered to the left.

"Reckless," Threat answered.

Cipher shared a look with Raze before turning his attention to Threat. "Are they alive?"

"Chance and Reckless are. Chance is in surgery with head trauma. Reckless is unconscious but stable. The other medic died on scene."

"That's a lot of damage for one suspect," Flare commented as he checked his weapon.

242 | LOLITA LOPEZ

"Unless it's an operative," Harm suggested. "Someone may have infiltrated the unit, took them out one at a time."

"Yeah, but why the pulmonary unit?" Fierce adjusted his shoulder mic. "Was it specifically those men? Or were they just in the way?"

"The gas?" Cipher offered uncertainly. "Reckless is the expert, right? He runs the pulmonary unit. Maybe this is an attack on our readiness?"

That became their working theory as they set up their plan for assisting the security team with clearing each floor. When they docked, the head of security and the captain of the vessel liaised with Raze while Cipher set up at the security station. While his teammates fanned out with the security team and a support group that had come in from the *Arctis,* he took control of the elevators, doors and cargo loading areas and started scanning the security footage for any glimpses of the perpetrator.

As he listened to his team clear the hospital ship room by room and floor by floor, he guided their movements and controlled the flow of patients and staff sheltering in place. He called in the *Mercy's* head tech for the security system and had him run the doors and elevators so he could take a better look at the footage.

"Anything?" Raze asked as he returned to the security station almost an hour later. "Our guys have nearly cleared the whole ship."

"There's nothing here." Cipher blew out an irritated breath. "Whoever attacked those three men is a ghost. There's no one going in or out of the unit after us."

"Us?"

"Brook and I," he clarified, rolling back the footage to the two of them leaving. "There's nothing after us until the security guard does his round."

"What about before?"

"Before what?"

"Before you left," Raze explained. "Maybe someone snuck in when the unit was unlocked to let Brook inside?"

Cipher wound the footage all the way back to five minutes before they arrived in the waiting area. He moved it forward slowly until Brook entered the unit. Again, there was nothing out of the ordinary.

"Do we have any eyes on the treatment areas?"

Cipher shook his head. "Only the hallways."

"Uh, sir, that's not exactly true," the security tech interjected. "Reckless had us put in a set of cameras near the tube. He likes to watch the footage of his treatments."

"That's against the security regulations," Cipher reminded the tech. "Patients are supposed to have privacy unless they specifically sign a waiver allowing their procedures to be recorded." Scowling, he added, "I know I didn't give permission for my mate to be recorded."

The tech shrunk back in his chair. "I'm sorry, sir, but Reckless can be…" He made a face. "Well, he knows how to make things painful if you disobey him."

"Painful?" Raze repeated. "How?"

"He has a lot of pull on this ship. He's one of the highest ranked officers. If you cross him, you'll regret it."

"Show me the recordings," Cipher ordered.

The tech leaned over and tapped in a code that opened a hidden file of recordings. Cipher selected the one for that day and let it play. He ran through most of the footage, scrolling quickly with his finger until he saw Brook and Chance. A volume mixer in the lower corner caught his eye. In disbelief, he asked, "This has audio?"

The tech nodded. "Yes, sir."

Cipher couldn't believe how many rules they were breaking on this ship. Nevertheless, he turned up the volume so they could hear what was happening in the chamber with his mate. When she went into the changing room, he narrowed his eyes at the tech. "If there's a camera in there, I swear I—"

"No, sir! There are no cameras in there!"

Relieved that at least Brook hadn't been recorded naked, he watched as she reappeared in the too big gown and surgical cap. His hackles raised the moment Reckless opened his mouth. The shit he said to Brook enraged him. How fucking dare he?

"Easy," Raze urged, putting a hand on his shoulder. "He's a superior officer. You can't go kick his ass."

"He's no superior," Cipher growled. "He's a piece of shit."

"Agreed," Raze said, his voice low, "but there are other ways of handling this." The boss arched his brows in silent communication. "Right?"

Cipher nodded, understanding exactly what Raze meant. "Right."

The thought of getting Reckless alone somewhere and planting his fist in the other man's face stilled his rage. As he watched Brook climb into the tube, his heart broke a little bit. She looked impossibly small inside the chamber and so scared.

I should have been there with her.

Speeding up the footage until after he had taken her home, he slowed it down when Reckless started to lay into Chance about something. He rolled it back a few seconds and let it play.

"Don't you ever question me in front of a patient!" Reckless pointed his finger at Chance. "And you sure as hell better never question me in front of a gash!"

Cipher's rage flared back to life at hearing Brook referred to so crudely.

"Sir, she's an officer's mate. She risked her life to—"

"She's nothing," Reckless interrupted nastily. "She's just some backwoods piece of trash who doesn't deserve to breathe the same air as us. None of these women that have joined our men are worthy of our seed. They're worse than the poppies." He made a disgusted face. "The only good thing on that skinny tunnel rat was her mouth. It's the only place I'd allow my seed to land."

"Sir!" Chance recoiled. "You cannot—"

"I can do whatever the fuck I want. This is my unit. I'm the one who makes the rules here. If you don't like it, go back to the *Valiant* where you soft pussies belong."

"Fucking gladly, sir," Chance snarled and turned on his heel. As he reached the doorway, he stopped. "You can take your other offer and shove it up your ass, *sir.*"

"Chance! Soldier! Get back here!" Reckless shouted

after Chance, but the medic kept walking until he was out of frame.

"What other offer?" Cipher glanced at Raze who seemed just as taken aback by what they had just witnessed.

"No idea." Jaw hardening, Raze said, "Make copies of that. Send one to me. Send another to Orion and one to Vicious."

"On it, boss." Cipher minimized the feed, grabbed the file, copied it and sent it to the admiral and general. He suspected Reckless would be on his way back to Prime as soon as he was discharged from the hospital.

"Wait. Where are they going?" Raze gestured to the screen where Chance had walked into frame along with another man. "Is that the dead medic?"

"Yes," the tech answered. "Talon. He is—was—the senior medical tech on that unit."

Cipher maximized the feed. Chance and the senior medic looked ready to confront Reckless. The audio cut out before Reckless appeared, robbing them of the chance to hear the heated conversation. The angle was too poor for Cipher to attempt to use one of the programs that read lips. The discussion grew more belligerent as all three men were pointing and shouting.

"Look at Chance's face," Raze said, his finger pointing at the younger man as Talon stormed after Reckless off screen. "He looks surprised."

Cipher agreed. "Something's not right."

"Wait! What the hell?" Raze exclaimed as the feed went black. "Did we just lose it?"

Cipher tapped away but couldn't retrieve any data. "It

was shut off inside the room."

"Reckless?" Raze guessed. "He walked out of view. He probably cut the audio when he saw them come back to confront him."

"Probably," Cipher agreed. Sitting back in his chair, he asked the obvious question. "Did those three get into a fight? Was this a workplace dispute?"

"Looks that way," Raze said quietly. "Shit. What a mess!" He scratched the back of his head and made a face. "Get Keen over here. This is a criminal matter. It's out of our purview."

"You got it, boss." Cipher keyed up his mic to relay the request. Raze stomped off to pull the team back and end the lockdown.

What followed was three hours of absolute bullshit. Cipher and the rest of SRU Alpha were forced to wait on the departure deck as Raze, Keen, the captain of the Mercy and Falcon, Orion's newly promoted second-in-command, argued about who had jurisdiction over the case and whether Reckless and Chance could stay on the same medical ship together. Until Reckless or Chance gained consciousness, there wasn't any way to get an idea of what had happened. Evidence in the treatment room might give Keen some clues, but he needed to interview both men.

"Listen, you three sort this out among yourselves," Raze said finally, throwing his hands up in exasperation. "I'm clearing my men back to the *Valiant*."

Without waiting for a reply, Raze whistled sharply and circled his hand in the air, signaling the team to round up and move. Cipher fell into step behind Flare and Harm.

When they stepped onto the dart, Blaze was waiting for them, leaning back against the door to the cockpit. "Clusterfuck, huh?"

Raze smacked Blaze's shoulder. "Brother, you don't know the half of it. Take us home."

Blaze nodded and returned to the cockpit. Cipher found a seat and dropped down in a tired huff. There wasn't much said on the short flight back to the *Valiant*. They all seemed lost in their own thoughts. Cipher had so many questions about what had happened between Reckless, Talon and Chance.

There was something strange about those final few seconds of footage. Whatever Chance had thought was going to happen when he confronted Reckless with Talon had gone wildly wrong. Considering Reckless was the least wounded of the trio, it seemed to Cipher that the doctor was likely the perpetrator. Unfortunately, with his rank and connections, even if guilty, he was unlikely to face any real consequences.

That thought irritated him as they docked and returned to HQ for their debrief. When they were finally dismissed, he trudged to the elevator with the rest of the team. The unmated guys stepped off on the floor where Cipher had recently lived. Raze had stayed behind for a meeting with Orion and Vicious so the remainder of his ride was quiet and alone.

As he unlocked the door to their quarters, he wondered if he would find Brook in bed or lounging on the couch. He didn't find her in either place. Instead, he followed the light coming from his workspace. They had been lucky enough to be allotted an apartment with a third bedroom. He had converted it to a place where he could bring projects and tinker away on new designs and ideas. He had encouraged Brook to spend as much time in there as she wanted, and he trusted her to treat his projects with care.

When he pushed the door open and found her kneeling by one of his more secret devices, he froze.

Fuck. Fuck. Fuck.

He hadn't told her about those designs yet. How the hell had she even found it?

His gaze moved to the goggles perched atop her head. Of course. She must have found the goggles in one of his desk drawers. They allowed the wearer to project blueprints over their surroundings and were standard issue to most engineers and techs. With those on, she would have been able to see that hidden cabinet tucked away along the wall.

Finally sensing him, she glanced toward the door. Her curious expression morphed instantly to one of pure happiness. She hopped up from the floor and rushed toward him. "You're home!"

He wrapped his arms around her and played her words over and over in his head. Home. He was home. With his mate. Was there any sweeter greeting?

"I'm home," he replied and kissed her lovingly. She responded with the same pliable softness she always did, letting him take and seek until he had his fill. When he pulled back, he brushed his thumb along her cheek. "Did you get some rest?"

"I did." She rubbed her hand across one of the loops on his tactical vest. "Are you okay? Do you want to talk about what happened?"

"I'm fine. It was a false alarm." He let his thumb move along her pouty lips. "And, no, I'd rather not talk about what happened right now." His focus drifted from her face to the device on the floor. "I'd like to talk about that, though."

"Oh." She bashfully dropped her gaze. "I found it with these." She reached up and tugged the goggles free from her head, making a mess of her hair as she did. "I'm sorry. I shouldn't have gone through your things."

"It's fine." He took the goggles from her and tossed them onto the closest chair. Smoothing her hair with his hands, he asked, "Do you know what that is?"

"A puzzle box?" she guessed. "I've been trying to open it for the last half hour."

He shook his head. "Not a puzzle box."

"Is it something classified?"

"No."

She threw up her hands. "I give up!"

"Do you really want to find out what it is?"

She narrowed her eyes as if trying to read him. "Why do I get the feeling that thing I found is something naughty?"

He smiled down at her. "Because it definitely is."

"Oh."

"Yes."

She bit her lower lip. "Will I like it?"

His heart thundered in his chest as he imagined her writhing on top of it. "Why don't you sit on it and find out?"

Chapter Sixteen

B ROOK GLANCED AT the strange black box she had discovered while snooping and then back at Cipher. He wouldn't do anything to hurt her, and the mischievous glint in his eyes convinced her she would definitely enjoy whatever it was.

"Okay."

"Take all this off." He touched her dress. "Everything. I want you naked."

She swallowed nervously and felt those first flutters of excitement and desire in her belly. "Yes, sir."

She stepped back and started to strip. She slowly peeled out of her blue dress and draped it over a chair. Her panties and bra followed next, joining her dress on the chair.

"Take down your hair," he instructed, his voice husky and dark.

"Yes, sir." She complied with his order, unraveling her braid until her hair fell in loose waves around her shoulders and back.

"Come here." He held out his hand, and she walked toward him as gracefully as she could manage, ignoring the urge to skip happily over to him. He led her to a chair. "I want you to sit here, with your legs over the arms. You're going to touch yourself and think about me." Taking gentle but firm hold of her chin, he gazed down at her and sternly ordered, "You will not come. Do you understand? I want you wet and aching when I get back from my shower."

"Yes, sir," she answered shakily. Following his instruction, she sat on the chair and lifted her legs until they were draped over the arms. His appreciative gaze fell between her wide-open legs. Only that morning he had spent half an hour with his face buried in her sex, licking and sucking until she was trembling and keening.

"No orgasm," he reminded her.

"I won't, sir." She watched him leave and then closed her eyes. Thinking only of Cipher, she slid her warm hands down the front of her body. She cupped her small breasts and played with her nipples in the way she had learned she liked most. It wasn't exactly the same as Cipher's rough fingers tugging and pinching, but it still felt good.

She let her right hand move lower, skimming along the slope of her belly until she felt the tuft of hair between her legs. Her fingers traced each side and then the seam, repeating the movement until she felt that tingle toward the top of her mound. She parted her folds and let her finger slide all the way to her entrance and then back up her clit. She rubbed the little nub in slow, easy circles and let all the memories of the wicked things Cipher had done to her come to mind.

Gradually, her arousal increased until she could feel the slickness when she swirled her finger at her opening. She breathed a little harder now and dipped her finger into her wet heat. With her fingertip now slippery, she strummed her clit while remembering the way Cipher's tongue felt there. She began to pant as the exquisite feeling started to expand and pulled her hand away from her body. She gripped the arm of the chair and waited for the sensation to fade.

When it had faded enough, she touched herself again. She was just starting to feel that wonderful trembling when she heard Cipher's footsteps approaching. Still rubbing her clit, she turned her face toward the doorway and met his burning gaze. She could practically feel his eyes moving over her naked body, lingering on her breasts and the hand between her legs. She returned the desirous stare and raked her eyes down his incredible body. The towel around his hips sat so low she could see the trail of hair that led right down to his thick cock.

"Cipher," she whispered and reached out to him. "Sir. Please."

He didn't make her beg a moment longer. Striding toward her on those long, powerful legs, he scooped her up out of the chair and carried her back to the device. "Kneel down next to it."

She slid out of his arms and did as he asked. He crouched down and slipped his finger along a hidden switch on the side of the innocuous black box. Feeling silly for not finding the switch earlier, she curiously watched as he lifted and set aside the lid. Inside the box, there was a black half-moon shaped mound. On the top, there was a shiny black plate with ridges and bumps.

"Touch it."

She glanced at him before reaching out with her finger. "Oh! It's so soft."

"It's made from a medical grade material. It warms up when it's pressed against your skin. It's impervious to fluids, and it molds to your unique shape."

"*Oh.*" It finally clicked. This was a something she was supposed to straddle, and the squishy ridges would rub up her in all the right places.

"It's never been tried," he admitted. "I've been tinkering with it for a while. I've made other machines for couples before," he confessed. "Most of them were simple thrusting attachments, but this one is a little different. It vibrates and rolls and massages. You can add a penetrating attachment here and here." He pointed out the hidden slots. "I've even got designs for different stimulation plates and several modes of vibration."

She couldn't help it. She grinned at him and started to giggle. "Oh, Cipher. You're so wonderfully you."

He cocked his head. "What's that supposed to mean?"

"That only an engineer like you would think to combine all the different ways to drive a woman wild in a neat little box like this," she explained. She slipped her arms around his shoulders and embraced him tightly. Nuzzling her face against his, she whispered, "You really are the most considerate man."

He kissed her, darting his tongue into her mouth to taste and tease. With his forehead against hers, he asked, "Do you want the first ride?"

"Yes, sir." She giggled happily and climbed onto the contraption. It was surprisingly comfortable, not too wide or high. Still wet and warm from touching herself, she pressed herself against the stimulation plate and gasped at how good it felt.

"You okay?"

"Yes."

"You ready for the next part?"

Hands on her upper thighs, she nodded. "Show me."

He reached behind her to the base of the device. A delicious vibration started between her legs. She inhaled a shocked breath as the vibration started to move back and forth along the stimulation plate. The firm jelly-like ridges felt like different tongues on her all at once, and she swallowed hard. She had never felt anything like this. In only a few seconds, she was on the verge of climax.

Cipher knelt in front of her and tangled his hands in her hair. He tilted her head back and claimed her mouth, stabbing his tongue inside and sucking on the tip of hers. She shuddered atop the device and whimpered against his lips. His sensual kisses were matched by the firm grasp of his hands, one staying in hair and the other moving down to clutch at her ass. He pressed her down against the device, and she shattered with a gasp, coming so hard she couldn't speak.

"That's it, baby girl," he urged. "Watching you come makes my dick so hard." He nipped at her lower lip as she trembled wildly. "Can't wait to feel your mouth on my cock."

"Yes, sir. Let me taste it," she begged. "Please."

He leaned around her to adjust the speed of the vibrations before rising tall and removing his towel. He tossed it aside and grasped his big, thick cock. His hand moved up and down the length of it before it settled just below the head. He nudged her lips with the tip, smearing the slick droplet of fluid gathered there on her mouth, before pressing it forward. "Suck."

She had only learned how to do this days earlier, but from the way he groaned, she was a quick study. Just as he seemed to find pleasure in using his mouth on her, she found it intoxicating to do the same for him. He was so big that he stretched her lips, and she couldn't even get close to taking all of him. He didn't care. He had told her as much that first time he had taught her how he liked it. He got the most enjoyment from the head and right below it so that's where she concentrated.

His hand tangled in her hair, pulling lightly and making her scalp tingle. She gripped his muscular thighs as she bobbed back and forth on his shaft, humming happily around it and making sure to use her tongue. He growled as she worked her lips over him, and he gently pumped his hips. She glanced up at him, his cock buried in her mouth and her legs shaking as the device vibrated her closer and closer to an orgasm. His eyes were stormy and dark with desire, and she had the heady realization that even in this precarious position, she was the one with the power over him.

"You look so beautiful with my cock in your mouth."

He stroked a finger down her cheek and thrust carefully into her. "You feel so good, baby."

She hummed around him and sucked him in as deep as she could, relaxing her jaw and trying to take more. He groaned, and the fingers tangled in her hair tightened. The vibrations between her legs were driving her crazy now. The biggest ridge rested right below her clit, and the waves were flowing through her in all the right places.

Cipher tilted her head back with the hair trapped in his fist and pumped shallow and short, sliding his cock over her willing tongue. "Are you going to come with my cock in your mouth?"

She nodded and moaned around him. Her thighs tightened around the device, and her nails scratched at his hips, leaving red marks as she clung to him. He reached down with his other hand and pinched her nipple, tugging it and rolling it. The spark of pain sent her flying over the edge. She whined around his cock as she rocked atop the device, riding wave after wave of pleasure until she slumped against him.

He pulled his cock free and moved behind her so quickly she fell forward onto her elbows. She gasped in shock and delight as he pushed her shoulders down and lifted her ass, spreading her for his coming invasion. The blunt head of his penis pressed into her pussy, and she cried out with desperate need.

"That's it, little mate," he growled. "Take it. Take all of it."

Her toes curled as he slid so deep that she could feel

him nudging against the entrance to her womb. He wrapped the long waves of her hair around his hand and started to thrust hard and fast. She gasped when his palm cracked her bottom. "Ow!"

"Naughty little girls get punished for snooping," he grunted and smacked her other cheek.

Heat blossomed on her skin, and she cried out with a mix of shock and pain. "Sir!"

"Are you my bad girl?" His hand bounced from cheek to cheek as he thrust into her. "Do you deserve to be punished?"

"Yes, sir!" She couldn't believe the words coming out of her mouth. It was as if she had lost control over her brain. She was completely at Cipher's mercy as they played their wild game.

Leaning forward and straddling the device, she was stretched wide open for him and her clit was in constant contact with the vibrating ridges. The mix of thrusting, spanking and vibrating was too much, and she let go, unable and unwilling to try to hold back a moment longer.

A howl unlike anything that had ever come out of her mouth echoed around the room. She sounded almost like an animal as she cried out with the passionate waves of pleasure that completely overwhelmed her. Cipher seemed just as lost in the moment, roughly taking her from behind. He gripped her hair and her hip, surely leaving bruises on her skin, and fucked her like a wild man.

Too soon, he shouted her name and thrust so deep, she slid off the device. He followed her to the ground, trapping her smaller body under his as he shuddered and filled her with his seed. She couldn't think and could barely breathe as her pleasure wrecked body trembled under his. He shifted on top of her, still buried to the hilt and kicked aside the whirring machine. It clattered loudly and stopped making noise.

He moved aside her hair and started kissing her neck and temples. "Brook," he whispered lovingly. "My sweet, sweet girl."

She closed her eyes and relished the feel of his lips moving so tenderly across her skin. She shivered when he grazed the stubble on his chin along her shoulder and giggled when he kissed that sensitive spot on the curve of her neck.

Finally, he rolled off of her and onto the floor. Propped up on his side, he stroked her back and smiled at her. His expression turned so loving and vulnerable as he confessed, "I'm falling in love with you."

Her heart stuttered in her chest, and she didn't even try to stop the grin that tugged at her mouth. "That's good."

"Yeah?" He drew a lazy shape on her skin. "Why?"

Taking his huge hand in hers, she brought it close and kissed the back of it. "Because I'm definitely falling in love with you."

Cipher's grin matched her own as he pulled her into his arms and kissed her. There were so many things she wanted to ask him, but right then, in that moment, she was content to press her cheek to his chest and just listen to his heartbeat. There would always be time to talk, but moments like these, quiet, gentle moments, were the ones to cherish.

Chapter Seventeen

"CI, WE'RE GOING to be late if you don't put that down and get ready," Brook gently chided from the doorway of his workspace.

He glanced at his watch and grimaced. "Sorry. I lost track of time."

"It's okay," she assured him as she swept into the room looking so beautiful she took his breath away. Earlier that day, Dizzy had sent over a bright pink dress that fit Brook to perfection. The color made her eyes seem even greener, and her hair looked so rich and dark against the fabric.

"You look amazing, Brook. Pink is definitely your color."

"You think?" She shyly brushed her hands over the fabric. "It's not too much?"

"No. It's just right." He rose from his drafting table and crossed the room. Cupping her face, he leaned down to kiss her. "You are going to be the prettiest woman at this dinner."

"I don't know about that," she modestly replied. "Ella was a muse back on Calyx. She's so gorgeous."

"She is, but so are you. Especially in this dress," he added, sliding his hand along the curve of her back to rest on her pert little ass.

"No." She flicked his chest and stepped away from his hand. "We don't have time for any of *that*."

"Fine," he grumbled, "but we're leaving early to make time for *that*."

She playfully rolled her eyes. "Go. Change."

"We're going four doors down," he pointed out as he left his office. "It's a twenty second walk."

"All the more reason to be punctual." She closed the door to his workspace. "I want to make a good impression."

"Brook, they're all going to love you."

"Well, I bet they'll love me even more if I'm on-time the first time I meet them." She shooed him with a wave of her hands. "Go."

"Yes, dear," he grumbled sarcastically. She stuck out her tongue at him, and he smiled, deciding he would give her an enjoyable punishment for that later.

In no time at all, he had changed out of his lounging clothes into the uniform required any time he was outside his quarters. He found her waiting near the entryway, nervously wringing her hands and fidgeting. It finally occurred to him that this was probably her first time to ever go to a dinner like this. She was about to meet so many new people and that had to be daunting for someone who had spent most of her life in a secluded cabin.

Sliding his arm around her waist, he dragged her close and cupped the back of her head. "Brook, look at me."

She lifted her gaze to his. "Yes?"

"You are smart, beautiful and brave. I know it, and my friends are about to learn it, too."

She offered a little smile and toyed with a button on his shirt. "I don't want to embarrass you."

"Don't think like that," he urged. "You could never embarrass me."

"I really could," she insisted. "I still haven't learned all of the rules about social interactions, and I've never even been on a date. This is all so new to me."

"I'll be right there with you." He traced her jaw with his thumb. "And I mean it this time. I'm not leaving you alone like I did with that asshole Reckless."

"That wasn't your fault. You were following the rules."

"Fuck the rules," he said harshly. "Especially where that bastard is concerned."

She reached up to stroke his face. "They were just ugly words, Cipher. It's not the first time someone has been nasty to me."

"It damn well better be the last." He turned his face to kiss her palm. "No one will disrespect you like that ever again."

"I'm sure they won't if they see you scowling like that," she teased.

He smiled and took her hand in his. "Ready?"

She nodded, and they left their quarters. They reached Raze and Ella's door as Vicious and Hallie came off the elevator. They were a striking couple, and Cipher secretly hoped Hallie would take Brook under her wing. The two women were similar in age and background. If anyone could understand the life Brook had lived before he claimed her, it was Hallie.

"Hello!" Hallie greeted with a warm smile. "How are you, Cipher?"

"I'm well, ma'am. You?"

"Very, very good," she said, sneaking a quick glance up at her mate. Vicious had his hand on the back of her neck, and his fingers brushed the area just above her stark white collar in a loving gesture. Turning her attention to Brook, she grinned. "I have heard so much about you from Vee!"

Brook anxiously glanced at the general. "Uh-oh."

Hallie laughed and wound her arm through Brook's. "All very, very good things. Now—let's get you introduced to everyone." She looked back at her husband and playfully rolled her eyes. "The boys are going to talk guns and other boring things, but Ella and Naya always have the best gossip from around the ship."

Left behind with the general, Cipher watched Hallie knock on the door and guide his mate into her first dinner party. Vicious clapped him on the back. "She's in good hands. Come on. Let's find Menace. I actually do want to talk to him about a new weapon I think we should acquire."

Cipher laughed at that and trailed the general into Raze and Ella's home. After a quick round of greetings, he gravitated toward the men who had taken up seats in the living area. He made sure to pick one that gave him a direct line of sight into the kitchen and dining room where Brook was surrounded. Dizzy and Naya were chatting with her about something that had all three of them smiling and laughing. Ella and Hallie milled around in the background, putting the finishing touches on dinner.

"Any word from Risk on Chance's condition?" Venom asked.

"Still in his medically induced coma," Vicious answered. "Risk assures me that he'll make a full recovery with all his cognitive and physical abilities intact, but keeping him cold and asleep is the key."

"We need to know his version of the story," Raze insisted. He glanced back at the kitchen, making sure none of the women were listening, and leaned forward as he spoke in lowered tones. "I don't believe a word that came out of Reckless's lying mouth."

"Nor I," Vicious agreed. "Orion also thinks he's the one who attacked the other two, but Reckless maintains that he was defending himself against Talon and Chance."

"None of that makes sense," Menace remarked. "Talon and Chance are twenty years younger. They're stronger, faster." He paused. "Well, Talon *was*."

"I heard that Talon and Chance went to medical training together," Venom said.

"Not just medical training," Cipher interjected. "They grew up together. Their dads served together. Chance's betrothed mate is Talon's younger sister."

Venom made a face. "And what does Keen think about that?"

Vicious shrugged. "Whatever he thinks, he isn't sharing yet."

"Typical," Raze grumbled. "What's the deal there? Is he

criminal investigations or is he Shadow Force?"

"I couldn't say," Vicious remarked, his gaze briefly moving to their mates.

Understanding that was a question that needed a certain clearance level to answer, they dropped it. Instead, Cipher asked, "How long is Reckless staying in the brig?"

"That's up to Orion." The general stretched out his long legs. "There's no love lost between those two. As soon as he can get this matter cleared up, Orion will likely bounce Reckless back to Prime to face a court martial or be forcibly retired."

"Good riddance," Raze muttered. Shaking his head, he asked, "How many other mates do you think he treated like that?" The boss glanced at Brook with sympathy. "He had no hesitation saying that horrible shit to her. He's definitely done it in the past."

Menace cleared his throat. He, too, made sure their mates were busy in the kitchen before admitting, "Naya heard some rumors about Reckless and some of the wives down in the enlisted men's section."

Vicious sat up at that. "What kind of rumors?"

Menace shot him a look. "What kind do you think?"

The general's jaw visibly stiffened. "Tomorrow, I would appreciate it if you would ask Naya to talk to Keen. If Reckless has been hurting women on this ship, we need to know."

"If he's been taking advantage of other men's wives, you're going to have a line of men ready to beat the shit out of him," Raze warned. "You won't be able to keep him alive in the cells."

Vicious shrugged. "Well, that would be a pity, wouldn't it?"

None of them had a chance to reply because Ella appeared and stood behind Raze, rubbing his shoulders as she announced, "Dinner is ready."

Raze took one of her hands and kissed it before standing and taking his place next to her. While the other men joined their mates, Cipher walked to Brook's side. Ella directed Vicious to the seat of honor at her right and Brook to the seat on Raze's right. The others filled in the spaces as they liked. Wanting to make sure Brook was comfortable, he took the seat to her right. She smiled at him, and he sensed that she had settled in nicely with the other mates.

"So, no worries about my cooking skills," Ella joked as she sat down at the head of the table. "I catered so you're all safe from food poisoning and having to chuck the burned bits under your chairs."

Laughter rounded the table, and they began to serve themselves family style. Ever the social butterfly, Ella kept the conversation light and funny. As Brook was drawn into conversation with Naya and Dizzy, he looked around the table and felt such gratitude for his friends and their willingness to welcome his mate.

Vicious frowned and glanced at his watch. "Raze, may I use your comm unit?"

"Of course." Raze gestured to the room he used as an office. "There's more privacy in there."

Vicious nodded. "Excuse me."

Not letting the general's abrupt departure dampen the mood, Ella said, "So, we received some rather good news today."

"Oh?" Dizzy grinned at Ella as if she already knew what was coming.

"Not *that* news," Ella said, pinning Dizzy in place with a look. She turned to Naya. "Do you want to tell them?"

Naya smiled. "Ella and I are going into business together. Today, we were given an alcohol import permit!"

"We are going to be the sole importer of beer, wine and spirits from Calyx to the fleet!" Ella wiggled in her seat and clapped her hands. "Go us!"

Amid the laughter and congratulations, Naya explained their business plan. "Ella has the contacts in the alcohol industry, and I already have the import logistics down with my shop. We decided to merge and bring the very best that our planet has to offer to the restaurants, bars, shops and clubs up here."

"When the skyport opens, we have a five-year exclusive permit for supplying every business on the port with alcohol."

Cipher didn't have to be a genius at math to figure out how much money the two women stood to make on their venture. Ella would have no problem funding all of her charitable works, and Naya would be able to establish the business empire she wanted to build.

"What did I miss?" Vicious asked as he returned to the table.

"Naya and Ella announced their liquor business," Menace explained as he gazed adoringly at his mate. After all the two had been through, Cipher was so glad to see them happy.

"Oh! Did your license come through today?" Vicious reached for his glass. "Orion mentioned that he had put in a good word for the two of you with the planning council."

"That's shocking to hear," Ella muttered. "During our meeting, he did nothing but scowl and ask questions that made us feel doomed."

Vicious shook his head as he sipped his drink. "That's just his default setting. Don't take it personally."

"Maybe he needs a reboot," Naya suggested wryly. "If ever there was a man on this ship who needed a wife…"

"He had one," Hallie remarked offhandedly in between bites.

Vicious snapped his attention to his wife. "Says who?"

"Says him," she answered. "He told me himself."

"When?"

"At your birthday dinner," she said, setting down her fork. "You had wandered off to talk to someone, and he sat down beside me and said that he missed having a woman look at him the way I look at you." She seemed a little embarrassed as she said, "I think he'd had too much to drink. When I asked him about the woman who had looked at him like that, he told me she had been dead for more than twenty years. Apparently they were teenage sweethearts, but she died before their first anniversary."

Vicious stared at his wife with an expression of won-der. "Terror was right. You would be an incredible interrogator. Everyone just spills their secrets around you."

"Not everyone," she said with a frown. "Especially not Terror."

Vicious sighed and sat back in his chair. "That's why I needed your comm unit, Raze." He gestured to his wrist. "I've been getting tracking alerts for Terror's new chip. He's still restricted until the psych board clears him so anytime he gets near anything too critical or classified, I have to override the system or send one of Torment's recruits after him."

"He popped out of a heat sink vent outside the shooting range this morning," Menace grumbled. "I almost shot him! Thought he was a stowaway or a Splinter assassin."

Vicious grimaced. "He's been spending hours in the hidden corridors of the ship. Savage is at his wit's end, and Orion is threatening to confine him to quarters."

Venom snorted. "Good luck with that."

"It's not the skulking around that's the real problem," Menace interjected. "The worst part is that he's walking around with ballistic plugs in his ears so he can't hear you when you yell at him for scaring you half to death," Menace said with an aggravated shake of his head.

"Ear plugs?" Raze frowned. "Do you think he has sensory overload after being held captive?"

Before Menace could answer, Brook interrupted. "He's just trying to be close to her again."

Vicious frowned at Brook. "Her? Who?"

Brook nervously glanced at him, and Cipher smiled encouragingly at her to continue. "The night I visited him in the hospital, when I gave him that orange, he asked me about a girl. A deaf girl," she added. "I got the feeling that she was important to him. I offered to go back to the mountain and ask around, see if anyone knew her, but he told me to drop it." Her expression turned sad. "If she was a captive like him, she's probably dead now or got sold by the same types of monsters who kidnapped me."

"I had no idea," Vicious admitted after a quiet moment. "He didn't say anything."

"He probably didn't want to tell you because he knew you'd ask him questions that he wasn't ready to answer yet," Brook said carefully. "Telling your best friend about someone you cared for and lost makes it painfully real."

Vicious's face softened. "I'll keep that in mind."

Suddenly, every man at the table tensed and lifted their wrists. Cipher glanced at his and felt relief when it wasn't a call for SRU.

"Torment?" Raze asked, flashing his wrist.

Cipher and the rest of the men nodded.

"We haven't even served dessert!" Ella protested as the men stood to leave.

"Sorry, sweetheart," Raze apologized and bent down to kiss her. "Save me some cake?"

She blew a raspberry at him. "Fat chance! Me and the girls are going to sit here and eat our feelings after being abandoned by our husbands!"

Raze leaned in and whispered something that made her smile. She grabbed the front of his uniform and dragged him down for a kiss.

Cipher glanced away and noticed the others bidding farewell to their wives in similar fashion. He took Brook's hand and pulled her closer. "Go straight back to our quarters when you're done here."

"I will."

"I may be late coming home so don't wait up for me."

"I don't mind."

"I know you don't." He kissed her softly. "Don't forget your treatment."

She made a face and sighed. "I won't."

"And, if there really is cake, smuggle out a slice for me," he requested with a playful grin.

She giggled and kissed him. "I'll do my best, sir."

He was still smiling as he fell into step behind Venom. He wasn't happy about being called away from Brook, but he had something to look forward to at the end of a mission—coming home to his mate.

Chapter Eighteen

"**Y**OU SURE YOU don't want to stay for a bit?" Ella asked as she sealed a slice of cake into a takeaway container.

"I have to do a breathing treatment every night," Brook explained while loading the last plate into the dishwasher. "It's a whole process, and it makes me feel like garbage after so I'd rather get it over with sooner rather than later."

"I've got a bottle of wine chilling," Ella wheedled. "Dizzy can't drink, and Naya has already gone home so that just leaves me and Hallie to enjoy it."

"Sorry," Hallie piped up as she swept under the table. "No wine for me tonight."

Ella narrowed her eyes. "And why is that?"

Hallie smiled and touched her belly. "The treatment worked."

Dizzy and Ella squealed with excitement and ran to hug her.

"A baby!"

"I'm so happy for you!"

"Congratulations," Brook said with genuine happiness.

"Thank you." Hallie beamed at them. "We haven't told anyone but Menace and Naya." She bit her lower lip and then confessed, "And it's not just *a* baby. We're having twins."

Another round of squeals erupted, and Brook was infected with their contagious excitement. Twins! That was an incredible blessing.

"How far along?" Dizzy asked, her hand cupping her more prominent bump.

"Eleven weeks."

"How are you feeling?" Ella asked.

"Tired mostly," Hallie answered. "My morning sickness is worse in the afternoons, but the nausea meds seem to work well."

"They were the only thing that kept me going," Dizzy said. "I was practically living in the bathroom until I found the right dose."

As Dizzy and Hallie shared morning sickness stories, Ella joined her at the sink. She bumped their hips together and smiled. "You and Cipher planning to try for a little bundle of joy soon?"

Brook blushed and shrugged. "We've talked about it for the future."

"I haven't known Cipher long, but I think he'll be an amazing dad."

"I agree." She had first-hand experience with his patience, kindness and love for teaching.

"They can be a little weird up here about fertility," Ella explained, her voice softer now. "Hallie and the general had to basically smuggle fertility drugs onto the ship for her." She looked sad as she added, "Raze has some medical issues that make it almost impossible for us to conceive. We've been working with Risk, though."

"I hope whatever you try works."

"Thank you." She shrugged and confessed, "We are already planning to adopt. A biological child would be a wonderful addition to our family, but our hearts are wide open and ready for a child that grew in another mother's belly."

"Are there a lot of orphans in The City?" She knew Ella was heavily involved in charitable works there.

"So, so many," Ella replied sadly. "We'll never be able to find families and homes for all of them, but we have to try. Every child deserves to be safe and loved."

Brook could see how important this work was to Ella. When she left a short while later, Cipher's cake in hand, she wondered if she had what it took to be an adoptive mother. It wouldn't be easy, especially if the child was older and had suffered neglect or abuse, but she imagined it would be the most natural thing in the world to love and protect any child.

Safe in their home, she placed the cake in the refrigerator for Cipher to enjoy later. Thoughts of sad and abandoned children led her mind to thoughts of Terror aimlessly wandering the ship. The fact that he was wearing ear plugs worried her. How much emotional pain was he in right now? How alone did he feel?

Knowing that she was the only one he had spoken to since his rescue and concerned that he was at risk of falling into a deep depression, she decided she had to try to find him. Her gaze moved to Cipher's workroom. The glasses!

She retrieved the glasses from the drawer where she had found them the other day and slipped them into place. She tapped the rim of the right lens until the correct overlay was in place. She could see the blueprints of the plumbing and electrical wires on each wall.

Cipher had explained that there were hidden access points on every floor of the ship. She just had to find the one on this floor to get into the secret corridors where Terror had taken up residence.

Fully aware that Cipher was going to be upset but unable to abandon Terror again, she left their quarters and wandered down the hall until she found an access door to the left of the elevator. She wasn't sure how to open it until she noticed a diagram of two wires leading to a single spot about four feet from the floor.

When she touched it, there was a soft hiss and then a click as a panel in the wall moved. She stepped through the small space created and found herself in a seemingly endless hallway. Miles of metal grate gangways stretched as far as she could see in front of and behind her. Looking down, there were multiple levels of walkways. Looking up, it was the same thing.

The panel slid closed behind her, and suddenly she was committed to her admittedly bad idea. She was in a labyrinth of metal with no idea which way to go. Left? Right? Stay on this level or move up or down?

Remembering what Menace had said about Terror appearing near the shooting range, she tapped the glasses until they displayed a 3-D layout of the ship. She found the armory and shooting range and noticed it was accessible if she walked the corridor for almost a mile and then took a ladder down three floors. Glad she was wearing flats, she set off on her impromptu adventure.

The longer she walked, the more she realized the hidden corridors and interior levels of the ship were almost identical to the mines she had spent her life inside. It was hot, cramped and poorly lit. There were strange smells and hazards like low ceilings and uneven flooring.

Lost in memories of the mines, she became suddenly aware of heavy footsteps. She froze and listened carefully. The footsteps were below her. Was it Terror? The possibility that it wasn't him kept her quiet.

A man came into view, and it wasn't Terror. It was Reckless!

Crouching down, she tried to make herself small and unnoticeable. Shocked to see the mean old doctor, she wondered what he was doing here. Wasn't he supposed to be in a cell? Why was he wearing a guard's uniform? And what was he carrying in that big first aid bag?

The answer to the last question came as he stopped near a blinking red sensor. He unzipped the large duffel bag slung over his shoulder and retrieved a small oxygen bottle and mask. He placed them over the sensor and taped them in place.

Her stomach dropped. If those were the gas sensors Cipher had placed as an early warning system, the clean air being blown across them would mask a gas attack!

Reckless wasn't just an asshole. He was a terrorist. He was in league with the Splinters!

And then it all made sense. He must have been in the mine that day she was on recon. He may have had his face covered and voiced muffled by a gas mask, but her subconscious mind had recognized him. That was why she had had the brief flash of a memory after her treatment in the chamber.

Torn between fleeing and trying to stop him, she chose the latter. If she could find out where the gas was stashed, she might have a chance to alert Cipher before Reckless could disperse it. If she ran and tried to get help now, they might not be able to find him in this maze of gangways and ladders.

The crazy bastard started to whistle as he walked on, swinging his duffel bag on his arm. She slipped off her shoes and left them on the platform, determined to be as quiet as possible. Staying behind him so as not to cast any shadows he might see, she trailed him through the ship, growing more and more worried every time he covered a sensor.

Thinking about the gas he might have hidden somewhere on the ship, she tried to imagine how he planned to disperse it. It couldn't be a coincidence that he was covering sensors here in the mated officers housing section. He wanted to kill families. He wanted to hurt the men on this ship in the worst possible way.

The HVAC system!

That had to be his endgame. It would be the easiest way

to widely disperse the gas. Was there a central control nearby? A main unit that served the apartments allotted to couples and families?

She tapped the glasses until she found the list of mechanical systems. She flicked her finger in front of her face, letting the lenses read her movements to scroll through the list until she reached the HVAC listing. When she found it, she tapped the air and opened the file. It gave the location and had a link to a navigational overlay that would take her there.

Her destination chosen, she quietly climbed a ladder to another level and let Reckless disappear from view ahead of her. She had somewhere else to be than trailing him like a shadow.

When she reached the correct level, she walked as fast as she could while staying as silent as possible. Her bare feet started to ache from the constant pressure of the sharp grates, and she prayed she wouldn't start bleeding all over the place. Leaving Reckless a trail of bread crumbs to follow wasn't going to help her get back to Cipher in one piece.

Before she reached the HVAC central unit, she found—to her absolute horror—an actual fucking bomb. Her horror increased when she realized there were more bombs placed along the gangway to the HVAC unit. He must have planned to cut off all access to the unit to prevent anyone from shutting it down to halt the spread of the gas.

Ripping off the glasses, she moved closer to inspect the situation. The lower grade explosives were eerily familiar to her. They were the sort used in the mines to widen tunnels or bring down a curtain of rock in an emergency situation. The brand was one her father had used many times, but it had been phased out of use by the time she started working on her own.

Knowing how volatile old explosives were, she gingerly approached the first device and quickly identified the parts. Explosives. Ignitor. Switch. Power source. It was a simply built bomb, very similar to the ones she had learned to build as a young child. It wouldn't be powerful enough to knock a hole in the wall of the ship, but it would be enough to cause the gangway to collapse. Eyeing the other explosives, she could see that was the intent. Each successive explosion would destroy the walkways and cut off the HVAC section where Reckless likely planned to disperse the gas.

Without any tools, her options were limited. She checked the device from various angles, pressing her body flat to the grate so she could see beneath and along the sides. Fairly certain it wasn't rigged to blow if moved, she held her breath and picked it up. When it didn't explode, she exhaled slowly and traced the wires connecting the power source to the switch and ignitor. Once she had a good idea of how it had been constructed, she grasped the wire connecting the power source to the triggering components and yanked it free.

She flinched, expecting the worst even though she was confident in her skills. With a sigh of relief, she tore the battery from the bomb and ran off to the next one. Without a power source, Reckless wouldn't be able to hastily fix them.

One by one, she deactivated the nine remaining bombs between her and the HVAC unit. Her arms were loaded with batteries, and her feet were bleeding from the pressure of the sharp grates as she reached her destination. She put the batteries on the first available flat surface and tried to get her bearings. The gangway expanded to include a huge platform with a massive air flow unit in the center. There were so many pipes and ducts arcing off of it. She couldn't even begin to make sense of where they all started.

But none of that mattered.

Her horrified gaze landed on the canisters of gas taped to the ducts. There were tubes connected from the tank regulators into slits in the ducts that had been sealed over with more tape. She rushed forward and checked the regulators to make sure they were closed. They were but it would only take a few seconds for Reckless to open them and set off his murderous plan.

"I thought I smelled a whore's perfume."

Brook whirled around to find Reckless standing behind her. His ugly face was contorted in disgust, and she shuddered as he leered at her. "I think you and I are going to have a lot of fun together on my ship."

"I'm not going anywhere with you!"

"Don't be ridiculous," he replied dismissively. "Do you want to stay here and die an excruciating death?" He shook his head. "You'll come with me and keep my bed warm until I find someone who wants to buy you."

"I'll take the excruciating death," she snapped.

"Suit yourself." He took a menacing step toward her, and she retreated. It seemed to amuse him. "You want to play a little cat and mouse? Have me chase you a bit before I catch and kill you?"

As Reckless taunted her, she spotted movement behind him, just off to his left side. She schooled her features, keeping her gaze on his nasty face as Terror seemed to materialize from thin air. The one-eyed operative stalked toward Reckless, and she did her best to keep him occupied. "Your explosives were garbage. I was building better charges when I was eight."

"I'm sure you were."

"You won't be able to isolate this room now. SRU will send in their techs and remove this gas."

"No, they won't." He seemed so very pleased with himself. "They'll all be dead soon. I saved the very best canister for them. They won't even smell it coming."

She narrowed her eyes. Had he rigged up something at a different HVAC unit? Maybe one that served the SRU? "You're insane. Killing all these innocent people? You need help."

Reckless snorted. "I'm insane? If I thought you had more than twenty minutes of your life left, I would explain to you how no one on this ship innocent. Not the soldiers and airmen. Not the mates. Not their grubby mix breed kids."

Behind him, Terror raised his arm to strike—and Reckless unexpectedly spun and sprayed him right in the face with a small vial of fluid. Worried it was deathly gas, Brook screamed, "No!"

Wiping at his stinging face and slinging the fluid from his fingers, Terror pointed at Reckless with one scarred finger and laughed, sending a chill down her spine. "Riot gas? Tor and I used to spray each other in the face with that as a prank at the academy."

Reckless's arrogance seemed to falter. "You won't get out of here alive."

"Maybe not," Terror agreed. "But she will." He held her gaze. "And she knows exactly what to do."

Instinctively, she backed up and gave the two men space. Something terrible and violent was about to happen.

I should have stayed home.

Chapter Nineteen

"**W**HAT WAS SO damn important you had to drag us away from dinner?" Vicious demanded as they filed into Torment's domain.

"If I miss out on cake because of some bullshit, I'm putting you in a headlock," Raze warned Torment.

Torment actually rolled his eyes. "Is proving Reckless has the stolen gas canisters bullshit?"

Cipher exchanged a look with Venom before asking, "How?"

Savage walked out of his office with Orion following closely behind. "The admiral sent Risk and Stinger over to the *Mercy* to look through the pulmonary unit. The cargo crash patients were there." Savage grimaced. "They were basically being used as human suitcases."

"For what?" Vicious asked.

"This." Orion held up a dummy gas canister exactly like the ones taken from the mine. "The bodies had depressions in them the exact same size as these." He shook his head in disgust. "He got some of the gas off the planet and onto the *Mercy* by implanting them in those patients."

Cipher recoiled at the depravity of it. His mind raced, and he remembered something from the logs he had checked the day they were informed about the missing gas. "One of our medical mission ships was on the planet's surface the day that Brook was in the mine doing recon. It was offering vaccines and medical care to a rural area."

"And guess who was leading it?" Torment asked dryly. "Our very own xenophobic asshole."

"That cargo ship had to have been brought down purposely." Raze pulled the pieces together. "It dropped down right near where Reckless and that medical mission were posted. He was the first on scene. He triaged the patients and performed emergency surgery, right?"

"Yes," Torment confirmed.

"Who were his medics?" Venom asked.

"Talon, Blitz and Rake." Savage tapped the massive screen on the wall and displayed their files. "Talon was killed in the pulmonary unit."

Raze crossed his arms. "The other two?"

"Blitz is dead." Savage pointed to an image of his body hanging in his quarters. "Rake went missing."

"After he killed Blitz," Cipher remarked, stepping closer to the screen. It was easy enough to see the angles of his supposed suicide were all wrong. "There's no way he hanged himself. Look at his boots." He gestured to the dead soldier's hands. "And his fingers."

Vicious winced. "He must have been clawing at his neck trying to get loose."

"Probably," Cipher agreed.

"Rake either fled, or he's come here," Raze said, his voice tight. "We have a real fucking problem on our hands."

"Brig to SFHQ. Brig to SFHQ. Code Red. I say again, 'Code Red.'"

Savage glanced at the radio unit across the room. "Is that Pierce?"

"Yes." Torment rushed over and pulled up the feed. "SFHQ to Brig. Go ahead."

Pierce appeared on the screen. He was covered in blood, sweating and panting. "We need HAZMAT to the brig immediately. Medical, too. Get SRU spun up and shut down the ship."

"What the hell happened to you?" Torment asked.

"I got stabbed," Pierce snapped. "Six fucking times." He groaned and moved his hand to his belly. "By Reckless," he added, wincing. "He requested a medic for stomach pain. Brig officer let him have one. The medic was his accomplice. He had gas. Killed all of the guards. I came out of the interrogation room when I heard the coughing and choking. Reckless got me with a scalpel." Pierce groaned again. "I'm locked in the interrogation room. It's sealed, but I don't know how long it will hold or how far the gas has gotten."

"Hold tight, Pierce. We're coming to get you," Torment assured him.

Raze was already headed to the nearest communication console. He opened a line to the SRU and sent out a ship wide call. "All teams report to SRU HQ. Code Black."

Orion crossed the room to the ship wide alarm. He lifted the lid and slapped the button before grabbing the red handset. The alarm started to blare as he ordered, "This is the admiral speaking. This is not a drill. I repeat. Not a drill. All hands to battle stations. All civilians shelter in place. I repeat. All hands to battle station. All civilians shelter in place."

While the order repeated on a loop overhead, Orion replaced the handset and raced toward the door. He was already using his shoulder mic to contact the bridge, giving orders to shut down and isolate all the HVAC systems. "What do you mean it's down? Get someone down there and fix it!"

"What now?" Vicious asked, stopping his own orders mobilizing the land forces on the ship.

"We can't shut down the HVAC systems. Our bridge control has been overridden."

"For fuck's sake," Vicious growled. "Let's go."

The general and admiral disappeared from the room, and Raze pointed at him. "Stay here. You're our link with Shadow Force."

"Got it."

Raze, Venom and Menace rushed from the room, and Torment tossed a gas mask at him. "Here. Weapons and gear over there. Take whatever you need."

Cipher needed only the mask and rushed to a computer. He used his credentials to get into the live security feeds of the brig, the bridge and SRU. They were all hives of action as soldiers and airmen tried to get control over the situation. With those displayed on a separate large wall screen, he started pulling up maintenance and security feeds from the HVAC units.

"Oh, fuck me," Savage all but shouted. "Is that Terror?"

Cipher turned to see the screen behind him where he had sent the feeds to be displayed. Terror had a knife in his hand and slashed at Reckless, cutting free the duffel bag he had slung over his shoulder. Small canisters of emergency oxygen fell out and rolled around on the floor.

His stomach dropped, and his heart skipped several beats as the last person he ever expected to see in the damn bowels of the ship appeared. "Brook!"

"Shit." Savage stepped closer to the screen. "Tor, get our boys down there. Immediately. Terror needs backup." As if remembering that Brook was his mate, he glanced at Cipher and said, "She's a smart girl. She'll stay out of trouble."

"Clearly not!" he snapped.

Why was she even there? He had told her to go back to their quarters after dinner. She had promised she would. She had promised she would take her treatment and wait for him. How the fuck had she ended up in the most dangerous place on the ship?

"Where is she going?" Torment asked as Brook dragged the bag of emergency oxygen away from the two fighting men. "What the fuck is he spraying at Terror?"

"Tear gas?" Savage guessed. "It's not fatal whatever it is. Reckless wouldn't be dumb enough to use something in close quarters without a respirator in place."

Cipher's gaze danced between Terror and Reckless and his mate. "She's moving back to the HVAC unit." He jumped back to the computer and took control of the cameras there. He moved the view to the right and managed to get a good look at the massive unit. "Oh, shit."

There were canisters of gas hooked up to the ducts.

"Are those active?" Savage demanded.

Cipher zoomed in as Brook rushed toward a canister of gas and started pulling on the tube that had been spliced into a duct. He held his breath as she tore it free. If there was gas flowing, she would be dead in a few seconds. When she moved to the next duct, he released the breath he had been holding. "No."

"But where is Rake?" Torment asked. "Unless he died in the brig attack, he's got to be somewhere on the ship."

Savage did a quick count of the bodies in the hallways of the brig. "No, he's not there."

"How many bodies were in the pulmonary unit?" Torment asked.

"Seven," Cipher said, his focus never leaving Brook as she bravely dismantled the gas tubes. "There are six canisters on that unit."

"So, where's the last one?" Savage wondered. "With Rake?"

"Probably," Torment agreed.

"Do we think it's the NA-9X?" Savage rubbed his jaw. "It would make sense, right? Keep the worst gas for another part of the ship?"

"The bridge?" Cipher suggested, still watching Brook. "Or maybe the central units that supply air to all of the mission centers? SRU, Bridge, pilot's deck, hangars?" He glanced away from the screen where Terror and Reckless continued to fight. He tapped on the security feed from that sector and made it bigger. "There!"

"Is that Rake?" Savage looked aghast. "Is he rigged with explosives?"

Cipher zoomed in on his vest. "Yes."

"Fuck," Savage swore. "He's blocking the only entrance to that unit?"

"Yes," Cipher confirmed, checking the other angles of cameras.

"We need EOD down there immediately. If he has a canister of gas rigged to that unit, and we can't shut it down remotely, we're all fucked," Savage snarled.

"Maybe not," Torment said, gesturing to the screen where Terror had taken down Reckless. Brook rushed forward to help, grabbing a roll of silver tape that had fallen from the duffel bag and hastily securing the doctor's ankles while Terror held him. "Is there audio in there?"

"No." Cipher's mouth went dry as Terror held his knife against the doctor's eye socket. Brook glanced away as she taped his hands together, using her slight weight to keep him from moving. A second later, a gush of blood erupted from Reckless's face and his mouth opened in a silent scream. The eyeball that had once been safely housed there flopped out onto the metal grate.

"Fuck," Savage groaned and made a face.

"It's effective," Torment murmured, his attention fixed on the doctor who seemed to be babbling as Terror took his blade to the man's ear.

"It's illegal," Savage reminded them.

"I don't think anyone is going to care," Cipher said, wishing with every fiber of his being that Brook wasn't there to witness the gory display. At the same time, he couldn't deny how much pride filled him as he had watched her dismantle the crude gas delivery system and help Terror secure the doctor.

"Where the hell are they going now?" Savage demanded as Terror and Brook shared a serious look before leaving the bleeding, howling but tightly secured doctor on the floor.

Cipher's blood ran cold as Brook placed the glasses from his office onto her face. "Toward Rake and the bomb."

Chapter Twenty

B ROOK REFUSED TO even think about what she had just witnessed. She pushed all the gruesome images and the gross sounds of Terror popping that eye out of the doctor's head from her mind. She tried to forget the smell of blood and piss as the doctor wet himself in agony and fear. There would be time to deal with all of that later.

Terror hadn't tried to discourage her from following him. He must have known that he needed her help. If what Reckless had told them was true—that Rake was rigged with an explosive vest and the canister of deadly NA-9X gas was on a timer—they didn't have time to wait for backup. She wasn't as skilled as the explosives techs on the ship, but she had confidence in her abilities. Reckless and Rake had rigged terribly simple bombs on the gangway so it was likely they had done the same with the ones on the vest. She could handle that.

Terror didn't need the help of the glasses as he raced along the gangway, but she did. She kept the glasses in place as they ran, just in case he veered off course or they got separated. Watching him in action earlier, she had understood that he had definitely earned his name. He was a terror. A walking, breathing nightmare to anyone who crossed him.

When they reached the first ladder, he hopped down and landed as gracefully as a cat. She wasn't about to try to hurl herself that distance, especially without any shoes on and her feet already bleeding. She would have tried to slide down, feet against the outside, but again, no shoes. Instead, she descended two and three rungs at a time.

Terror hadn't waited for her, and she didn't mind. Time was of the essence. She raced to catch up to him and inwardly groaned when she saw him jumping down another ladder chute. Glad for all the hundreds of times she had climbed and descended ladders as a miner, she descended as quickly as possible and sprinted after him. They descended three more ladders and must have covered at least three-quarters of a mile before they finally neared their destination.

Terror raised a hand, silently telling her to slow down and stop. Trying to control her breathing, she did as he instructed and sidled up close to him. He crouched down, using a wide chute for cover and motioned for her to join him. He moved so close she could see the beads of sweat on his upper lip. His mouth brushed her hair as he hissed, "I'm going in this way. I want you to follow those condensers until you find the service entrance to the compressor. You're as small as some of our maintenance robots. You'll fit. Get inside the compressor room and look for any other explosives. If you find the gas, try to disconnect it."

More nervous than she had ever been in her life, she nodded shakily. "Yes, sir."

"Brook." He grabbed her upper arm and forced her to meet the stare of his single eye. "If we fuck this up, everyone dies. You. Me. Cipher. Our friends."

The reality hit her like a load of bricks to the chest. Lifting her chin, she promised, "I won't fuck this up."

"Good girl." He roughly patted her back. "Go."

With shaking limbs, she grabbed onto the first bracket securing the huge condenser lines and hauled herself off the deck. Her lungs weren't happy with all the exertion required to climb without ropes or a ladder. The treatments had helped, but she felt herself breathing harder and harder as she ascended. Her arms started to burn, and her fingers ached from grasping the hard metal brackets. She didn't even want to think about her throbbing feet. She could feel the blood smudging the cold metal of the condensers.

When she finally saw the flat top of the compressor room, she heaved a grateful sigh. She glanced down, but Terror had vanished from sight. Certain he was about to put the hurt on Rake, she pushed him from her mind. She was about to drop into a room that might be rigged with explosives and poisonous gas. She didn't have enough space in her brain to worry about him, too.

There was a grated cover over the ventilation space similar to the ones she had encountered in the mine. It was so heavy, and she had to strain every muscle in her body to lift it a few inches out of its grooved seat. Panting and sweating, she pushed it as hard as she could to slide it out of the way and make enough room. When it was out of the way, she stuck her head through the slim opening to check out the situation. Terror was right. It was a very small space, but she could fit. For once, her thin figure was going to be very useful.

With trembling arms, she lowered herself through the hole and grabbed onto a beam. It was so noisy inside the compressor room, and the smell of grease and dust made her wrinkle her nose. Worried she was damaging her hearing being so close to all that noise, she cautiously swung her feet forward until she felt a bracket strong enough to hold her. She stretched out her right arm and took hold of another beam. She was barely tall enough to keep her toes on the bracket and her fingers on the beam. She cursed her petite stature and prayed to any deity listening that she wasn't about to fall and break her neck.

Seeing a spot where she could descend, she lowered her arms to her sides and took a steadying breath. Her bloody feet protested as she stepped from the bracket onto a thin beam running parallel to the floor. Trying to stay as balanced as possible, she walked the unnervingly long length of the beam. She wobbled three different times, and her heart clattered in her chest.

Don't fall. Don't fall.

Somehow, she managed to make it safely to the other side. She crouched down carefully, her thighs shaking and her stomach lurching with fear, and took hold of the beam under her feet. Not very gracefully, she lowered one leg and then the other. Dangling too high from the ground to jump without hurting herself badly, she stretched out her left arm toward a ladder-like structure of welded metal holding up various pieces of the compressor.

It was so loud next to the compressor that she could feel her brain rattling in her skull. She clenched her jaw and growled as she swung herself to the metal bars. Her hands slipped as she grabbed hold, and she only just managed to catch herself. Panting and clinging to the metal as if her life depended on it, she carefully climbed down until she made it to the floor.

Wincing at the incredibly loud cacophony from the machine, she started examining every place she could see for any signs of a bomb. She didn't find anything that looked out of place until she followed the giant pipes running from the condenser to the blower unit. When she walked around to the front of the blower, she spotted a canister of gas, this one stamped with a skull and crossbones, attached to the blower and fan. There was a single tube running from the canister into the blower unit box.

That would be easy enough to remove, but there was another problem.

A really, really big problem.

The canister was rigged to explode.

In less than seven minutes.

She didn't hesitate. Lifting the glasses onto crown of her head, she rushed forward to examine the small metal case holding the canister and explosives. She could remove the case from where it had been screwed into the wall of the blower unit, but she couldn't remove the canister from the explosives or case. There were too many wires, too many decoys and not enough time.

She checked the explosive device, the canister and the case for any sort of pressure or movement switches. Years earlier, her father had taught her how to build that sort of explosive charge. Back when their people had first settled the mountain, the miners had accidentally dug into the burrows of underground creatures, terrifying man-eating monsters that could see in the dark. They had used explosives triggered by movement to trap and kill the monsters and make the mines safe.

There weren't any of those monsters left, just the occasional set of bones in an abandoned shaft or newly opened mining section. Still, her father had wanted her to know how to build that kind of device, just in case. She silently thanked him for being so thorough and prayed that he was somehow looking after her now, guiding her from wherever the soul went after death.

After her third check, she was relatively sure that there were no pressure or motion switches. She looked around, desperate for a tool to remove the screws bolting the case to the wall of the blower. An idea struck her. She reached up and grabbed her collar, unbuckling it and studying the silver buckle. It looked to be close enough to the correct size.

With hands that were surprisingly steady, she started unscrewing the bolts. She hissed when she tore her fingernail on the sharp metal but ignored the pain and kept going. One bolt. Two bolts. Three bolts. She was working on the fourth when she heard a man screaming in pain. He was so loud she could hear him over the clang and hiss of the compressor. She glanced toward the nearest door. It was closed, but she suspected Terror and Rake were fighting on the other side of it.

Hurry. Hurry. Hurry.

Her nimble fingers twisted the buckle of her collar, loosening that final bolt. She was just about to wiggle it loose when it happened.

A blast.

In a split-second, all the air in the compressor room seemed to suck away from her body. Not even a heartbeat later, it was rushing back at her with such pressure that her lungs felt like they were being crushed under her ribs. The force lifted her from the ground, flinging her across the room and into a metal chute as if she were lighter than a feather. A scorching wave of heat kissed her skin and singed her hair as she screamed into her arm, hiding her face and desperately hoping she wasn't about to burn alive.

As quickly as the blast began, it stopped. Ears ringing and head throbbing, she pushed up on shaking arms to survey the damage. There was fire and smoke everywhere. Her eyes stung, and she coughed, wondering if it was the smoke or if the gas canister had been damaged in the explosion. The door to the room had been blown clear out of its frame and had landed against the blower unit, denting the side of it.

She spotted the case holding the gas bomb. In a panic, she clambered toward it, crawling over metal shards and stumbling over broken pipes until she reached it. Somehow, the damn thing had survived without being detonated or damaged. There was a slight ding in the case, but that was it.

The timer was still counting down.

Are you kidding me?

In that moment, the reality of her situation became crystal clear. This bomb wouldn't be as powerful as the one that had just rocked the ship, but it would be deadlier. It would kill everyone. The gas would be blown into the air and that would be the end of every life on the Valiant.

Cipher.

And Hallie and Dizzy and their babies.

Ella and Naya and their dreams of becoming powerful businesswomen.

Raze, Venom, Menace and the general. Risk. Men. Women. Children. All of them, murdered in the most horrific way, strangled and choked by an invisible assassin

NO.

She remembered her promise to Terror who was likely dead after that explosion.

I'm not going to fuck this up.

She scanned the place where she had been tossed by the bomb and found the glasses. They were a little cracked but still worked when she slid them into place. She brought up theblueprints of the ship and flicked her fingers until she found the closest space vent. There was a cargo bay, a small one meant for medical waste, not far from here. She would have to run faster than she ever had in her life, but she could make it.

Not wasting another second deliberating, she snatched

up the explosive case and canister and sprinted out of the compressor room, through the burning doorway and onto the destroyed gangway. There was a hole in front of her, not too wide, and she bravely jumped it, leaping over it and landing on the other side. The metal was hot beneath her feet, and she cried out in pain as her tender soles were burned. She cast a glance on either side of the gangway, hoping to see Terror. She couldn't see anything but smoke and fire and some sort of strange white foam spewing from broken pipes.

Hugging the case to her chest, she sprinted as if she were being chased by some great and evil monster. She ignored the pain in her feet. She ignored the burning ache in her chest. She ignored the throbbing in her head. None of it mattered. If she didn't reach that cargo bay in time to vent the bomb and gas, she would be dead.

All around her, there was collateral damage from the explosion. Ceiling panels dangled precariously. Smoke filled the air. Pipes had fractured. Torn wires sparked. She dodged each hazard as the bomb's timer continued to tick away the seconds. She looked down and winced at the sight of one minute and seventeen seconds remaining.

Up ahead, she spotted the cargo bay and kicked up her pace, sprinting with every ounce of energy she had left in her battered body. She slapped the door button but nothing happened. Realizing it had been damaged, she set the case on the floor and growled as she tugged on the heavy door with all her might. It slid open just enough for her to squeeze through with the case.

She rushed inside the dimly lit the cargo bay. It wasn't very big, maybe forty feet by forty feet. The pale green glow of emergency lights powered by batteries illuminated the space. There were sealed bins of medical waste stored all the way to the ceiling. Many of them had fallen over in the blast, spilling out used needles and empty vials. In the far corner, she spotted a familiar device. It was the broken hyperbaric chamber that had necessitated her traveling to the *Mercy* for treatment.

She found the control panel just to the side of the door. When she raced over to it, her heart sank. It had been damaged in the explosion. The screen was broken, and there was no power to the unit. She slapped it angrily. "No!"

Seeing the seconds ticking by on the bomb's timer, she glanced frantically around the room. Her eyes lit up on the emergency ejection button. She had read about the system for ejecting damaged sections of the ship in the event of an attack. Each section could be sealed off from the ship, maintaining hull integrity and giving the ship a chance to stay in the sky until repairs could be made.

She glanced back at the door she had squeezed through to get into the cargo bay. There was an emergency lever to close and lock the door from the inside. She looked back at the emergency ejection button as a wave of crushing sorrow overwhelmed her.

Was there really no other way?

An image of Cipher looking down at her as they cuddled in bed, his strong hands stroking her face as he gazed at her with such tender adoration tore at her heart. The days she had spent with him had been the happiest of her life. She had finally found the one person in the entire universe who liked her just as she was. She had found her life partner, her mate.

I love him.

I love him so much.

It was that love she had for him that spurred her into action. She had one final act of courage left in her.

She put the bomb and gas canister on the floor. The timer had ticked down to twenty-eight seconds. It was now or never.

Crying and shaking, she marched to the broken door and gritted her teeth as she pulled it shut. Her bloody feet slipped on the slick floor as she tugged with every bit of muscle she had. It slid into place, and she reached for emergency lock handle. She had just started to push it down, irrevocably locking herself inside when someone appeared in the small window there.

"Brook!" With panic in his eyes, Cipher slapped the window with his bare hand. "Brook! Open the door! Now!"

She stared up at him, taking in his handsome face and committing it to memory. Those dark eyes, the strong line of his nose, his square jaw. She wished more than anything that she could kiss him one more time. She wished she could hold his hand and tell him how much he meant to her.

Praying he would understand her actions as a vow of love, she forced the emergency lever down all the way. It locked with a clang, and he reacted with shock on the other side of the door. He started to beat on the glass. "Brook! No! No! Open the door! OPEN THE DOOR!"

She placed her dirty, bloody hand on the glass as if to stroke his face. With tears clouding her vision, she said, "I love you."

His eyes widened, and he touched the glass where her fingers were. "I love you."

Crying harder now, she nodded and stepped away from the door. Unable to look at him a moment longer, she turned her back and ran. Her gaze flitted to the timer on the bomb. Thirteen seconds.

She scrabbled over the bins of medical waste and reached the emergency ejection button. Not allowing herself to hesitate or second-guess her decision, she lifted the clear cover and pressed it. It took more force than she had expected, probably to make sure it was never hit accidentally, and then it locked into place. Instantly, the emergency lights in the room shifted to red. A ringing alarm sounded.

I don't want to die.

She wanted to live. She wanted to grow old with Cipher. She wanted to experience all the wonderful delights the universe had to offer.

As the venting doors started to hiss behind her, her focus shifted to the broken hyperbaric chamber. An idea struck. If it still sealed, she might be able to survive the explosive depressurization. Maybe. Possibly.

It's a chance.

She ran toward it, clambering over the medical bins and stabbing herself on discarded needles. She didn't care. She ignored the pain. It didn't matter. Nothing mattered except getting into that chamber.

She hefted the lid and scrambled inside, grabbing the handles on the inside of the lid and tugging it closed. She slid one lock into place, sealing the lid, before the venting door was blown from its hinges.

She was thrown forward in the chamber, smacking her head on the clear lid. Screaming with fear, she moved the second lock into place as the chamber started to skid across the floor. Medical waste bins whizzed out of the hole and into space. The bomb and gas canister flew by the chamber and bounced off the frame of the missing door before being sucked out into the cold emptiness.

Then the chamber was flying. She screamed again, even louder, and wondered if this was it. Something slammed into the chamber from behind, probably another piece of discarded equipment, and she rocked forward and barely avoided knocking her face on the lid. She started to panic as a strange sensation gripped her lungs.

There's no air.

I'm going to suffocate.

Chapter Twenty-One

"**B**ROOK!" CIPHER BEAT his hand against the window as she turned away from him and scrambled over the medical waste bins to the emergency ejection button. "BROOK!"

When he tried to grab the handle, strong arms wrapped around him and jerked him away from the door. He kicked and snarled, trying to free himself as another set of arms grabbed him. "Let me go! Fucking let me go! Brook!"

"It's too late!" Raze shouted, holding him back from the door with Venom's help. "It's too late."

"No! We can get the door open! We can get her out!" He struggled against his friends, hating them for keeping him away from her. "Brook! BROOK!"

A blast rocked the ship as the doors were blown free. Desperate, he bit down on Raze's arm, and the boss hissed as he let go. Cipher shook off Venom's hold and rushed back to the door. He pressed his face to the glass, letting his eyes adjust to the red emergency lighting. Everything in the room was being sucked out of the hole.

"She got into the tube," Torment said, his finger pressed to his earbud. "Savage watched her get into it before the door blew. She's inside it still."

"In space?" Cipher asked dumbly. "Is it pressurized?"

"I don't know," Torment admitted. "If the seal holds, she has a chance until…"

"Until she suffocates from the lack of oxygen," Cipher finished. Squeezing his eyes shut, he couldn't help but imagine her gasping for air and choking to death while clawing at the lid of the chamber.

"Ci," Raze said softly and put a hand on his shoulder. "You did all you could."

He roughly shrugged off Raze's hand. "No, I didn't. I promised I would keep her safe."

"She made her choice," Torment insisted. "She chose courage and bravery. She made the hardest decision any person can make. She chose to sacrifice herself for you. For me. For everyone else on this ship."

Cipher's eyes burned, and he blinked angrily. "She can't die. I can't lose her."

In a move that shocked him, Torment gripped the back of his neck and drew him into an embrace. "I'm sorry, Ci. I really am."

A wave of devastating grief tore the air right out of his lungs. A sound he didn't know he was capable of making escaped his throat. He clung to Torment as he unleashed a ragged sob that came from the very depths of his soul.

Over and over, he replayed the moment she had touched the glass and spoken her love for him. He hadn't been able to hear her voice very well through the glass, but he could see in her eyes how much she loved him.

As much as I love her.

It was a painful blow to lose her just moments after declaring their love.

"What?" Raze said harshly. "Say again. Your transmission is breaking up." He paused. "Where?" he shouted. "We're on our way."

Raze snatched Cipher by the shirt and jerked him away from Torment. "She's alive. Move!"

"What?" Cipher stumbled after Raze, his shirt still clenched in the boss's hand. "How?"

"Hazard," Raze said, starting to run. "He was approaching on a cargo flight when the first explosion happened. He saw the door blow and intercepted the chamber when he heard Savage's call go out to all stations."

"Hazard?" He repeated in shock, racing to keep up with Raze.

"That wild son of a bitch," Raze remarked with a relieved laugh. "He's the only who would be crazy enough to try a mid-air retrieval on a cargo ship."

Cipher's panic and grief gave way to such intense hope. Was she hurt? Was she still breathing? Had she inhaled any of the gas?

Please be alive.

He silently begged the universe over and over as he rushed through ship, following Raze with Venom just behind him. His legs were shaking from the adrenaline and the fear that Raze was wrong, that Hazard hadn't grabbed the chamber and recovered her alive.

Please. Please. Please.

They burst into the medical bay with such force that

the doors rocked on their tracks. A medic took one look at him and indicated the major trauma room at the rear of the hall. Cipher pushed by Raze and sprinted to the room.

"Hold on!" Stinger caught him before he could rush to the metal slab where she had been laid out by medics. Risk didn't even look up as he treated her, his full focus on saving her life. "She's alive. Cipher!" Stinger demanded his attention. "She's alive. She's a little banged up, but she's alive."

Cipher sagged with relief. His legs crumpled under him, and he dropped to the floor, slamming his knees against the ground. He didn't even care about the pain. It felt good. It was a tiny bit of what his incredible, awe-inspiring mate had experienced tonight.

Stinger squeezed his shoulder. "You're a lucky man, Cipher. She's a hell of a woman."

"Yes," he said, his voice thick with emotion. "She is."

HOURS LATER, SO late he couldn't decide if it was still night or early morning, he sat at Brook's bedside as she endured yet another breathing treatment. She grimaced behind the mask, holding it to her face with one hand and clinging to him with the other. Their gazes met briefly, and she smiled at him. He smiled right back, his heart thumping wildly in his chest. "I love you."

She laughed into the mask. He had been saying it to her every few minutes since she had awoken in the trauma bay.

Stinger had been right. She was banged up. Both of her feet were covered in a skin healing gel and wrapped in bandages. The medics had pulled a small pile of metal slivers from her feet before cleaning and treating them. She had a bump on the back of her head, and a gash on the hairline up front as well as a mild concussion. Her hands were a mess of cuts and scrapes. She had to take two bags of IV meds to protect her against any viruses or bacteria she might have been exposed to through the used needle sticks.

But it was her lungs, her damaged but healing lungs, that had saved her life. In the most bizarre twist of fate, she had gotten so used to a lower concentration of oxygen that she had been able to survive longer in the broken chamber than a healthy person.

It seemed almost poetic in a way. Her hardscrabble life as a child miner had all but saved her tonight. From the bombs she had dismantled to the climbing and crawling through tight spaces to the quick-thinking that convinced her to take the gas to a space vent, she had used all the skills of her childhood to save everyone on the ship.

"They're calling you a hero," he said as she finished her breathing treatment and handed the nebulizer to the medic who had come to check on her.

She rolled her eyes and coughed. Shaking her head, she protested, "I'm no hero. If anything, I'm the biggest dummy on this ship." She gestured to her battered body. "What the hell was I thinking? I'm not a soldier!"

"And yet you kept pace with Terror and saved everyone," he insisted.

"Has he woken up yet?" She glanced at the long window that looked out across the infirmary. Directly across the hall, on the other side of the medic station, Terror had been admitted for his injuries sustained in the explosion. He had a broken leg, some cracked ribs and quite a few gashes, but he was alive.

"I don't know." With a wry smile, he said, "When he does, we'll probably all hear about it."

"You should go down to the shops and get him some oranges if they have them."

He thought she was joking. "You're serious?"

"Yes."

He sighed. "Okay. I'll go down in the morning when they open."

"Thank you." She cleared her throat and made a face at the taste of the nebulizer treatment clinging to her mouth. "What about the other one? Pierce?"

"That man has the worst luck in the entire universe. At the rate he's going, he'll be twenty-percent original parts soon. If they don't force him into early retirement, I'll be shocked."

"Poor guy." She frowned. "I hope he recovers quickly. Being stabbed like that has to be awful." She looked back toward the window. "What about Chance?"

"Still in his medically-induced coma as far as I know." Cipher bent down to unzip his boots. "I'm not sure how things will shake out for him or his family."

"Or hers," she remarked. "If her family or his were working with Reckless and the Splinters, his whole life will be flipped upside down."

"If he didn't know," Cipher replied, standing and toe-ing off his boots. "He might have been in on it all along."

She shook her head. "No, he's not that kind of man."

"You hardly know him."

"True," she allowed, "but I saw his face when he talked about Nika. When we were on the *Mercy*, he was upset on my behalf and tried to stop Reckless from being so nasty. He wouldn't have done that if he was secretly some racist Splinter nutbag."

"I guess." Cipher decided to reserve his judgment until there were more known facts. He closed the door of her hospital room and activated the privacy setting on the window. With the glass frosted, he peeled out of his uniform shirt and undershirt and took all his gear from his pockets. Exhausted, he tugged his belt free and turned toward the bed where Brook had wiggled over to make room for him. "Ready for bed?"

"Only if you come over here," she said, holding out her hand. "I need you."

"Not as much as I need you," he replied and slid into the hospital bed.

"Is it a competition?" she asked with a little laugh.

"Maybe," he said, sneaking in a kiss. Pulling back, he gazed into her beautiful eyes and felt emotion well up inside him. His voice cracked as he said, "When I thought I lost you…"

Unable to continue, he dropped his gaze. She traced his lower lip with her thumb and ducked her head until she captured his attention. "I know."

It was a simple statement, just two words, but it meant so much. She knew exactly what he had felt because she felt the same thing. It must have been the hardest thing in the world for her to choose death to save him and the rest of the ship.

"You are everything to me," he whispered. "I love you so much."

"I love you." She pressed her soft lips to his. Smiling, she confessed, "It makes me feel giddy to say it."

"Same," he admitted as he slipped his arm under her shoulders. Leaning back against the pillow, he sighed and enjoyed the peace of their quiet, intimate moment. "We're going on vacation," he decided rather suddenly. "As soon as I can get you out of here, we're going to Blue Shores. You. Me. Sunshine. A beach. Lots of water."

She drew her initials on the skin of his chest. "I think we've earned it."

"Hell yes we have," he agreed. "Damn war council should pay for it," he grumbled. "A little rest-and-relaxation stipend after the way you risked your life twice to help us."

"We'll be lucky if they don't send me the bill for blowing a hole in their perfectly good ship." She laughed and snuggled in closer. "You think they might give me a medal? I could hook a medal onto my new collar." She glanced up at him with a saucy smile. "Maybe then *you* can call *me* sir."

Cipher snorted and kissed her forehead, being careful to avoid her stitches. "I'll call you whatever you want, baby girl."

She giggled and sighed happily. After a few moments of stroking his bare chest, she quietly confessed, "I want a baby, Cipher."

Surprised, he glanced down at her. "Like right now?"

She swatted his chest. "Be serious!"

"I am being serious." He gestured toward the door. "If you want one right now, I need to go lock that door."

She laughed as he nuzzled her neck. "Not *right now* right now, but soon."

"Little one, you just say the word and I'm there."

She placed her small hand on his neck. "Promise?"

He took her hand in his and threaded their fingers together. Hoping she could read the love in his adoring gaze, he vowed, "Promise."

Chapter Twenty-Two

WITH AN IRRITATING limp, Terror left the Departures deck where he had just seen Cipher and Brook off on their well-deserved vacation. He had used his clearance to fast track her mate paperwork and nullify the travel waiting period.

It hadn't taken nearly as much arm-twisting as he had been expecting to get their stay in Blue Shores comped by the war council. A mate saving an entire ship by blowing herself into space with a nerve gas canister rigged to explode had a way of getting people to move their asses.

Seeing Brook smile and practically vibrate with excitement as she waited to board their ship had been worth the discomfort of moving his aching, bruised body from one side of the ship to the other. He didn't even try to hide his enjoyment of her. There was something incredibly pure about Cipher's mate. His approval was hard to earn, but Brook had managed to do it easier than anyone else, even Hallie.

Even D.D.

The memory of her beautiful face and innocent smile made his chest hurt. Not D.D. Her real name was Maisie. It had taken him a few visits to get that out of her. She had finally given it to him the last time he had seen her.

It had been her regular visit to clean his cell, but she had been sporting a black eye and a busted lip. There had maroon fingerprints on her neck. He had been enraged at the realization that someone had beaten and strangled her. She was like him, a captive under the care of her sadistic stepfamily, and never seemed to do anything except what she was told.

She had refused to tell him who hurt her. She had only told him two things, tapping out the messages in code on his back. Firstly, Devious had been exposed and was in trouble. Secondly, her mother had named her Maisie. The cruel nickname was just another way for people to abuse and humiliate her.

She had left him another orange that morning—and then she had vanished.

Deep down in the dark parts of him where he still allowed a sliver of hope to reside, he pleaded for her to be alive somewhere safe. He wanted to believe that she had escaped, maybe with the help of the Red Feather or with a contact Devious had left her. She deserved to be free and happy.

Of all the regrets Terror had—and there were many— one of the worst was that he hadn't been able to thank Maisie for all she had done for him. Her kindness and decency had saved him. She had given him the strength to endure. She had given him a bright spot to anticipate. He had counted down the days until her next visit, forcing himself to suffer through whatever horror the Splinters had in store for him so he could see her incredibly blue eyes and feel her shy hands on his body.

If she was still alive, he would find her. If he had to travel to the ends of the galaxy, he would find her. If she was happy and safe, he would leave her be. If she was in trouble, he would save her and set her free.

He just needed the right piece of intel. One little bit of information that would give him an idea of where to start looking.

And he planned to get it from Reckless.

Secure in the Shadow Force unit, he traversed a long hallway and a series of doors to a thick, black slab. It was the entrance to the cell they called The Hole. The disgraced doctor had been brought to The Hole after Stinger stabilized him. While Terror had been forced to recover in the hospital for two days, Torment had taken custody of Reckless. No doubt, the doctor had learned exactly why his friend had been given that name.

He scanned his good eye on the retina screen and waited for the door to unlock. With a hiss, it unsealed itself and opened outward, the hinges squealing under its weight. He stepped inside the dank, dark room and let his eyes adjust.

In the center of the room, Reckless had been forced into a stress position. He was squatting low, shackled to a bolt on the floor with his arms restrained behind his back and shackled to a bolt in the floor. Judging by the antiseptic smell in the room, Grim had given their prisoner a hasty spray down to clean him up before Terror's arrival.

Unable to crouch with his broken leg in a brace, Terror

motioned for Grim to get their prisoner on his feet. Reckless howled and whined as Grim roughly dragged him upright and moved his arm shackles overhead, securing him from a ceiling ring. The older man's legs shook as his abused muscles tried to accept the flow of blood they had been denied so long.

Standing in front of Reckless, Terror simply stared at him. He had learned in his earliest interrogations that silence and a steady look were the most unnerving things to a prisoner. He let his gaze rake over the eye patch covering the doctor's empty socket and the bandage that had been slapped over gash in the side of his head from his missing ear. There hadn't been much point in Stinger fixing the man's wounds. He wouldn't be alive long enough to heal.

"Apologies for making you wait," Terror finally said. "I trust my friends treated you to a level of hospitality you've yet to experience."

Reckless gulped. He wasn't stupid enough to say anything.

"You know, my friends tell me that they discovered your little handbook of nightmares in the files they took from the mine." When Reckless flinched, he smiled. "I had no idea you liked to freelance as an enhanced interrogation expert. Perhaps you'd like to give me an honest opinion on our techniques?"

Reckless started to shake. "Please, I'll tell you anything."

"Of course, you will," Terror agreed. "After."

"Please," Reckless cried. "Please! I'll tell you about the

mole! I'll tell you about Devious. What do you want to know?"

"Grim, how many times did the good doctor here stab Pierce?"

"Six." Grim stepped forward with a wickedly sharp scalpel in his hand.

Reckless panicked as his gaze fell on the gleaming scalpel. "No! NO!"

"Yes." Grim closed the distance between them.

"I know the locations of all the safe houses on the planet. I know the sympathizers on the colonies," Reckless babbled. "I know about the skin traders they use to fund their operations."

"I haven't heard anything new," Grim said, shifting the blade to the other hand. "What do you think, boss?"

"I think our guest needs a little encouragement to dig deep into that brain of his and give us the really good intel we deserve."

"Encouragement?" Grim grinned almost evilly. "That just so happens to be my biggest talent."

"No!" Reckless screamed as Grim began to demonstrate those talents.

A long time later, Terror rinsed the blood from his hands at the sink in the corner of the room. It hadn't taken nearly as much knife work to get what they needed from Reckless. Many of the things he babbled in a desperate bid to make it stop had already been uncovered by Savage and Torment while going through the doctor's extensive notes and files. Like so many assholes, his arrogance in his own abilities had left his notes poorly encrypted and easily deciphered. Safe houses, ships, names of skin traders, names of friendly politicians, names of other Splinters serving in the Harcos land and sky forces…

Much of that had been confirmed during their session today. Much more would be confirmed in the coming days and weeks as they worked to untangle the mess left behind by Reckless and the untimely death of Devious. There were still assets lost in the wind. There were still critical missions that had to be completed.

But he had other places to be.

"What do I do with him?" Grim asked, wiping his face with a cloth. He coldly eyed the blood on the towel before tossing it in the trash.

Terror glanced at Reckless who had slumped over against the wall, crying and bleeding everywhere. "Clean him up. Get him dressed. Let Orion know the good doctor is ready for the noose."

"Got it." Grim studied him for a moment. "What about you?"

"What about me?"

Grim's mouth settled into an annoyed line. "You heard what he said about the girl. About *your* girl," he clarified. "You going after her?"

"Yes."

"You need help?"

Terror considered Grim. He was the best assassin the Shadow Force had ever produced. He would be an asset on a job like this. "Sure."

"Lethal is bored as fuck. He's useful in a tight spot."

"Bring him."

"What about a pilot?"

"I've got that handled." Down at the Departures deck, Zephyr, the same pilot who had shot him out of the sky all those months ago, waited to repay his debt. "One hour. Docking Station 12."

Grim nodded. "I'll be there."

Terror left The Hole and returned to the main offices of the Shadow Force HQ. He was surprised to find Vicious waiting for him. His oldest and dearest friend wasn't wearing his usual general's uniform. He was in tactical clothing and strapped for battle. Frowning, he asked, "What the fuck are you doing, Vee?"

"The fuck does it look like I'm doing?"

"Getting us both in trouble with your pregnant wife," Terror stated matter-of-factly. "I just got out of the hospital. I'd like to not end up there again when Hallie kicks my ass for getting you hurt."

"I'm not going to get hurt." Vicious rose from his chair. "And Hallie knows I'm here."

Terror wavered. "Vee, I've got other men willing to go."

"Great. The more the merrier."

"That's not my point."

"I know what your point is," Vicious replied. "I'm here because I want to be here." He stepped closer and placed his meaty paw on Terror's neck. "I'm here because you're my best friend, and I almost lost you again. I'm done almost losing you."

"Impending fatherhood has made you soft," Terror gruffly said.

Vicious laughed and then said, more seriously, "I hope someday very soon you have the same experience."

A vision of a small child with bright blue eyes and freckles taunted him. Was that even a possibility for someone as fucked up as he was?

She might not even want you. She might hate you now.

There was only way to find out.

"Come on, Papa Bear." Terror slapped Vicious on the back. "Let's go piss off Orion by stealing one of his ships."

The End.

About Lolita Lopez

The alter ego of New York Times and USA Today bestselling author Roxie Rivera, I like to write super sexy romances and scorching hot erotica. I live in Texas on five acres with my husband, our two mischievous girls, a pair of Great Danes, a couple of cats and various fish.

You can find me online at www.lolitalopez.com.

Also by Lolita Lopez

GRABBED

Grabbed by Vicious

Caught by Menace

Saved by Venom

Stolen by Raze

Claimed By Cipher

Dragon Heat

Dead Sexy Dragon

Red Hot Dragon

Wicked Dark Dragon

Renegade Dragon

Printed in Great Britain
by Amazon